HUMAN

Red Fever Book 3

C R MacFarlane

ISBN 978-1-7753564-4-8

www.blueponypress.com

For Avery, who has always been there.

HALUD DEGAZO, FORMER POET LAUREATE of the United Earth Central Army, clenched his hand over his stomach and fought back a wave of anxious nausea.

Across the dark ante-chamber, lit by a single, red, incandescent bulb so their vision could adjust to the dark, a dozen rebels drew their hoods and secured black masks. All their clothes were black, and they nearly blended into the dark wall behind them, except for gaudy, blue tassels that hung from their shoulders, the significance of which he had yet to understand.

"Ready, Poet?" the leader, Athos, called to him.

Halud forced himself to nod. "Yes."

The door opened and they slipped into the street. A handful of stars lay scattered across the purple-black night, the lights of the Central City obscuring all but the brightest constellations—the sky here was nothing like the unfettered views from the freightship.

The freightship. A wave of nausea stopped him in his tracks. Gal, Kieran, Sarrin—oh Gods, Sarrin! He pressed his five fingers to his heart, praying. It was his fault. Finding his sister had been a set up. If he hadn't gone to rescue her, walking right into Hap Lansford's trap, they would still be alive.

But she would still be in the prison on Selousa—his mind flashed the vid Hap had shown him of her strung up, screaming like an animal—a prison he never should have let her sit in.

What a fool he'd been, politicking, playing 'the game.' How clever he thought he'd been, strategizing, gaining favour, playing at alliances. He'd lived in his luxurious apartments in the Speakers' compound, while his sister rotted in Evangecore. Gods only knew what they had done to her.

"Are you coming?" Athos stood in the street, turned to face him, while the others had all disappeared ahead.

"Yes, yes, sorry." Halud shrugged, adjusting the pack on his shoulders, and pulled on his own mask. "Ready."

"You don't have to come with us."

"I do though," he said, much as it terrified him.

"Your information should be enough to get us in and destroy the lab."

Halud shook his head. "I have to. For her."

This was his plan after all. In his last broadcast for the Speakers, he had reported on a vaccine for *Xenoralia nervosa*—the Red Fever. It was meant to protect infants from acquiring the disease, but Halud had seen the first child inoculated, watched its eyes turn from murky, dull brown to crystalline pale blue—identical to those of his sister and all the other Children of Evangecore. The vaccine wasn't protecting against new Augments, it was creating them.

Athos nodded. "I understand."

Halud sprinted with Athos after the others. The mask over his face restricted his breathing, but it only made him feel stronger, more determined. The pumping of his arms and legs, and the thrashing beat of his heart, exhilarated him. This was what it felt to be alive, to take action, to actually do something instead of sitting at his Poet's desk.

The Hospital of the Gods—the most advanced medical building in existence—loomed ahead, a big, concrete, blocky building at the base of the Speakers' tower. Halud clutched the pendant around his neck—a gift from years and years ago that had been given to him by his father, as his mother lay on her deathbed with Red Fever and he fled into the woods with Sarrin. A pendant he had long considered too dangerous, but now seemed exactly right. The gold casing was carved—something abstract, not at all in the taste of the Artist Laureate—and the jewel held in the centre was a deep red, casting the medallion in flickering fire. The very existence of something so beautiful, so full of colour, was defiance, and he tucked it under his cloak, letting the flames fuel him.

The rebels spread out around him, separating into groups. Halud's team clustered behind him, the backpack of explosives shifting on his back. These were not the same rebels as there had been ten years ago when John P led them; these were kids. John P had disappeared years ago—dead, according to Gal—but small cells of the rebels lived on.

He'd been lucky to find the lair, following the old symbols carved into nooks and crannies of buildings that led him there. Lucky that they still used the hideout, and lucky that they'd taken him in, believed him when he told them everything he knew, and luckier still that they were willing to help him.

He tapped his fingers against the timer in his pocket, pausing as the other teams got into position. After so many years of being idle, even this small waiting seemed too long. He could never undo what had happened to his sister, but he could stop it from ever happening again.

From across the square, Athos held his hand up in the air, signalling they were ready. The other team leader did the same. The rebels beside Halud took off running, all three teams planning their incursion simultaneously.

He hesitated. Was this what John P would have done? Not for the first time, he wished the old leader was still around. John P had been a legend in his time. No one before or since had ever given the Speakers such pause, no one had come so close. For a while, Halud had thought maybe John P still lived, was still in hiding—foolishly, he'd thought Galiant Idim, the washed up starship captain, was John P—but it was clear the old rebel leader was well and truly gone.

So the fight fell to him. Blood rushed in his veins as he ran after them, putting on a burst of speed to overtaking the others. He was not a trained soldier like Sarrin, but he had been infected with the virus all the same, his strength and speed augmented far beyond that of the regular folk.

Breathless, he reached the East entrance, and followed the ramp down to the service door. He nodded at each of them once, waiting to see their response that they were ready.

Was he ready?

He clenched his fists and exhaled. Yes. His heart beat around in his chest, and for an instant he felt like he might pass out. But this was the time. This was the moment.

A faint glow lit up the access pad beside the door, and one of the rebels carefully entered the sixteen digit code they had been provided by an inside operative. It took forever, Halud shifting foot to foot, but the pad beeped, flashed green, and the door slid open.

One of his team let out a nervous laugh. She tried to stifle it, but the others teased and giggled. A smile broke on Halud's face.

The corridors under the hospital were pitch-black. He followed the wall by hand until his eyes had a chance to adjust, one doorway, two doorways. At the seventh doorway, he stopped, the team fumbling around behind him. Once again he approached the door controls, this time pulling a plastic key from his pocket. The door sprung open, and they slipped inside. A faint glow illuminated the end of the long, small corridor, and they ran towards the seldom used room.

In the light coming from one of the hospital's large power generators, Halud shifted the small backpack to the floor, unclipping it to reveal the shining home-made bomb. Two of the rebels bent, taking the bomb, and went to attach it to the generator, right beside the structural support at the back of the room, the same as a half-dozen other teams were doing throughout the building.

"Done," they announced.

The woman guarding the door let out a nervous squeal. Halud couldn't stop himself from smiling. After all their careful planning, this would finally be a blow the Speakers wouldn't see coming. Maybe it would change things, maybe not. But if they made enough noise, if the hospital crumpled even partly what they predicted, people would start asking questions. And if enough people started asking questions, maybe just maybe some truths would start to surface.

Halud nodded. "Set the timer."

They moved like shadows, their faces distorted in the glow of the generator. Halud lifted his backpack, now empty, and followed them down the long corridor. The minutes until the timer detonated, and the bomb on the generators ripped apart the structural support, hopefully collapsing this very corridor. One of the rebels let out a cheer.

Lungs burning, Halud revelled in each pump of his arms, each slap of his feet on the damp concrete floor. Here they were, alive, powerful. It reminded him of Sarrin, a sudden suspicion that this must be what the Augments felt like in the war, and it felt as though the two of them were connected.

He clutched the pendant at his chest, holding it to his chest as he ran. When this was all over, he would find Sarrin, and they would run in the woods, brother and sister again. It would happen, she was still alive, he had to believe it.

Dim light filtered in from the main corridor, outlining the door they had come through. He raced towards it, ignoring the niggling fact that the lights had been off when they entered—they were so close. He threw his weight into the door, pushing it open.

The others nearly crashed into him as he stopped abruptly. In front of him, in the dim light, stood a wall of grey-clad UEC soldiers. They wore a strip of black with the insignia of Strength —Hap's soldiers, elite soldiers. A dozen las-rifles pointed their way.

Halud swallowed dryly as the door swung shut behind them.

They had been too noisy, too confident, celebrating before they were even out. But this was the basement of the hospital in the middle of the night, they had studied the security systems and patrol routes, no one should have been there to hear them.

Raising his hands in a gesture of peace, Halud stepped forward. He modulated his voice, turning it so the pitch and timbre dug into their subconscious and made them want to listen.   "Gentlemen, I believe there has been a misunderstanding. There's no need for laz-rifles."

But the laz-rifles did not drop.

A dark cord dangling from one of the guard's ears caught his eye: earpieces. They couldn't hear him. But it wasn't a standard part of the uniform—protections against the explosions, maybe?

He reached for his mask, pulling it off to reveal his face: the trump card. He was still the Poet Laureate, hadn't been denounced publicly, Hap knew he was still the face the folk trusted. "My friends," he said, taking another step to be sure they could see him in the dull light.

Laz-rifles lifted with a uniform precision, the guards bringing the sights to their eyes. "Down on the ground," yelled the one in the centre.

Behind him, one of the rebels whimpered, and he heard all three of them shuffle to the ground.

Halud brought his hands up. "I am the Poet Laureate of the First Speaker —," he tried.

"Get down!"

His limbs went cold. "I am Halud DeGazo—"

"I know who you are. Now, get down."

He looked across the line. They did know who he was, none of them had so much as flinched when he pulled off his mask. They'd come with ear plugs. Whoever led them, knew Halud would be there and knew the power he wielded with his voice.

The door to the small corridor clicked open, causing Halud to turn involuntarily, his heart thumping erratically in his chest. The figure that slipped through from the dark was tall and lithe and terrifyingly familiar.

"Commandant," Halud breathed, leaning as far away as he could manage before he stumbled to catch his balance.

Her lips pressed into a thin line, the explosive device bouncing carelessly in her one hand. "You're really not very good at this, Poet." Her fingers dug into detonator, pieces clattering across the floor. "The hospital was an obvious target, although I was surprised that you would resort to this level of violence."

He found his voice, maybe too loud: "What are you doing here? The Comrade left a week ago."

She faltered, a frown creasing her otherwise placid features. "Yes. My services were required elsewhere."

"You were demoted," he surmised, a sudden strength surprising him. Rumours had floated around the Speakers' compound, passed along by none-other than the ever-smiling receptionist Joyce. "I heard you let the freightship go. I suppose I should thank you for that."

"Don't," she said coolly. "I'll kill you and your sister the instant I get the chance, but the Speakers have requested you alive." She signalled the soldiers. "Prepare them for transport."

The elite guard surged forward, almost too fast for Halud to comprehend even with his heightened reflexes and the massive dose of adrenalin coursing through him. The commandant grabbed his wrist, forcing him to the ground. Soldiers grabbed the rebels, dark covers tugged roughly over their masks, and lifted them up, half-carrying, half-dragging them deeper in the hospital's labyrinth.

"Wait," said Halud, "where are you taking them?" He's struggled to pull away, but her grip was too strong.

Instead of answering, Amelia gave him a feral grin, her iron grip tightening until something snapped in his wrist and he cried out in pain. A heavy sac was pulled over him, obscuring his vision completely. Something pricked his shoulder, and the noises and movement around him faded as much as his sight, and he slumped to the ground.

The commandant's cold voice was the last thing he heard: "The First Speaker wants him in the Rehabilitation ward."

ONE

Sarrin Degazo blinked, eyes rapidly adjusting to the familiar shadows of the room around her.   A soft blue glow was the only light in the room. Her sleep had been unusual, soft, and gentle. Her dreams had featured wide woods and ungulate creatures.

Glowing blue goo sloshed in the tank beside the bed as the occupant twitched uncomfortably: Kieran Wood.   The engineer. Her friend. She twisted around to get a better look at him, peering over the glass sides. The bio-resonance gel covered his body, only a small air bubble covered his mouth and nose allowing him to breathe.

It wasn't clear in her mind if she could see or hear or feel him wince, but she reached her hand into the tank and took his. His palms were one of the few areas that had been spared from second and third degree burns when the freightship exploded around him, and she rubbed them comfortingly while his fingers twitched, clutching desperately.

Pain washed through her where his skin met her overly sensitive flesh. She bit her lip, fighting down the urge to snatch her hand back—her strange ability to draw energy from those around her had killed, but Kieran was proof it could do good too.   Instead, she pushed soothing calm through the connection, ignoring the monster that pulsed in the recesses of her mind.

A minute later, calm pulsed back through Kieran's hand, and his grip loosened. His body relaxed, and she knew he had gone back to sleep. She held his hand a little longer. He needed it, to help with the pain.

Still holding him, she laid her head on the pillow, pulling up the blankets with her free hand.

This time, Kieran was in her dreams. He held her hand, laughing as they ran. He couldn't run as fast as she could, Sarrin half-pulling him as they leapt over roots and branches. Tall ungulate creatures, with flowing manes and tails, galloped through the woods beside them, weaving in and out, close enough to touch, their warm breath puffing over her neck and arms.

She put on a burst of speed as the creatures surged past. Kieran tripped, his legs flailing as he pulled them both down. Instead of being angry, he laughed, the corners of his green eyes crinkling. "Sorry," he puffed, then he pulled her close, wrapping his body around hers. To her surprise, she liked it, leaning in. Too soon, he pulled away, smiling. "Go on without me."

The last of the creatures' hooves crashed by, long tails disappearing in the dense trees. If she didn't go now, she'd lose them. But she couldn't leave Kieran.

"It's okay," he said. "I'll be here when you get back. Promise."

She nodded, jumping onto her feet, too excited to hold back. Kieran flashed another grin, nearly pushing her, and then she was sprinting through the woods again, chasing creatures that were at once entirely foreign and completely familiar. She spared a single glance back, looking for Kieran's reassuring smile, but he was gone.

She snapped awake, her hand free-floating in the thick bio-gel.

Someone stood at the foot of the bed: Leove. She hadn't even noticed him come in. She snapped her hand from the tank and skittered across the bed, heart racing.

The doctor only smirked and stepped close to the regen-tank to examine the sleeping form inside.

She forced her breathing to slow. Kieran was still here, his hand had merely slipped away from hers in all that blue gel. A good thing too. How foolish she had been to leave it in the tank, to leave it touching him, for so long and while she was asleep. There was no telling what could have happened, what the sick, twisted part of her mind could have done if she hadn't been there to stop it.

Kieran sat up, rubbing his face gingerly to clear the goop from his eyes. He turned to her, blinking twice before he flashed a smile, not as free as it once was but a smile nevertheless.

Leove drew his attention away from her: "How is it this morning?"

Kieran quirked his lips up, the effect somewhat gruesome with the lines of scar tissue and the bio-gel still covering his face. "Good'nough."

Leove raised a single eyebrow. "Good enough for what?"

Kieran shrugged, goo sliding off his naked back into the tank. The shrug must have hurt because he winced, and then he slowly flexed and drew his shoulder blades apart.

Sarrin caught herself staring and looked away.

"Good enough for whatever you have planned for today."

Leove laughed once. "Pain score, I'm here to check on you. Then I'm sure you'll want to go check on Cordelia and the engines."

"Pain's fine," Kieran said.

"Really?" Leove flicked him in the shoulder

"Ow!" Kieran reached over to cover the spot, but he

moved too quickly and made himself clench in pain. He sighed. "I don't want any more of those opioids. They scramble my brain."

Leove nodded. "Sure, Kieran, but you let me know if it hurts. There's no shame in it. I've never seen a non-Augment heal this fast, or be this stubborn about it."

Kieran snorted once. "I've got things to do, places to go, people to rescue." He turned, quirking an eyebrow at Sarrin.

She found the corners of her mouth tugging up at the familiar mischief in his eyes.

"Actually, that's the other bit of good news," Leove said. "Cordelia says we've arrived."

"So quickly?" Kieran spun his head back, wincing again.

It had been two weeks since the accident, but only a few days since they had left the spot where they had first encountered Cordelia as a planet. They had to wait for Kieran to wake up, and then he insisted on several days of testing to ensure Cordelia fully understood the mechanics of grav-jump travel before they left.

But four days? Even the messenger ships or Speakers' warships couldn't make it that fast. And Kieran had been adamant that Cordelia take the recommended cool-down breaks between FTL jumps.

Leove nodded.

"How long have I been asleep, I'm losing track of days."

"Sixteen to eighteen hours," said Leove. "That's good, most people would still be in an induced coma right now. Or dead."

Kieran's energy shifted. He nodded his head solemnly.

"Let's get you out of there, so you can tell Cordelia what's what as we coast into Etar," Leove said with a grin. "She's getting antsy."

At that moment, a figure appeared in the doorway. The door hadn't opened, the woman appeared to simply materialize from it. "I don't like this at all." Cordelia paced across the room.

Kieran's lips quirked into a smile.

Today, Cordelia wore a full set of battle armour, and a set of white, fuzzy slippers with stitched on faces and long, floppy ears.

"What are you wearing?" Kieran said.

"What?" Cordelia paused, indignant. "These people destroyed Cornelius. I must be prepared."

Kieran grunted, as he stretched one leg in preparation, Leove reaching into the tank to help him. "I know, but the slippers."

"I'm trying to stay relaxed." She started pacing again, the heads on the slippers bobbing with each step. Her arms flung up into the air and she spun on her heel towards Kieran and the doctor. "Ugh, here."

Kieran was suddenly standing, the goo gone from his head and body, and he was fully dressed. His eyes sought out Sarrin again, the scarred skin at the corners crinkling.

It wasn't abnormal for Cordelia to shift things around them —after all she had made the entire ship, her ethereal body able to become whatever it was they needed—still, Sarrin felt a wave of annoyance pass through her.

"How far out are we, C?" Kieran asked.

She raised an eyebrow. "We're here."

"In orbit?"

"Relax, Sarrin," the woman turned her eyes to her briefly before turning back to Kieran. "Of course."

Sarrin tucked herself further away, quashing her growing annoyance with Cordelia and her presumptuous, overfamiliarity with Kieran. Her skin felt hot, and she fought an urge to bury her face under the bedsheets.

"But how did you bypass the security nets?" asked Kieran, oblivious.

"I modulated our frequency so the sensors couldn't detect us."

"You can do that?" Kieran turned to Sarrin, his eyebrows both raised in surprise.

"I asked Gal, he knew how." Cordelia waved for them to follow as she strode out the door.

Kieran reached out, startling her. She stared at his outstretched hand for just an instant before he grabbed her and pulled her behind him—the same way she had pulled him in her dream. They chased Cordelia down the corridor, Leove trailing behind them. Kieran's excitement spilled over into her where their hands touched and she found herself quickening her step to keep up.

Cordelia led them to the Bridge. It was more a crew comfort than a necessary structure, Cordelia herself controlling everything in the ship. Still, Gal sat in the captain's chair, Isuma at Flight Control, Thomas at Navigation, and Rayne at Tactical.

Gal scratched his arm nervously as he stared out the massive window at the planet below.

Rayne spent as much time staring at Gal as she spent staring at her console. The expression on her face suggested he was as much a tactical threat as anything out there.

Sarrin stared out the window at the green and purple planet: Etar 1.

Kieran squeezed her arm once. "Ever been here?" he asked, his voice low.

"Just to transfer ships." After she'd survived the exploding Earth, it seemed the best thing to do was get as far away from the central planet as possible, as quickly as possible.

"It's gorgeous," he continued. "The sea is purple because of the high manganese content and the specialized bacteria that feed on it. The view from the southern mountain range is incredible. We should go there." He squeezed her arm again.

She caught the corners of her mouth turning up as she turned to look at him. But a sensation of regret and pain crept across their touching skin. Kieran's too shiny skin already looking tight and dry, his lips pressed into a line. She fed soothing through the place where they touched.

His face relaxed. "Thanks," he smiled at her. Still the subtle hum of pain was there.

Gal grumbled, leaning forward in his chair. "Where are you taking us?"

Isuma lifted her hands off the flight console to show she wasn't in control.

Cordelia had a hand on the back of Isuma's chair. She watched the window with interest but made no move to the physical controls. "The forest preserve."

Gal's face blanched. "The forest?"

"Mhmm." Her fuzzy slippers bounced as she tapped her foot.

"They want to find the Poet, not a bunch of… trees." Gal's face had gone white.

Cordelia looked back at him, quirking an eyebrow. "It's a good hiding spot for someone that doesn't want to be found. And it's close to the Central City."

Gal started to argue but she stopped him.

"Besides, they'll know the second Galiant Idim drops into their city."

His eyes opened wide. "I'm not going."

"Yes, you are."

He gestured around. "We have to go find the other Augments, the settlers on the outpost planets; there are plenty of people who need help. Away from Etar."

She raised her eyebrow again. "The others can do that. Your mission is down there. Isn't it? Truly?"

He stood, stepping towards her, his finger raised as though

to make his point. "Cordelia, I—." But he didn't finish, a hole opened in the floor and swallowed him up.

Kieran let go of Sarrin's arm and rushed forward. "Where did he go?"

"To the surface." Cordelia looked around. "What? He wouldn't have gone on his own. Who's next?"

"Is it safe?"

"You wont go splat at the bottom, if that's what you're worried about. Think of it like a big slide."

Kieran shook his head, sharing a bemused grin with Sarrin and rolling his eyes.

But satin was intrigued by the easy access to the planet hundreds of kilometres below. When they had talked about it before, not many had volunteered for the mission. It was better that way. A small group could travel unseen.

Gal and Rayne would go. Grant had volunteered immediately, so had Alex, the young boy Sarrin had saved so many years ago in Evangecore, and another named Luca. And Kieran. They would be able to find Halud and bring him back.

Alex stepped up to the edge of the port and jumped in, followed by Luca, and then Rayne.

Grant walked up behind Sarrin, nearly landing his hand on the small of her back before she flinched away. "You're next, Sar."

She stared at the opening, that presumably would carry them safely through the atmosphere and to the planet below. The planet where Halud waited. She took Kieran's hand in her own and stepped forward.

Kieran's hand tugged back, his feet rooted on the floor. The twinge of regret turned into a throb. "Sarrin," he said, his voice heavy, "I'm not going with you."

All of her breath escaped her, her body suddenly numb as she stood in the middle of the bridge.

"I can't. I can't be out of the tank more than a few hours."
He turned his gaze to the exposed skin on his arms, red, raw,
and scarred.

Her eyes darted wildly—he never talked about his burns,
never even hinted they might be a problem. Until now.

"But you have to go." He turned his bright eyes on her.
"Rescue Halud."

She gasped, air rushing in. "But you're getting better.
We'll bring the regen-tank."

He shook his head. "It's part of Cordelia."

She gulped. "Then I'll stay with you."

His lips turned up, but he shook his head, no.

"You need me." She looked to Leove, for the doctor to
agree.

"That might be true," he told her quietly. "But I'll be okay.
Your brother needs you more. I need to stay here. I wish I
could come with you, but I'll be here when you get back." He
stepped back, pulling his hand away from her. Separating
them.

Her breath caught in her throat, nearly doubling her over.
Suddenly, Grant was there, his arm wrapping across her
middle, tugging her. She took a confused step back, closer to
the hole in the floor.

Kieran set his gaze on Grant. "Remember what we talked
about."

Grant swallowed dryly and nodded.

"Find him," Kieran said, meeting her eyes for what felt like
the last time.

But how could she?

Her gaze fell to the floor, blinking at the hole, until it
swallowed her whole too.

* * *

Galiant Idim landed with both feet on the ground and
promptly fell over, rolling across the soft forest floor. He

huffed, biting back the urge to scream Cordelia's name, knowing it would only bring him more trouble. As he lay flat on his back, breath heaving, he took in the tall, narrow trees stretching up into the blue-purple sky.

Two Augments appeared a few metres away landing steadily. They looked around, scanning their surroundings—the fools had been wearing clothes provided by Cordelia, but they seemed unperturbed by their sudden nakedness. Rayne appeared shortly after, landing in a defensive crouch, neat and ready as always.

But she had no idea what was waiting for them here. Gal hauled himself to his feet, his heart already racing. Of all the places, why did Cordelia have to drop them here? When his shuttle had crash landed here twenty-odd years ago, they had let him go only because he had promised never to come back, and to never tell another soul what he had seen.

They had to find the fence at the edge of the city—if Cordelia had any sense, she would have put them right next to it. He looked around for any hint of the twenty-foot construction, but didn't pick out the glint of metal alloy in any direction.

Rayne craned her neck to look into the trees. She shivered once. "We should get out of here, the Speakers won't be happy if they find us here."

"They won't be happy to find us anywhere," said Gal.

Sarrin appeared amidst a rustle of leaves, Grant immediately behind. She scrambled to her feet and stared into he sky.

"This is all of us," Grant said.

"Good," snapped Gal, although he still couldn't see the way out.

Grant spun around, taking in his surroundings. "Where are we?"

"Somewhere we shouldn't be."

"The forest preserve on Etar," answered Rayne. "Eighty hectares of trees and wild lands. The Gods forbid us to enter."

Gal's heart dropped. "Only eighty?"

She spared him the barest of glances. "Eighty."

"Four years ago, it was two hundred. When it was Indaer, the planet was almost entirely forest."

"The cities are expanding, they needed more space for the folk." Rayne fidgeted, working her hands like she was itching to hold a laz-rifle.

"Still…." Gal shut his eyes. He half-expected Aaron to show up with some snide remark, but he was gone, had been for weeks. If he were here, no doubt Aaron would have said something about the disappearance of the forest preserve, but he wasn't, so the edge of regret was entirely Gal's. He sighed. "We need to get moving."

"Central City lies at the eastern edge of the forest preserve," said Rayne. She pointed to a pale fungus growing on one side of the tree. "That's this way."

"We should see how far it is," said Grant, "there's no guarantee we're on the edge, or the right edge." Before Gal could stop him, the Augment jumped ten feet into the air and started scaling one of the trees like he was climbing a ladder. A piece of bark broke off in his hand, tumbling to the ground.

The tree swayed under Grant's weight, leaves rustling, and Gal gritted his teeth. A branch snapped somewhere behind him, sending his heart into his chest. The naked male Augment broke off part of a leafy bush and used some vine to tie it around himself. "Don't," Gal tried, but it was too late— they would know.

Grant landed beside him, the impact sending a shudder through the ground. "Not far," he said, "maybe five kilometres. I can see the Speakers' Tower, same as it looks on the feeds."

Gal picked his way quickly across the forest floor, keeping a careful eye on the path in front of him. Five kilometres to the fence. The village would be farther away than that. Maybe they could make it before anyone had time to notice they were here. That would be best.

Never mind the danger that waited on the other side of the fence. Another place he had said he would never return. One thing at a time.

Bessie him, Grant suddenly stopped, beat his chest, and let out a loud whoop.

"What are you doing?" Gal hissed.

Grant shrugged, strutting backwards and flinging his arms out. "We've been cooped up for a long time."

"Don't." Gal tried to grab his arm but missed.

"How long have you been on that ship. It must feel good to stretch your legs. There's no UECs here. Live a little, while you can."

Gal groaned. He might not be living that much longer. This stupid forest preserve. What would his life have been like if his shuttle had never crashed here all those years ago. If he hadn't been trying to sneak away early and meet Aaron in the city before they were returned to the Academy on Earth. If he hadn't chosen to fly the restricted airspace above the forest.

He heard a peel of laughter behind him.

Grant and the other Augments ran through the trees. It was the girl who squealed.

Gal stared, frozen.

Grant and Alex turned, swatting at each other, running faster than Gal could ever hope to. They yelled, and came to jump at Luca. She leaped away, rolling fluidly, before getting up and giving chase.

"Hey," he shouted.

Grant spared him a glance.

"Stop it!" Gal waved his arms frantically.

Grant switched directions and leapt past the other two, who now seemed to be chasing him. "Come on, Gal. We're just blowing off a little steam."

Gal looked at the young men and woman. Kids really, they weren't any older than twenty. They deserved to run around and be young for once in their lives.

He shook his head, "It's not safe here."

Grant frowned, and then sighed. He muttered, "You're lucky Kieran likes you, for whatever reason." But he waved to the others, and they fell in line.

Gal resumed his path, watching carefully where he placed each foot.

The others stayed behind him at least.

"You've been here before," a familiar voice in his head said. Gal whipped around, looking for Aaron.

A loud snap sounded in the trees, and suddenly the ground jerked away and he found himself hanging in the air, upside down.

* * *

Sarrin clutched the net reflexively, tough vines pressing into her legs and shoulder as she tried impossibly to pull away from the others.

Gal beside her muttered, "Oh no. Not again."

Her heart was beating too fast, too erratic.

"What is this?" said Rayne, her voice higher pitched than normal.

Gal only groaned, pressing his forehead into the netting.

Sarrin's skin crawled. They were all wrapped up in it, squished and tumbled against each other. The others started to panic, she felt it welling up around her like a cloud. She tucked he hands protectively into her chest, trying to make herself as small as possible. But Gal was right beside her. She couldn't keep her skin from touching his, no matter how she shifted. The last time she had touched him she had taken his energy, all his pain and hurt, and nearly died of it herself.

All that radiated from him now was a kind of defeat, an eerie calm taking over. It was enough to keep the black clouds from taking over completely. Enough that she could still see, knew they were in a net, and knew that whoever had set the net hadn't yet arrived.

"Damn UECs," Grant grunted. His elbow jarred her in the side as he tugged on the vines. "Help me with this, Luca." The girl beside him shifted, and they both grabbed onto opposite sides of spacing in the net, pulling and ripping, but the material—whatever it was—was too strong.

Sarrin turned away, her eyes searching -- there was always a way out. Escape routes… there! Her eyes focussed at the top where the sides of the net came together, tied with more of the vine-material. She could undo the knot. They would fall, there might be injuries, but it wouldn't be fatal.

Pulling herself up, she wedged her shoulder into the narrow opening, and started to work the knot. Her fingernails started to bleed as she picked at the cord, but she couldn't feel them, her hands numb from the wrist down since experiments in Evangecore had stripped the nerves away. She pressed down images of Halud and Kieran, even of Grant and Luca and Alex, and picked at the strand that had already started to come loose. If the UECs found them here, there would be no way to help anyone.

Slowly, the vine started to unweave. She pulled frantically, so close and yet there was still more to undo. Knots upon knots. Almost there.

Without warning, they fell, flying through the air and crashing to the ground with a thump, bouncing over one another. Sarrin coiled into herself, rolling to her feet. She hadn't been fast enough; they were surrounded. But not UECs after all. Her eyes took in the scene rapidly: Wild men, pieces of animal hide tied around their loins, tan and leathered skin covered in designs made with dark paint. Each held a sharpened spear, the glinting, dark tips pointed at them.

They outnumbered them three-to-one.

"Galiant Idim." The words rolled unnaturally off the tongue of a tall male, inky designs rolling all the way down his arms.

Gal swallowed noisily and dragged himself to his knees.

"You were never to return. You have broken your word."

Beside her, Grant signalled, his hand barely moving as he communicated a plan.

But it wouldn't be safe. These warriors were strong—she could see it in the way they moved, the subtle and continuous twitches as their muscles readied and rebalanced. She gave subtle shake of her head, motioning for him to stand down.

Grant frowned.

She shook her head again. If they were to engage, she guessed, there would be no option for her but to release the monster that churned inside of her. And who knew what it would do—what she would do. Not for the first time that day, she closed her eyes, imagining Kieran had been able to come with them. He would have stuck a big grin on his face and shouted 'Howdy,' turning them, however unlikely, into his friends.

Like he had done to her.

"It's a simple misunderstanding," said Gal. "We were just trying to make our way out of your forest when we stepped in the net. We wouldn't have even crossed paths, except." He was still kneeling, and he gestured at the fallen vines around him.

The leader grunted. "You had to access the forest somehow."

"Ah," Gal frowned. "It's a long story. Our, um, ship

dropped us off here by accident."

"Another shuttle malfunction?" the wild man asked skeptically.

"Urubane, I'm not a threat to you or your people. Please, bring Ruel, she'll—"

"Ruel is not well."

"Oh."

The one Gal had called Urubane shifted his spear.

Gal threw his hands up. "Ruel said I could be trusted, right."

"We also said you were not to return."

"I know. But I'm telling you, accidents happen. I can be trusted, and these people, they're friends of mind, and they can be trusted too. Just let us go. We won't even see the village, there won't be anything to tell."

Urubane frowned. "I cannot do that. Our way of life is already threatened." He lifted his spear.

Gal shuddered. "Don't kill them."

He sighed, cold eyes frowning down at them. "It is not my decision. We will bring them."

"Wait," Gal said, jumping to his feet. "Are you sure?"

One of the warriors grabbed Sarrin around the shoulders and lifted her up. She flew a short way through the air—almost as if she was too light for him—and landed on her feet. Around her, the other Augments did the same.

"There is no choice now. You have brought them this far," said Urubane, his deep voice rumbling through the trees.

"I'm telling you, we didn't mean to enter the forest. We were just trying to get out." But at a quick signal from Urubane, Gal quieted and hung his head. He glanced back at the others quickly, almost apologetically, and followed the wild men as they led them deeper into the forest.

Grant's eyes met Sarrin's, worried. She shook her head again, and fell into line, the others doing the same. The dark edges of her vision crept in, the trance reminding her that, if she allowed it, it could take over and destroy everything in sight. But that wouldn't be wise. There was no way to stop her once it took over, no way to tell it who was friend or foe.

If only Kieran had come.

"Gal," Rayne squeaked. She side-stepped her way to the captain, dodging a spear tip. "What's going on? You know these people?"

He smiled faintly. "When I was sixteen, my shuttle crashed in these woods. They call themselves the Uruhu. They live here, outside the city walls. They're very secretive. I was lucky, I think, that I was so young and they trusted me not to tell anyone else."

"I've never heard of anyone living in the woods."

Gal nodded. "I know."

The warriors prodded them through the trees until a faint path began to appear. Shuffling on the increasingly worn path, Sarrin marched, somehow a prisoner once again. Maybe that was just how it was supposed to be. At least they weren't in UEC hands again; these people might even be hiding from the UECs themselves. Perhaps, once they explained, they could work together. And instead of running, instead of counting escape routes, she found herself inexplicably drawn forward.

A crunching noise sounded far in the woods. She turned her head towards it at the same time as the warriors did. A flash of movement, a dark, rough shape, moving. The texture and colour looked like the hide the man in front of her wore.

There weren't supposed to be animals in the woods either.

Where had they come from? Escaped stock from the luxury meat farms?

The leader nodded once, passing a similar but unfamiliar signal, and two of the warriors left the formation, running in the direction of the noise.

She almost went with them, but a tap on her arm with a spear reminded her to stay in place.

The footpath twisted around a corner, and suddenly they were on the edge of a village. People paused to stare at them, turning from their tasks. Fifty or more. Sarrin's step faltered. Gal had said village, but this was a sprawling community.

The warriors herded them past short huts that couldn't be meant for more than sleeping, and large, open communal areas where folk sat and children played.

They brought them to a cage.

Gal entered willingly, easily.

Sarrin, behind him, stopped. The monster flared. Grant was right, they should have fought their way out, back in the woods, when it was easier.

She looked over her shoulder, her mind painting the fastest path back to the tall trees that surrounded them. She would run, she could. She could move fast enough to evade the guards, and then escape through the village. In the forest, she would run, in any direction. Away. Forever.

She took a step, exploding to the right, faster than they could track.

But a hand grabbed her out of mid-air. Reflexively, she jerked to free it, but the hand held firm. Her breath caught as her eyes went wide.

Flashes of memory flooded her: the woods, a sleeping hut, a woman with a newborn child. Her eyes locked onto the guard who held her, his hand nearly burning her flesh where he gripped. She dropped to her knees. He held her wrist tight, squeezing the bundle of nerves, pain and everything else shooting up her arm.

Her own life flashed: Halud in the orchard, her bunk at Evangecore, the hunt, isolation, and endless combat drills.

His face paled, and he pushed her into the open door of the cage, throwing her with enough force and speed she slammed against the far side.

"Sarrin, are you okay?" Grant crouched down in front of her, as the door slammed shut behind them.

She lifted herself up onto her elbows, nodding. But the cage was too small. Two-metres square. Her mind started to whirr. Small spaces were a trap. For her, for them. The edges of her vision started to close in.

"Sarrin," Grant said, calling her back into the bright daylight that shone into the uncovered cage.

"What are they going to do to us?" Rayne gripped the bars and shook.

Gal went to her, placing a hand on her shoulder. "Rayne, I —"

She turned on him, anger in her dark eyes. "This is your fault."

He backed away, head hanging.

Alex strained at the bars, trying to break them open, but it was no use. They were wood, yes she could see, but the wood had been coated in dried sap, making it black and hard. The beams were tied with vines, but a similar coating covered the knots, making them unbreakable.

She fought to control her breathing, her vision swimming in and out of focus. But she couldn't lose control, not here, not now.

Escape routes: zero.

The guard who had caught her spoke to the others, hind hand gestures frantic. His gaze met hers.

Probability of survival: zero.

TWO

THE SOUND PULLED HER from an erratic dream, and she blinked furiously in the daylight. They had been four days in the cage, without food or water. She could still run if she had to, but there had been no opportunity for escape.

Still half in the dream, she flinched as another target flew at her. There were too many, and they slammed into her while she was too weak to dodge effectively. The projections were only light, but in the dream they burned, each hit followed by a neural shock they used to punish her for failure.

She collapsed under their weight.

A pair of blue eyes met her. "Sarrin?" It was Grant. He had a hand outstretched as though to shake her, and she flew backwards, her spine pressing up against the walls of the cage.

The bars soared up to the sky and then cut across on the roof. The criss-cross of beams made perfect squares against the bright sky. It looked too much like the tangent lines on the walls of the holographic training chamber at Evangecore.

Her body started to prepare, the muscles becoming taught and springy, her vision more acute, her thoughts moving quickly.

There were five targets in the chamber with her.

No, not targets. People. Gal and Rayne and Grant and Alex and Luca.

Her heart rate was too high.

Grant stared back at her. "Sarrin, relax. But he was not relaxed with his tense muscles and his wide watching pupils. He was already standing up, already backing away.

"You're dreaming," he said steadily. "You're going to hurt someone." She looked around at the others, pressed to the far side. Initially she had tried not to fall asleep, but with nothing to do but sit, and no food or water, eventually she had to succumb.

Monster.

Beyond the cage, a group of the Uruhu warriors stood, spears in hand. She felt their eyes on her, watching. They had watched all of them, but especially her.

She hadn't seen the guard who had touched her, the one with the cozy hut and the newborn child, since the first day. They hadn't seen Urubane either.

She drew her legs up tighter to her chest, rolling over on the ground.

"Sarrin," Grant said again. This time more urgent.

She looked up and the warriors had approached.

"Filthy," one said, in the odd guttural tones they all seemed to speak in as though they normally spoke something other than the standard dialect.

Another kicked dirt into the cage. An image flashed in her mind of his knife cutting across her throat.

The edges of her vision clouded in.

"Sarrin," Grant called her back.

She shook her head, as though it would fling the black clouds away.

Grant stepped up to the bars, putting himself between her and the guards. "Stand down," he ordered them.

The Uruhu looked at each other.

"Back off. Go away," he said.

The men didn't. "This is our land."

Grant put his hands on the bars and pulled. "Sorry you dragged us here."

"They should have killed you," said the one.

"You were sent to destroy us, and they argue your fate," said the other, waving his hand flippantly at the large hut at the edge of the clearing.

"Why would we be here to kill you? We didn't even know you existed until you trapped us in that net and brought us all here. We're trying to escape them, same as you guys."

The Uruhu suddenly paled and stepped back.

Grant preened.

But the Uruhu were not looking in his direction, they had their eyes fixed to the ground, heads bowed.

The door to the large hut opened. First exited Urubane, and then four others, all heavily decorated and heavily marked. Last to come was a withered old woman, leaning heavily on a walking stick.

Sarrin felt her attention fixate on the old woman, as though she could do nothing to control it. The woman's spine was stooped, her heavily marked skin wrinkled and sagging, but her body must have stood tall and strong in her youth. The power she exuded gripped her like a solid wave, and had Sarrin been standing, she would have dropped to her knees. She wore stacks of wooden bands, and jewellery made of greying white bone, and as she walked, she held a swaying crystal pendulum in front of her.

The woman paused, her failing body writhing as she coughed, the hacking echoing through the silence that had descended on the village. Her pendulum swung toward the Uruhu warriors by the side of the cage, and they fell back in the dirt as she watched, the creases at the edges of her eyes crinkling.

Gal stood. "Ruel?"

She hobbled toward him. "Galiant," she said, a faint smile coming to her face. She reached through the bars and cupped his face. "You've grown. Twenty-two years. What will they say about you?"

Gal bent his head.

Ruel laughed, her voice weak and gravely. "Galiant Idim, destroyer of worlds—is that what you think?"

Urubane was beside her in a flash, reaching in to pull back her hand. "Careful, Ruel."

She raised a single eyebrow. "You think to caution me, young Urubane?"

He pressed his lips tightly, but continued anyway, hissing under his breath, "These are demon creations, sent by the Others to destroy us. You know how they plot."

"We have not yet ascertained their reason for being here," she said pleasantly.

"We found them in the woods, near their city," said Urubane.

Gal interjected quickly. "It was a mistake, just a misunderstanding." He caught his breath, looking wary. "Our ship… it dropped us off in the wrong place."

"Or the right place," said Ruel.

"No, no. Definitely the wrong place. You told me not to come back."

Ruel shook her head. "There are no mistakes, only turning points of fate. Each of you is exactly where you need to be."

Gal blanched.

Urubane hissed, "They've come for us."

Ruel's pendulum flung out to the side, pointing at Urubane. A pointed wave rippled out from its tip and hit him in the arm.

Sarrin shook her head to clear her imagination.

"I have been awaiting your return, Galiant," Ruel declared.

"Pardon?" Gal sputtered.

Calm child. Sarrin gasped, pressing against the bars as the words echoed clearly in her head, strong and powerful.

You are powerful too. In greater ways than you think. Sarrin's gaze met Ruel's, even as the old woman continued to speak to Gal, and in an instant knew the voice in her head was the old woman's.

Ruel turned from the cage, to Urubane. "Galiant has been our guest here. These children need water. They need food. They need clothes."

Urubane opened his mouth to argue, but the old woman held up her pendant at him.

"You do not have eyes to see they are afraid. Feed them, or they truly will have a reason to want you dead."

The warrior set his shoulders and gestured to his men.

I see the reasons for your arrival, said Ruel. *You will not find what you are looking for here. Never mind though, all will work out as it should.* The pendulum swung at Sarrin, a ripple shooting forward.

Sarrin squeezed her eyes shut, unable to dodge before it crossed the small cage. But instead of a punishment as Urubane's had been, this arrow filled her with a glowing serenity. The dark clouds blew back from the edges of her vision, and her heart rate returned to normal.

Ruel smiled at her, a teasing flash in her eyes, before she turned back to Gal, stroking his face and talking quietly to him.

Sarrin stared. Even the monster had no answers, had no way to comprehend what she had seen, and felt. She stood, her mind still thrumming with the glow of whatever Ruel had some to her, hoping to speak with her to… take her hand and hold it, clutch it to her chest.

Ruel met her gaze, smiling, but she pulled her hand away from Gal and out of the cage, turning away.

The guards pushed food and water and some basic clothes through the bars. Gal took them from the guards, frowning once at Sarrin, before he passed the supplies to the others, who leapt hungrily, chugging the water and tearing at the meagre bread and dried meat.

But Sarrin gripped the bars, watching the old woman. They were still in the cage, but her claustrophobia was gone, the panic and fear was simply gone. The monster was quiet. What was this place? More importantly, who were these people?

* * *

Gal pulled at the thin, dry bread, breaking off a piece before putting it into his mouth to chew.

He kept his eyes on the ground, refusing to look at Aaron who stood in front of him.

Aaron tapped his foot impatiently.

Beside him, too far away, Rayne sad huddled, chewing fervently on the hard bread. She looked terrible, subdued and sunken, and he wanted nothing more than to wrap his arms around her, break them out of this cage, and take her far, far away.

But, she wanted nothing to do with him.

"Want to talk about it?" Aaron said.

"Go away," he murmured.

"Come on, Gal."

"Go away."

Rayne turned to him, her dark eyes glaring.

Too loud.

For a time, Aaron had gone. When they were sitting on Cordelia, when he'd go between forgetful moments of relaxation and empowering thoughts of delusional grandeur, Aaron had left him alone.

Until he'd shown up in the forest and Gal had missed stepping into the trap.

"So this is where you were that day?" said Aaron. "The day you were late and almost missed the Academy transport?"

Gal looked up. How much did Aaron know?

Aaron laughed. "I know everything. I'm in your head. But the real Aaron never knew, and it helps to have him to explain it to, isn't it? Or else how would you keep it all straight in your own head?"

Resignedly Gal admitted, "It was the first time anyone had ever told me they didn't believe in the Gods or the Speakers. The first time I'd ever thought a person could question it."

Rayne turned her gaze on him, her voice cutting, "The Speakers tell us the Will of the Gods."

He stared in shock at her, at her beautiful face. At least she was talking to him.

Aaron still loomed.

"You've been here before," Aaron confirmed. "In a secret village in the woods."

Gal nodded his assent.

"Why are they really here? The Speakers would never allow this." Aaron gestured to the Uruhu.

Gal shut his eyes. He couldn't answer out loud. Rayne was already staring at him. Not that he could really answer anyway—how had they escaped annihilation when so many others had succumbed?

He scanned her again, now that she'd gone back to picking at the bread. Beautiful and dark. The light brought out the richness in her skin in a way the artificial ship lighting never could, in a way he almost didn't remember.

He smiled in spite of the situation.

"Gal?"

"What?" he snapped, spinning his head around. Aaron was gone. In his place stood Grant, the gruff one who had an implant in his back that would give him a protective second skin at a moment's notice. He had a burn mark by his eye, the only trauma he'd suffered while Kieran, his engineer, had been burned to a crisp.

Rayne would never forgive him. Not for the part that he'd played in the ship explosion. Definitely not for the part that he'd inadvertently made her play.

"You have some pull with these people."

Gal squirmed. That wasn't quite true.

Grant continued anyway, his voice quick, frustrated. "I can make an explosive with some of the items I see in the village. If you can get them to bring them to us without them realizing what I'm building, I might be able to get us out of here."

Gal raised his eyebrows. He looked at Rayne, who still sat curled up against the wall, her expression dismal. "Do you think it will blow through the bars?" He'd watched while the Augments took turns first pulling on the wooden bars, and then trying to cut through them with a sharp rock—all to no avail.

Grant glanced behind him at the dark wood coated in layers of strong sap. "It's the best option we have," he shrugged.

"A bomb, Gal?" a second voice caught his ear. Aaron had reappeared.

Things died in explosions: Aaron, Cornelius, Kieran nearly, heck, even Earth died in an explosion.

But they couldn't stay. Ruel had told him that, when she'd muttered sweet, hopeful things into his ear.

The Uruhu had planned to kill him when he had come before. Ruel had said he was worth trusting, and so he got to live. But they had told him what would happen if he ever returned.

The Uruhu had a secret—no one knew they were out here —and they wanted to keep it that way. They were warriors. They had no qualms about killing to suit their needs.

He nodded once at Grant. "What do you need?"

                          * * *

"Hey, Urubane." Gal's heart beat quickly in his chest as he called to the man.

The tall warrior stepped up to the side of the cage.

"Is this really necessary?" Gal gestured at the cage around them. "You know me. I mean, Ruel said—"

"You were told never to return."

"I know, I know." He held up his hands. "I swear to you it was an accident. I had forgotten all about you and your secret life here. Otherwise I wouldn't have come in through the forest. It's just that we didn't want anyone to see us coming."

Urubane lifted a single eyebrow. It made his eyes dance, and Gal realized with a start they were each two different colours, split down the middle: blue and white. How long had they been separated from the rest of the population? Genetics had done some odd things in that time.

"You would not forget."

Gal gulped. No, how would anyone forget the simple little fact there was a group of people living with their own rules inside the forest preserve.

"Say, I'm curious what that is." Gal pointed to a nearby jug, forcing his voice to stay relaxed even while his heart threatened to jump out of his skin. The warriors would take turns going to the jug and rubbing some of the liquid on their lips and their hands. Some kind of oil, Grant guessed.

"The firewater is not for your kind."

"But what is it? I just want to know."

Urubane grunted and turned away.

Gal stepped back from the bars.

He caught Rayne staring at him, an unreadable expression of disappointment on her face. She shook her head and turned away.

He reached up and tugged on his hair. At least he was trying. He might have gotten them into this mess, but at least he was trying to help get them out of it.

"You plot something," Urubane said. His voice booming so all the other guards could hear. He was warning them.

Gal hung his head.

Urubane turned back to face him. "Do not insult me so, Galiant Idim."

Suddenly, Urubane pushed back from the bars, looking up. "What is this?" he hissed.

It took Gal a minute to hear it: the thumping of a hovercraft, and looked into the sky. They would be nearly overhead—it was the only place you could hear the whump-whump of the otherwise silent machines.

Urubane yelled. "You have brought the great burning beast with you," he shouted at Gal before running away. "Ruel was wrong, you have come to destroy us."

The centre square was in motion, guards running back and forth, ushering women and children into the small huts. At the same time, Gal felt and saw the thin white gas being dropped from the hovercraft. It spilled out, starting on the edge of the village. They pulled out cloths and tied them over their faces, disappearing into the huts and slamming the doors.

The mist settled upon Gal's skin, cool and wet, like water. His breathing felt heavy, but clean, not unlike after a rainstorm on Earth. "It's okay," he shouted out. "Hey," he bounced to his feet and called out after the retreating Uruhu. "It's okay."

"It's protective for the forest preserve," Rayne shouted beside him. "It's safe."

Gal shared a look, and for a second they were a team again, until she turned away.

He ran a hand through his damp hair. What could he ever

say to her?

Sarrin coughed.

He turned.

The Augment was on her knees.

Grant ran to her, his lungs chortling as he went.

The others too winced and started to cough, softly at first but building.

Gal frowned. It was common knowledge that the Army sprayed the forest once a month, a mix of minerals and water to keep it healthy. It was safe.

Rayne, for the second time, met his gaze, as equally uncertain as his own. But she didn't cough.

Grant's limpet suit sprung out of his body, enveloping him.

Gal took another deep breath, but a tickle caught in his throat. Maybe the gas wasn't benign after all. He pulled his shirt-neck over his mouth and nose.

Sarrin's skin had gone pink. She dropped to the ground as the first blister began to show, more boiling up all over her body. Her eyes sprung open and she inhaled sharply—painfully. She coughed again, blood and sputum splashing on the ground.

Gal stood. Something in the mist was hurting them specifically, whether because of their metabolism or their physiology. "Hey!" he shouted out. Who knew how bad it would get. He threw his shoulder into the door of the cage.

Grant had a hand on Sarrin. His suit seemed to protect him, but the others had all started to bubble too.

"Help me with this," Gal shouted.

Grant took a second to look over—the exposed skin around his eye was freshly red and blistered—but he nodded and came to help. Together they rammed the door.

Rayne pulled strips of cloth from her old uniform and tied them across the Augments' mouths and noses, the same as Urubane and his warriors had done. She tied a strip across her own mouth.

The coughing didn't stop.

She looked over helpless at Gal.

"Hey!" he tried calling out again. "Please."

The door to one of the huts opened and shut quickly. From it slipped Ruel, limping as she did on her walking stick. Her pendant swung wildly ahead of her. Her skin flared red, but she persevered, slow and determined. She reached the door, somehow moving the massive brace aside.

The cage swung open.

"I've waited a long time for your return," she croaked, her pendant swinging wildly.

The Augments pushed through, Grant and Rayne dragging Sarrin.

Ruel snatched the pendant out of the air and held it to her chest. "Now my turn is done and it falls to you. You will return, and they will see," she said. "Now, go."

Gal stumbled forward, running with the others to the edge of the village. He owed his life, their lives, to Ruel. Again.

He looked back. She was still in the centre of the village, holding her pendant, her walking staff raised high in the air. Her skin had blistered until it was all white with cracked red lines. She muttered something, thumping her chest.

With one last beat, she met his gaze, her unnatural blue-white crystal eyes burning into him. Suddenly, she collapsed, falling to the ground. Her staff rolled away across the dirt, the pendant falling lifelessly, just like its owner.

* * *

Sarrin's own breathing rattled around in her ears deafeningly. Ahead of her, Grant called out, but she couldn't hear over her own wheezing and the high-pitched ringing in her head. Her skin was on fire.

Rayne kept looking back at her, frowning. Sarrin knew she had to go on—she had fallen too far back already; in

Evangecore, she would have been shot—but she couldn't, not anymore.

She paused, resting her hand against a tree. Her hands were red and oozing, probably just as badly as her face, but she couldn't feel it in the cold, dead, nerveless things.

Ahead, the others stopped at a wire fence, nearly thirty metres tall. Grant stopped, bending down, and Luca stepped smoothly into his clasped hands as he boosted her up. She flew into the air, clinging partway up the fence.

They were at the edge of the forest.

Somehow that milestone bolstered her for an instant and she stumbled forward.

Grant was still covered in his mottled grey-brown limpet suit, only the one eye exposed. With a gulp, Sarrin remembered when she had agreed to spar, lost control, and ripped the suit apart. "Sarrin, let me help you." He bent down again, his fingers interlaced for her to step into.

She felt sick as she stepped up, relying on the rote memory of hours of practice drills in Evangecore, and flew into the air. Her body moved automatically, catching then climbing.

Something tugged her hand, breaking the automatic rhythm. She paused, looking down. The nerveless, ulcerated skin had caught on part of the wire fence and ripped. Beneath the rent, she saw a flash of silver. She nearly lost her grip, but the good hand latched on, keeping her from falling.

Rounding the top, she let herself half-jump half-fall down the other side, too tired to climb. The landing set off a new round of coughing. For a minute, she knew nothing but the cough. When she came to, she was on her hands and knees.

"Sarrin?" Rayne's worried face appeared before her, her dark skin blending in with the growing dusk. Her eyes turned from Sarrin's face to her hands, and she rushed to cover the tear and the horrible silver skeleton.

Rayne's pupils were dilated fully in the dim light, but the

tension around the eyes showed her true panic. "Second degree chemical burns. We need to wash them and dress them immediately." She glanced around behind her. "We'll get there soon. Can you keep moving?"

Sarrin nodded. She could keep moving, even if she'd prefer to curl into the fetal position and wait for the inevitable, such a thing would never be tolerated in Evangecore.

"Come on." Rayne extended a hand.

Sarrin looked at it, but shook her head. What would happen if Sarrin were to touch Rayne in this state? A memory of Nurse Adelaide collapsing to the ground, dead, turned her stomach.

She pushed herself back onto her feet. And her feet miraculously continued forward.

There were no trees on this side, only bare shrubs and sparse grass that had managed to push its way through the con-plas slabs that lined the ground. It immediately felt hot and dusty, even in the descending night.

"Why is it fenced?" Alex's voice drifted back. At least her ears were getting clearer.

Gal grunted in response. "To keep the folk out, and the trees in."

"But isn't the forest meant to be a reminder?" asked Alex. "To keep us in touch with Earth?"

Sarrin stumbled, falling to the ground. Her breathing was hard and she fought to catch her breath.

Grant appeared, reaching out to grab her arm.

"Don't," she managed.

He pulled back. "Let me help you."

She could only shake her head.

"You look terrible," he said. "I don't understand." He reached for her again.

She flinched away.

"This is bad, Sarrin." His hand ran nervously across the

top of his ugly limpet suit, and he flinched as though he'd forgotten it was there, recoiling from the slick feel where his sandy hair should have been.

"You can barely walk. Let me help you." He reached out again. "Alex and Luca, they've got a cough, and my eye hurts like crazy, but you…." He shook his head.

"They've built weapons against me before," she said, forcing it all out in one breath and fighting for oxygen after.

"You think that nasty fertilizer-spray was designed against you." He pointed back in the direction of the forest.

The fence, she noted abjectly, couldn't be more than fifty yards behind.

"You're cracked. Gal thinks it's because our metabolisms are faster. And yours is faster than most, if I remember."

That was true. She'd been infected young, very young. That made everything the virus did more significant in her. It was why they chased her.

"They've got no way to know we're here. Unless they find your corpse out here on the concrete." He reached his arm out again.

She nodded and took it.

The slimy, slick skin under her fingers started to move and bulge.

"Whoa. It's never done that before," said Grant, staring down at his arm. "Ow."

Sarrin snatched her hand back. Stupid. She'd been distracted thinking about the UECs and weapons and metabolisms. She'd forgotten the biggest change the virus had made to her system: she could kill people with a touch.

"Don't touch me," she growled.

Grant stared down at his limpet-covered hand. Then at her. Then at the hand. Slowly, he reached out, testing. He pulled back with a yelp when the suit told him he had gotten too close.

"Sarrin…?"

She could do nothing but stare up at him and hope he didn't guess what a monster she truly was.

He sighed. "Come on, we have to keep moving."

She stared at her hands as she walked. The tear in the one kept flapping open, revealing a glimpse of the silver skeleton.

She wasn't even human.

Part virus. Part titanium.

She'd killed too many people. She couldn't even help it anymore. If Grant hadn't been wearing his protective suit, what would have happened?

Up ahead, Gal stayed low as he approached the first of the buildings: squat, two-story grey blocks lined up in perfect rows. It had been a long time since Sarrin had seen a UEC city. But she had not forgotten the standard layout, always the same pattern, and she followed Gal and the others as they dodged from cover to cover.

There were still a few people out on the streets. Curfew hadn't descended on them yet, which would bring with it patrol drones and more cameras. All they had to do now was be inconspicuous enough not to raise suspicion, and not to get the attention of any of the drones.

"Sarrin, come on," Grant whispered, waving his arm.

She braced against a building for a minute, drawing in breath.

"Gods," said Rayne, turning to Gal, "she needs oxygen, a hospital."

Gal pressed his lips together but shook his head. "We can't."

"But my father."

He shook his head.

Sarrin knew she was slowing them down. They waited in a tight little group for her to stumble up to them.

Alex watched her with concern. He'd come because he

thought she was a hero, the way she'd saved him during a training exercise in Evangecore. But she hadn't saved anyone —they didn't let any of the kids die in Evangecore without their saying so—she'd only damned herself.

Some hero she had to be right now, panting and gasping her way through the city. He'd been a fool to follow her here.

They'd all been fools.

Gal slipped away, angling them closer to the city centre, to the tall Speakers' tower with its smooth glassine dome raised above everything else like a beacon.

The Gods were probably laughing at her.

She slumped against the wall, letting her legs slide out from underneath her.

"Sarrin, we have to go," said Grant.

She shook her head. Her eyes started to close. The Speakers saw everything.

She'd had a chance to leave with Kieran on the Observer ship and escape. That was their plan anyhow. But now she was here and he was thousands of light-years away.

It had been wishful thinking anyway, an attempt to ignore the inevitable. She was a monster, an enemy, and she was better off dead. The breathing and gasping was just another reminder that she was still, annoyingly, alive.

She would spend her life like this, sneaking around, praying to the Gods that their Speakers wouldn't see them—like they did now.

Grant leaned down, shouting in her face, "Sarrin. Get up!"

The Speakers were too powerful. They controlled everything—from the drab buildings in their predictable layout, interstellar ships, newsfeeds, medicine…. If she was an enemy, she was an enemy. There was no way to overcome that.

Medicine?

Her eyes focussed, past Grant's shouting face, to the vid-screen plastered on the wall behind him.   A smiling news anchor, her smile broad enough Sarrin could tell it had been surgically altered, reported another medical breakthrough, something about children.   The screen cut, and it flashed to Halud, sitting calmly surrounded by medical equipment.

It was a re-run, she had seen it before, picked up on the feed-capture device Kieran had built for her. But she watched her brother, leaning forward.

Her breathing came easier.

Halud had tried.   He had summoned Courage and tried, he'd not succeeded, not entirely, but he'd gotten her free. Now it was her turn, she owed it to him to try, no matter what.

"We have to find him," she whispered.

Grant glanced behind him so see what she meant.   He nodded at her. "You have to get up first."

She braced, gritting her teeth against the pain.   The monster flared, but for once their goals were the same, and it lifted her to her feet.   She looked to the vid-screen. We're coming, Halud.

THREE

"SOLDIER, RELEASE ME." HALUD PRESSED his hands against the clear permaglass, banging it twice. He was in the Speakers' rehabilitation facility—a little known aspect of the prisons. What the folk did know was that sometimes a person could get confused, could start to doubt the Gods, and they were taken for a special re-education to be shown again the incredible power and goodness of Faith, Prudence, Strength.... Some of these people returned to the folk peacefully, others, they were told, fell so deeply in love with the Gods that they chose to join one of the struggling outer-rim colonies—their inevitable death due to starvation was the Will of the Gods. And the folk rejoiced. Too often, Halud had been the one to bear the news.

The guard glanced dolefully over his shoulder, giving Halud only the briefest of considerations.

Halud screamed louder. If he could get the guard to listen to him, he could convince him to release the seal and take Halud to the rebels. Probably even convince the guard to join the cause himself. He'd always had that gift. But the ensign was defactly ignoring him. Still, eventually, he would have to give in. For days, Halud had been banging and shouting at the clear barrier. Someone would hear him. Someone.

He stopped as the door to the anteroom slipped open, the guard coming to attention as he acknowledged the unannounced visitor.

Commandant Amelia Mallor strode in, an ostentatious cloak billowing behind her. She wasted no time and stopped directly in front of the ensign. Three words came from her mouth, though Halud didn't know what they were. And she made a quick hand gesture.

The soldier nodded and stepped to the control panel quickly.

The permaglass separated, the smooth door to his cell pulling back.

"Poet," she barked.

Halud gulped.

"Honourable Hap Lansford has requested your presence."

"Hap?" His brow furrowed in surprise. "What does he want with me?" He'd sat in front of the first Speaker often enough, but always as a friend, always on the same side. This new type of meeting, well, nothing good could come of it.

The commandant's only reaction was a subtle frown. "My duty is to transport you."

He crossed his arms. "Tell the Speaker I refuse."

The commandant marched into the cell, taking impossibly quick strides, and latched her hand onto his arm. Just above his elbow, she pinched, and he nearly doubled over. "You will comply with the demands of the Gods." She pushed him ahead of her, holding him by the elbow, and he was powerless to resist.

"You don't have to keep pushing me like that," Halud said, tugging his arm from the commandant's grip as they marched through the twisting maze of corridors. "I know where I'm going."

She sighed, shoving him, but she did let go of his arm.

"What did you do with my friends?" he asked, "The rebels

I was with?"

No answer.

"Even you must be able to see that this is wrong."

"Pathetic," she mumbled.

"It seems beneath you to be escorting prisoners."

Silence, again.

Pleased, Halud pushed on. "I thought you would have been out hunting in your warship. But maybe you changed your mind."

She slammed him into the wall. "Do not play your wily word tricks on me, Poet." Her voice rose, "I hate Augments, and I would kill every last one if my ship hadn't been taken. You and your pathetic sister. She stopped me. Somehow. I don't know how."

The quick expression of confusion surprised Halud.

"Now I'm here, babysitting you, a man whose only strength is his words. Useless. I should be hunting that insidious freightship full of Augments. 005478F is a far more dangerous adversary than any of the others."

Halud blinked. "The freightship? Sarrin? She's alive?"

She pushed away from him, slamming him into the wall, striding away as Halud fought to catch his breath. He glanced at the empty hallway leading back the way they came. If Sarrin and the others were still alive….

"Don't think about running," the commandant's voice was cold and demanding.

He followed her, suddenly bolstered. "Hap is wasting his time. I'm not his puppet."

"You certainly seem like one."

"Not anymore."

"We'll see."

"What do you care anyhow? I thought you wanted to destroy Augments."

"I serve the Gods."

"Why?"

"The Gods look after us. It is because of them that we thrive."

"Is this thriving? You want to destroy hundreds of children who have been captured and tortured, lost their parents, and who knows what else. My sister, Sarrin, she couldn't even speak. I've seen videos of them electrocuting her until blood poured from her eyes."

A hand twitched up to her chest, her five fingers together at the centre. The harshness in her features softened, only for an instant. Then, as though remembering herself, the scowl returned, ten times deeper than it had been. "Silence. Your word games and inflections will not work on me, Poet."

But he hadn't imagined it—the commandant had a heart, a weakness at least. He opened his mouth again, but she clamped her hand down on the nerve running over his elbow. "Do not speak."

He couldn't even if he'd wanted to.

She pushed him through the familiar halls, the grey-on-grey walls that grew lighter and lighter the higher in the tower they rose until it was nearly white at the upper floor and paintings from the Artist Laureate decorated them.

Joyce smiled at him from behind her receptionist desk. "Hello, Halud," she sang sweetly.

He groaned. Idiot.

The commandant pushed him up the staircase and into Hap's office. She pushed him right to the desk at the far end of the room, and forced him to sit in the chair. She released his arm but continued to stand half a step behind him.

Hap Lansford turned from the window, previously hidden by the overly-large wings of his chair, and placed his interlaced hands not he desk, ready to begin. It occurred to Halud that the man always started their meetings like that, his back turned while Halud entered and then he would spin around dramatically. The Speaker must have spent an awfully long time waiting with the chair turned away from his desk.

It had always intimidated Halud in the past, but now it just seemed absurd. "You're a fool, whatever you're going to ask for," Halud said before Hap could open his mouth.

Hap grinned at him. "You don't know that I'm going to ask for anything."

"But you always do," Halud spat. "I won't do it. I won't say whatever you want me to say. I don't support you and there's no reason for me to pretend."

"Oh, no?" Hap raised a single eyebrow. "I agree."

"You—what?"

Hap laughed. "Certainly not after last time. Although the folk still seemed to follow your words and not your dreaded thoughts. But I can't take that risk. Instead, I brought you here to tell you what part you are going to play. And then I'll let you sit in the rehabilitation facility with nothing but time to think."

Halud's blood ran cold. "I won't do anything you ask. You might as well send me to a colony." But his voice wasn't as strong as before, wasn't as sure.

"My dear Halud. Here's the beauty of it: you don't have to do anything."

Hap motioned to the commandant behind him, and she turned swiftly, marching from the room. Halud found himself missing her terrifying presence.

When she had gone, Hap continued, "You did do one thing for me, and I thank you. Hundreds of children have received the *Xenoralia nervosa* vaccine. You know what that means."

Halud shut his eyes.

"I'm making new soldiers. They will be better, stronger, faster than the last. We made errors with the first generation, but we have learned."

"What are you going to do with them?"

"With who? The Evangecore children? There's no use for them anymore. They'll be destroyed."

Halud shook his head. "You don't need to destroy them, just let them go."

"I can't do that. They're dangerous and unpredictable." Hap grinned wickedly. "The commandant tells me 005478F is still alive—fastidious, like a parasite—but she won't be for much longer."

Halud closed his eyes, he couldn't let Hap see how pleased the confirmation made him. "She doesn't want to fight. You know that."

Hap shook his head. "No, you know better than that. She is a fighter, a destroyer. She can't help it. Your sister was almost exactly what we needed. But she's uncontrollable. And that's why she needs to be destroyed."

"You told me she had already been destroyed on Junk, along with everything else."

Hap's face turned an angry red, and Halud allowed himself a little bit of hope. "I have been informed she is alive. Floating around somewhere in that ridiculously fortunate freightship I gave to Galiant Idim."

So she was alive, and they didn't know where she was. Halud gripped the chair to keep himself from grinning.

"Unpredictable and completely unaccounted for," Hap grumbled. "But no matter." He grinned again wickedly. "This is the part where you come in. You're here. She will come here to save her darling brother, if I know the subject at all. And then we'll destroy her."

Halud sputtered. "She won't. She's not stupid. She's millions of parsecs away by now." But his heart crashed around his breathless chest.

Because Hap was right. She would come for him. And the most selfish part of him wanted her to.

Hap called out for the commandant.

Halud would have to do something, find a way to get a message to Sarrin and tell her to run. He would escape, find her so she wouldn't have to find him. But the commandant was there with an iron grip on him, and he wasn't going anywhere.

FOUR

GAL GRASPED THE FAMILIAR HANDHOLD, pulling himself over the smooth parapet. Aaron was already standing on the rooftop, watching. "Do you think it's still safe, Gal? We haven't been here since we were cadets."

Gal grunted. "It was the only place I could think of."

Aaron walked around, stretching his arms. "Hard to believe it's still here, after all these years." He grinned at him. "Hard to believe you'd bring your new lady friend up here, like a teenager."

"Quiet, Aaron."

The apparition shrugged.

Gal went to the edge, helping Rayne over the lip. She was flushed, and her arms trembled. Next came the two Augments, Alex and Luca. Followed by Grant. Grant spun around, peering down the wall they had just climbed.

"Gal, what are we doing here?" Rayne said.

"We needed somewhere to stay." He leaned over the parapet; Sarrin was still ten feet below.

"She's not going to make it," Rayne said.

"She's a good climber," said Grant.

"She needs a hospital."

Gal held his breath.

"I offered to carry her, but she wouldn't let me," said Grant.

Slowly, Sarrin hauled herself over the edge, as they all watched. She rolled over the lip, collapsing onto the con-plas roof, breathing heavily.

Grant's Gods-awful suit had finally retracted, and Grant crouched on the ground next to the blistered girl.

"Don't," she croaked, struggling to her knees. A cough caught her, and she kneeled there, hacking, until finally a wad of clotted blood and pink foam splattered over the ground.

"Galiant," Rayne said firmly—at least she was talking to him, "she needs a hospital. She's dying."

The girl did look absolutely terrible, but out here at least she had a chance. "We can't," he said finally. "You know what will happen to her if we do." She would be captured. He would be captured.

"At least take her to the general's house," she said. "Let me talk to him, tell him what we know about the Augments."

Gal ran a hand over his face. He didn't want her to survive Evangecore and Selousa and Junk only to die on a rooftop, but the general was Hap Lansford's First General, involved with the Augments in more ways than one.

Sarrin braced herself on her elbow, half-sitting up. The Augments were tough as nails, that had never been in question, but he'd never seen one look so ragged.

"Gal, look at that."

Gal jerked his head up, eyes following where Aaron's long arm pointed. Across the chasm of streets and lower buildings, painted against the side of many buildings so that the picture would only be whole when you looked at it from a certain angle, was a symbol.

Gal stepped to the side to see it more clearly, cold disbelief washing through him. A circle with two parallel chevrons.

"Someone's still using the old mark," Aaron smiled.

Gal swallowed, nearly choking on his own saliva.

"We could go there," said Aaron.

He turned away.

"We stay here tonight," he told the others, giving Rayne a pointed gaze. There was a little cubby, a sort of frame made against the roof access door and the half-wall that ran around the edge, and Gal reached in pulling out a worn blanket. The last time he'd used it, he had been a teenager hoping some girl would give it up. It was where he brought all the girls back then; with the blanket spread out on the roof, they'd lay on it while Gal traced star patterns in the sky. Instead he brought it over to Sarrin, shaking out the dust, and laid it over her.

"Where did you get that?" Rayne asked.

He arranged the blanket over the girl, careful not to touch her. He met her wary gaze, hoping to convey how sorry he was he couldn't do more, that he knew if she died it would be on him.

She nodded, opening her mouth to speak, but another coughing spell overtook her.

"We could take her to the rebels," said Aaron, unasked. "They could get her medical assistance, a doctor. They can help us find someone who won't go to the UECs."

She coughed again and again, the wounds on her face oozing fresh, sticky serum.

A sinking pit opened in the chasm of his stomach. Was she that ill? Was it worth it? He closed his eyes, the painted symbol with its parallel lines fresh in his mind.

He opened his mouth to offer, but she spoke first:

"We need to find Halud." Her voice was grave and raspy.

"Sarrin, you need to rest." Grant crouched down beside her.

She shook her head. "Where is he? The newsfeed…."

"It can wait," said Grant, reaching his hand out gently.

She flinched away, tipping over and spilling across the floor.

"We'll go tomorrow. When you feel better."

"He's in trouble," she rasped. "He wasn't on the feed, that was a recording from weeks ago."

"Tomorrow, Sar. You can't do anything for him tonight. Sleep. Let your body heal."

"The general will know where he is," Rayne said softly.

Sarrin eyed Rayne, calculating, considering.

"Absolutely not," Gal snapped.

He regretted it instantly when they all turned on him. Rayne put her hand on her hip. "Why not?"

"We need to find Halud." Sarrin sat up, coughing.

Gal closed his eyes and shook his head. It was a fool's errand. When he opened his eyes, they were still staring at him. He noted a flash of grey demons, seated on the half-wall, just like they were enjoying a show. They clapped at him mirthfully.

He gestured at Sarrin. "She can't go anywhere."

"If you hadn't dragged her up on this roof." Rayne turned, heading for the wall where they had climbed over. "I'll go. The general can tell me where to find Halud and I can come back with some medicines."

"No."

She spun angrily.

He started before she could: "It's not safe." He wanted to tell her she could be taken, jailed, tortured, killed, wanted to tell her what he suspected her father had done, but his mouth wouldn't let him, it just stopped.

"My father is safe," she said coldly.

"You can trust the rebels," said Aaron.

Gal whirled around. "No. We can't trust anyone! We're in a city full of people who hate us. They don't give a damn about anything we have to say. And we will not be announcing our arrival to anyone, especially not Hap

Lansford's war general."

Rayne stepped back, shocked.

Sarrin coughed up another glob of blood.

"No one is safe here. There is no one we can trust." He turned his voice, for the first time in years, to the tone that made people listen. "Sarrin is going to feel better in the morning. We are all going to sit here, sleep if we can. No one is going to go anywhere. And maybe, we'll survive a night in the Central City." He spun away, blindly moving to a section of half-wall on the other side of the roof. He gripped the cool con-plas in his hands, imagining ripping it apart with his bare hands.

He had left Indaer when it became Etar, when the Speakers learned things about him they never wanted to know, and he had planned never to come back. Planned to die a peaceful old death out under the stars, having never uttered a single word again.

In the far corner, as distant from him as she could make herself, Rayne crouched in the corner. She didn't cry—she never cried—and somehow that was worse. Because he could see just how much he had hurt her, could watch as she bundled every little piece of it up and tucked it away.

She had followed him so far from home, barely visiting the planet because he had wanted her with him, and now she was so close but further than ever. Her life was ruined, all because of him. And what did he know anyway? What business did he have wrecking everyone around him?

"I think you need to tell her the truth."

Gal glanced warily at Aaron.

"About everything."

"Shut up." Gal pushed himself off the wall and marched pointedly to the centre of the roof, where he laid with his head against the hard con-plas, staring up at the stars. Blatantly refusing to meet the gazes he felt boring into his skin, he forced himself to sleep, drifting off against a backdrop of muffled coughing and his own regret.

* * *

Sarrin dreamed of ungulate creatures, of a forest, of a place where everyone knew everyone. For the first time, the dream-world held people. They were scared, but she couldn't figure out why. She went from person to person, but they each pushed her away.

She rolled over, coughing.

Her eyes slammed open as she gasped for breath, taking in the grey con-plas stone that she had been laying on. Events from the day before came flooding back as she hacked out a large clot of blood and tissue. She leaned against the wall, breathing deeply. Her lungs were sore, but they felt clear. She reached up to her face, it was dry and didn't sting nearly as much when she touched it.

It was still early morning, the wan purple light of night was just beginning to clear. Gal had slumped in the middle of the rooftop, and was now dreaming fitfully. Rayne was curled up in a far corner, making herself as small as possible.

Grant caught her eye and rose up from where he sat. He came to her. "How are you feeling?"

"We have to find Halud." The hoarseness of her own voice surprised her.

He scanned her critically. "Your skin is starting to heal."

She nodded.

"But it still looks terrible."

"They were showing video clips of him that were weeks old," she said—Grant would understand. Normally, Halud taped a new promo every day when he was in the Central City. If they had no newer material, it meant he was either away, or....

And he didn't have anywhere to go.

"I'll go look for him," Grant said. "I think you should stay here. Your face, it will draw too much attention."

"We have to find him," she said, her voice coming stronger now that the vocal cords were warming up.

Grant held a finger to his lips and pointed at Gal. "I will," he promised her. "You stay here and rest, you need it. I'll go out and see what I can find."

She shook her head. She needed to be out there, finding him. Grant didn't know him, not like she did. He was her brother. Plus, it was the only way to make up for what she was, everything she had done. It was the only way to show him she wasn't a monster. Not entirely.

"I have to —," she started, but a quiet clang close-by interrupted her.

Grant crouched, ready to leap into action. If the UECs found them here, could she run?

She scrambled to her own feet, although the effort was harder than it should have been and left her gasping.

Luca flipped over the half-wall, followed by Alex.

Grant relaxed.

Sarrin realized she hadn't even counted them missing when she scanned the roof.

"Hey," said Alex.

Grant shushed him and pointed to Gal's sleeping figure again.

Alex nodded in understanding and the two crept closer. They each had a large sac tied over their backs, which they deposited in front of them silently. Alex whispered, "I know Gal said to stay here, but I figured we needed food."

Luca reached into her bag and pulled out fruits and a loaf of leavened bread.

Alex opened his bag next, which was not really a bag but a twisted up sheet. Grey fabric flopped out. "We have to go into the city to find Halud, right. It will be easier if we can blend in."

Grant held up one of the pieces. It was a long robe, the kind that Halud wore, but less ornate. "Where did you get them?"

Alex shrugged. "Borrowed." He glanced at Sarrin. "They're from a communal laundry. We weren't seen."

But Sarrin didn't care. She eyed the fabric readily.

"And…," Alex threw her a crumpled grey ball, "a worshippers cloak, with a hood."

Sarrin set the fruit aside and pulled open the fabric.

"That looks sore," said Alex, gesturing to her face. "Ours are almost healed, but we didn't get it half as bad."

She shrugged, the fabric felt light and hopeful in her hands. With it, she could find her brother.

"We better hurry," said Luca. "I don't want that old common to try to stop us." She pointed at Gal.

Sarrin pulled the cloak over her head, tugging the hood low to cover her face.

"Where should we start?" asked Alex, looking at her expectantly.

She paused—surely they weren't thinking of coming with her.

"Hiding the back of your neck." Grant reached out, wrapping a twisted swatch of grey fabric around Alex's throat like a scarf.

Alex grinned. "Oh right. Thanks."

Unnaturally blue eyes and barcodes tattooed over their bodies—the only things that would give them away. Sarrin's neck was covered by her hood, and by her hair after that. But the cloaks couldn't hide their eyes, not if they wanted to be able to see. It would be too risky.

"I'll try to infiltrate the Speakers' Compound," she said. "The rest of you stay here."

"Sarrin —," Grant started to argue.

"He's my brother. The probability of detection and

capture is high, especially with more of us on the ground."
She didn't add that if they were captured, it would probably
be because of her, debilitated as she still was from the mist in
the forest. And if they were captured, her only escape would
be to trust in the monster, and it was doubtful the rest would
escape that. "I won't ask you to come."

"You're not asking," said Alex. He had already half slipped
over the wall. He gave her a quick grin and disappeared.

Luca followed and then Grant, leaving Sarrin standing by
herself at the parapet. She glanced at Gal, still sleeping in the
purple-grey half-light of the pre-dawn morning. Flipping the
long hood over her head, she sent Halud a silent apology for
turning her back on the captain he had so supported, and
stepped over the half wall, descending the jagged handholds
far more easily than she had climbed up.

* * *

The Augments were gone. Not that Gal was surprised.
He'd woken at the crack of day and watched them slip over
the roof. He hadn't even tried to stop them, not with the way
he'd acted.

Rayne still slept as far from him as she could get, curled up
uncomfortably tight in the little alcove that must have made
her feel a little safer.

Aaron was nowhere to be seen.

Gal rose to his feet, stiff in the cold. Sunshine bathed his
face, and he turned into it, away from the spot the others had
slipped away. This was their fight anyway, they would do
what they did. It was out of his hands.

The grey stone buildings were painted with even greyer
paint. The first of Etar's three suns flashed in the thin space
between buildings for just an instant, blinding him. When he
turned back, his eyes fell to the symbol painted across a half-
dozen buildings, to the circle and the chevrons.

Gal's hands had gone grey where he gripped the stone wall.

Below him, sounds of the folk going about their day rose up. The symbol was painted in a way such that you would never see it unless you looked from just the right way. How many of the folk walked by it and under it every day without knowing it was there? How many had never even thought to look?

"I can't believe it's stood all this time." Aaron was suddenly beside him, staring out at the clandestine array of buildings.

Gal only grunted.

"What does it mean to you? What do you see when you see that symbol now?" Aaron asked.

He'd seen the symbol burned, slathered in mud, covered in blood. Found it in rubble from bombed buildings, seen it sliced in two by laz-cannons, pulled it off corpses. "Death. Despair. Destruction."

Aaron raised an eyebrow. "It used to mean something different."

"It's stupid. Just some lines some kid drew."

"The circle was meant for unity, for protection. The chevrons for strength, life. They pointed up to show where we were going, the first over the second to remind us there was always more we could do, always a next step. It was there to remind us to work to be better."

Gal sighed, letting his shoulders slump over the ledge. For a minute, he remembered the kid. Long before the Earth was destroyed and the kid with it.

A noise—a pebble rolling cross the concrete roof—startled him. Rayne was two strides away—close enough to see the lines on the buildings. Hopefully not more, unless she came closer.

He pushed away from the wall, coming to meet her.

The bags under her eyes were puffy and dark, her hair loose and lopsided. Beautiful. She crossed her arms across her chest and stared at the ground as she spoke. "Where are the others?"

Gal gulped. "Slipped out in the night. Fools."

"Looking for the Poet," she surmised.

"Probably. Nothing we can do for them now. They'll be caught by sunsdown."

She pursed her lips, chancing to look at him for the first time. "The Gods are good, Gal. And we're good. We just need to have Faith." She brought her five fingers to her lips, kissing the five Gods, then tapped the fingers against her chest.

Yes, Faith, and Knowledge, Prudence, Strength, and Fortitude—a surefire way to dig your own grave. "Rayne, please." He took a deep breath. "I've been doing this a long time. We're marked as traitors now. If they see us, it won't end well."

He braced himself for an argument, but she didn't give him one. Instead she turned and leaned against the wall, looking out. She said simply, "What else are we going to do while we're here? Sit around and wait for Cordelia?"

He rubbed his boot into the con-plas roof. "She shouldn't have dropped us here. There's nothing we can do. We're just going to have to wait for her to come back."

Rayne frowned. "You don't know that. We know what the Augments are truly like now. They might not all be dead, but it doesn't mean we have to have another war. If we're caught before we can see my father, we'll just explain it. We can fix this for everyone."

She said it so earnestly, he let it strike a spark of hope in him. Just explain it. Fix it for everyone. Simple.

"Look," said Rayne, turning to the parapet, her voice filled with awe. Her chin tilted toward the tallest building in the skyline, tall and narrow and covered at the top with a perfect glass dome.

"The Speakers' Tower." He stepped between her and the damning circle with two chevrons, afraid she'd see it if she took just a step back and looked to the left.

"It's a symbol," she said. "A pillar for the folk to look to. A place of guidance." She sighed. "It's good to see it again. I think it reminds me who I am, my duty to the Gods."

"Duty?" he heard himself asking.

She wrapped an arm across his back, smiling sweetly. "We need to help these people. And help the Augments. And help your friends in the woods."

Gal frowned. "I thought…."

"What did you think?"

His heart sung, the way she looked at him. He loved her more now than he ever had before. But, he hung his head, reason returning. "I don't think we can."

"Of course we can," she said, taking his hand and patting it like a small child. "We'll do it together. You and me."

He met her deep brown eyes, let himself be swallowed by them.

"We just need to explain it to my father. The General can help us." She took a step toward the wall where they had climbed over the night before, tugging on his hand.

He let her fingers slip away from his. "Rayne. We can't."

"You don't know him like I do. I'm sure if he knew—if the Speakers knew the truth—we could stop all of this."

He shook his head, an alarm ringing somewhere in his mind behind the love-struck haze. "It doesn't work that way, Rayne. Please."

She frowned, the sweet look sliding off her face, replaced by dark eyes, angry, calculating. The smile slipped back on her features.

He wanted to melt back into it, almost let himself. He loved her. Loved her even more when she talked about the two of them changing the world, like she might one day understand. He would do anything for her.

She stepped again toward the half-wall, was only a step

away from climbing over.

"Rayne, you can't."

The false smile slipped away again, this time permanently. "You can't tell me what to do, Galiant."

He pressed his lips together. "You can't go down there. Your face is as recognizable as mine."

"I'm going to see my father."

He stepped toward her. "If you go out there, I don't know what will happen to you. I don't know anymore what they're capable of."

"Probably a lot more than you think," her voice scolded him.

And a lot more than she thought. "Listen to me," he started.

"You listen to me," she shouted. "We need to help these people. We're doing nothing, holed up here like prisoners."

His own anger flared. "We are helping. Can't you see? I'm just trying to keep everyone alive"

"No! You had me set a bomb! A bomb, Gal."

"You don't understand!"

"Yes, I don't understand. I nearly killed Kieran. Why would you make me do that? I trusted you. Even when no one else would, I did. But you cracked it."

He gasped, because it was true. "I'm sorry," he said quietly. "You can't trust anyone, Rayne. I want you to see that. Not the Speakers. Not your father. Least of all me."

His head turned of its own volition, and he caught sight again of the not-quite-aligned chevrons and circle, feeling it like a physical blow that sent him staggering back.

Aaron rounded on him. "It's calling to you. Mocking you."

Gal seethed.

"That symbol is inevitable. It's part of you, and you will never be free of it until you see it through."

Gal pushed him back. "No! We can't go! Too many people will get hurt. It's in the past. Leave me alone." He stumbled as he fell through the empty air.

Rayne had a leg over the half-wall where she paused, staring at him intently, angrily, shocked. They stared at each other, across the growing chasm between them. Then she started to move again, quickly. She swung the second leg over and made to drop.

He rushed forward. Before thinking, his hand was on her wrist, the other firmly on her elbow, and he pulled. He tugged her up and over the wall, throwing her across the rooftop.

His heart pounded in his ears. He blinked at the sight of her, just starting to pick herself up.

She blinked back. Her face was pale. Afraid. Afraid of him. A trickle of blood started from a cut on her temple. "You are cracked, Gal, just like they said. Cracked, spread, raging mad, and I'm sorry I ever trusted you."

"Rayne, I...." What had he done? Even when he was trying to protect people he hurt them.

And the last thing he could bring himself to care about closed her eyes on him and turned away, forever.

FIVE

Sᴀʀʀɪɴ ꜰᴏʀᴄᴇᴅ ʜᴇʀꜱᴇʟꜰ ᴛᴏ ᴡᴀʟᴋ calmly despite the overwhelming crowds of people that filled the streets. A nervous person would draw attention. They couldn't afford that. Instead she bobbed along in the sea of grey.

Grant caught her eye from the opposite side of the street and made a subtle gesture. He was pointing ahead at a group of workers. They all had a fleck of blue stitched somewhere on their uniforms.

She had seen a different group with a similar accent, all scholars, flutter by her earlier.

She shook her head slightly at his question to say she didn't know either.

It was strange. It was daring. It reminded her of the Augments and their bare-backed shirts on the Ishash'tor when they thought no one was watching.

But someone was always watching.

Her ears picked up on the whirring motors of a surveillance drone and she ducked her head again. She turned into a small cafe, pretending to read the posted menu as the drone passed behind her.

"Oh my!" she heard a shrill voice exclaim. "Oh, you lucky thing. You are just gorgeous." A woman, the owner of the voice, was suddenly in her face. She reached her hand up to the hood.

Sarrin jerked away, pulse ripping in her ears. The woman was going to reveal her. But the words didn't match.

"It's okay," said the woman. "I had my treatment last month. It totally rejuvenated me. I can see it working on you already."

Sarrin's head swam.

"It's important us girls take care of our appearance, what with our limited choice of wardrobe." The woman was tugging on her own baggy, grey, work outfit, showing it off grimly. "I love what you've done with your hair." Sarrin flinched as the woman grabbed for a rope of hair that was hanging loose from under her hood.

The woman had her own hair done up intricately, piled on her head so smoothly it gleamed in the light. She had also marked up her face with a bit of dark powder, making her eyes exotic.

"Oh my word," exclaimed the woman, "those are just exquisite." Sarrin's eyes flared wide, her body stiff, as the woman reached a hand around her back and encouraged her forward. "Forgive me dear, I'm being so rude. Please, come in, take a seat." The woman was the server at the cafe. And she was already showing her to a table. "You must tell me where you got your contacts," said the server.

"What?"

"Your contacts." The woman pointed at her own eyes. They were an iridescent green—they reminded her of Kieran, only not the same. Her eyes had a strange, uncomfortable quality about them, highlighted as they were by the kohl: the pupils were fixed, artificial, the result of coloured lenses. "It's okay, dear," the woman assured when Sarrin didn't answer, "They give us these grey clothes, but you and I both know it was the Gods who gave us beauty, after all.

Why not celebrate it?" She laughed, pulling a tablet out of the back pocket of her coveralls. "What will it be today?"

Sarrin caught sight of Grant watching her from the street, and knew she had lingered too long.

"Uh, nothing." Sarrin stood to leave. "I have to go. Sorry."

"Oh."

Sarrin felt the need to explain, holding her empty hands out to the sides. "Out of credits."

The woman broke into a knowing smile. "I see. Fashion doesn't come cheap. I had to save for my own facial treatment for months. Don't worry though, us fashionistas need to stick together." She winked, pulling back the inside of her lapel, revealing a flash of colour. Enough to have her arrested for treason. "I'll be right back."

Too stunned to move, Sarrin stared at the woman's retreating form and then at the dark, empty hall she'd disappeared down. Almost immediately, the woman returned, waving for Sarrin to follow her to the back of the cafe.

Sarrin cast a weary eye to the street, to where Grant stood watching her. He wouldn't be happy, but she followed the woman all the same. They passed through a hidden door and up a narrow stair, emerging into a tiny, cramped living quarters above the cafe.

"It's so nice to meet someone of a similar mind, you know. 'Don't heed the superficial,' 'We're meant to be serving the Gods,' and all that. But, I can't help myself." She made Sarrin sit at her little kitchen table while she washed a fruit and sliced a piece of bread for her. "You understand, don't you?"

Sarrin didn't.

Kieran had once told her the first rule of observing, of gaining information from people, was to get them to like you.

First, smile, he had said. So she did, pressing her face into an approximation of the shape Kieran had once teased her into.

The woman smiled back, handing Sarrin the bread and fruit. "I just have to show you something." She went to the far side of the room, into what was the sleeping area, and reached for her tall wardrobe. "It's dangerous, but I just knew I could trust you." She flung the wardrobe open. There were flecks of colour in every shade imaginable. Long ropes of it, small circles and squares, dangling jangly things that tinkled as the doors settled. There was even a UEC uniform, dyed purple.

The woman ran her fingers lovingly over every bobble. "One day, I'll be brave enough to wear some of it."

Sarrin stared, the question slipping out as barely a breath. "Why?" Why so blatantly defy the Speakers? Why set yourself apart? Why ask for them to hunt you?

The woman shrugged. "Before he disappeared, the Poet told us to be who we were. Individuals."

Sarrin's mouth dropped open.

"Not in so many words, I suppose. But when he speaks, I hear him. I hear what he's really saying." She smoothed the pieces lovingly and shut the wardrobe. "He always fills my head with these cracked ideas. Only, from him they don't seem so cracked, you know."

Sarrin snapped her mouth closed again, heart pounding in her chest.

The woman laid back on her bed, wrapping a pillow in her arms. It was grey, but there were faint designs in coloured thread covering the entire thing. Colour was for the Gods. Even the Artist Laureate was forbidden to put colour in his work unless he was illustrating the Speakers or the Gods themselves.

"But when you walked in, I just knew. You almost look like him." The woman sighed again. "Halud is—I mean, the

Poet Laureate is always telling us to do what feels right. To follow our hearts. I had to show you this."

Her pulse pounded so loudly in her ears, she could barely hear herself think, had to rely on instinct to know if the words she spoke came out loud. "Do you know Halud?"

The woman blushed. "Oh, no, no. I just love hearing him speak." She sat up, brushing the pillow carefully as she put it back, entirely grey side facing out. "I wish he would come back," the woman continued. "He's disappeared for such a long time again. What are we supposed to do without him?"

"How long has he been gone?" she asked, rising to her feet.

The woman sighed. "It's been three weeks since I've heard him speak. They play the recordings on the newscasts, but it's not the same. We want to hear the words of the Gods, of Halud."

Sarrin frowned. This woman thought Halud spoke the words of the Gods.

"I have an idea," the woman said suddenly, jumping to her feet. "There's a party tonight—well, not a party, but several of us are going to walk through the same place at the same time, each of us wearing a fleck of blue. I think it's really going to be something."

"Blue?" Sarrin blurted, as though that was the most shocking thing the woman had said.

"Yes. For Halud. Many of us are wearing the colour to show our support. Do you have some?" The woman turned into her bright wardrobe, fussing through the colours that hung there. "It can't be too much to draw attention, just enough for someone who's looking to see."

"I've seen others wearing blue," Sarrin said, stilling as the woman reached for her cloak and tied the smallest blue thread into the fabric. "Are they… rebels?"

"No, no, dear." The woman's eyes crinkled. "Those dangerous rebels disappeared years ago. We are simply people of fashion waiting for our beloved Poet to speak. Nothing so dramatic as the rebels."

And in her simpleness, Sarrin knew the woman had no interest in anything more than fashion. But still, they were rebels to wear a flash of blue and organize a type of rally, no matter how quiet it may seem.

"I need to get back down to the cafe, dear." The woman had a hand on Sarrin's shoulder before she realized it, and turned her to the stairs. "I hope I'll see you tonight."

* * *

Sarrin pulled the hood down covering her face as much as she could while still being able to see. Grant trailed her, three steps behind. The words of his earlier protests still rung in her ears: They don't know where Halud is. You're going to trust this woman you just met? Anything could happen tonight, Sarrin. It's a protest; we're going to join a protest. The UECs will come. Still, she led them through the streets.

Two of the three suns had set, leaving a subdued glow that cast long shadows as they approached the intersection the woman in the cafe had whispered in her ear. In the open square where several streets came together, folk bustled back and forth. They kept their heads down, their feet on a steady, set path as though they were about their regular business, but their eyes danced furtively, the very corners of their lips turning up. Flecks of blue flickered around them.

This was the party. Dozens of folk streamed past. A woman pretended to stumble, a man helping her up. A third joined them. Quick words were exchanged between tight lips.

Sarrin took a deep breath and plunged into the crowd. It was a long shot, but if the people were willing to rebel even in such a small way, maybe there were people willing to do more. Maybe there was someone who knew something about Halud.

The group of three departed from their almost-certainly-coordinated accidental meeting, and Sarrin paused.

Grant pressed in to her shoulder, and she ducked away. "There's too many people here," he said.

"Someone might know about Halud," she whispered back.

"They're all folk, followers."

She shrugged. "The blue means they're followers of Halud."

"We're drawing too much attention," he said. "This whole place—this many folk out this close to curfew. We have to go."

"You can go," she said, stepping away. "I have to find Halud."

"Sarrin." A hand landed on her arm, staying her. "Kieran said to trust you, that you knew what you were doing, even when things went...wonky. But this is cracked. Surely you can see what a bad idea this is."

She turned to respond, but something caught her attention, like a hand snapping her gaze across the square.

"Sarrin?" Grant seemed far away.

A young woman, a fleck of blue in the sleeve of her coat, scurried through the crowd pushing a grey pram in front of her.

"Sarrin?" Grant called more urgently, as she felt herself take a step towards the mother and baby.

The woman paused, peering into the pram. She reached in, and pulled out the mewling infant, lifting it to her for comfort. But the baby's eyes cut across the square, meeting Sarrin's across the distance and the throng of people. Crystal blue eyes, pale and burning and completely inhuman. A perfect reflection of Sarrin's own.

Only when the mother shifted the baby, putting it back into the pram, did Sarrin start to breathe again.

"Sarrin?"

"It's an Augment," she breathed.

"What?" Grant stepped in close, following her gaze.

"The child."

"That's impossible. Xenoralia hasn't been seen in twenty years."

"I know what I saw." What she didn't know was how, or why. Or what would happen to the child.

A shrill voice called out from close behind, making Sarrin jump. "Oh, there you are! I wondered if you'd come." The woman from the cafe reached out, fingering Sarrin's cloak where she had woven in the tiniest blue thread. "And this"— she laid a hand on Grant's chest—"must be your lover. Oh my, what an attractive pair."

"We should keep moving," Grant said into her ear.

"Oh yes, dear, you're absolutely right." But the woman didn't move. She reached for Sarrin's hood, pulling it down. "You shouldn't hide such a pretty face. You've healed marvellously. We mustn't be afraid to let our beauty show!" She reached next for Sarrin's hair, but Grant caught her wrist in mid-air.

He flashed Sarrin a warning look. The woman didn't seem bothered by her eye colour, but the barcode at the back of Sarrin's neck would be a dead giveaway. He was right: too risky.

The woman snatched her hand back and glared at Grant.

Sarrin pressed her lips together. What was it Kieran had said—be friendly, find common ground. But how could she ask her for more information about Halud, or if she knew anyone who might know.

A hand on her shoulder roughly pulled her away before she could find a single word to use, the woman disappearing behind a stream of folk as Grant tugged her back.

She twisted away from him, finding her footing far too slowly. An edge of grey surrounded her vision.

"Don't get upset. She was drawing too much attention to

herself." Grant brushed a hand through his sandy hair. "This is a bad idea. Did you see what she was wearing? We don't need that kind of attention."

The folk parted around them, throwing them curious glances. "We're already drawing attention."

Glancing around him, Grant nodded, dropping his voice. "Put your hood back up."

Sarrin frowned, but covered her face once more. "She didn't know."

Grant stepped into the crowd, blending in with their pace and direction. "What's gotten into you? What if someone had seen your eyes? Or the code on your neck?"

She frowned, crossing her arms as she followed him. "But they didn't."

"Alex is right there. We'll get him and Luca and then go. I don't like this place."

"There might be someone who knows where Halud is."

"Maybe. But what are you going to do? Shout it out across the entire square? 'Hey, has anyone seen my brother, the traitorous Poet?'"

Her step faltered.

"Sorry." He led them to a sheltered alcove where one building jutted up against the next.

She drove her toe into the dusty, grey ground. "There are too many emotions here. Too many people. They all feel heady and reckless."

"You used to give me a hard time for being too reckless."

When she looked up, he was smiling. It reminded her of the countless days and weeks they had spent together—the missions, months spent hiding, finding food, shelter. They survived the war leaning on each other, more than anyone, Sarrin had trusted him.

"We used to be so close." His hand came up to her shoulder, and she flinched away. "You've changed."

Facing into the crowd, she said, "We all changed."

"Ever since I came aboard, you've wanted nothing to do with me."

Her shoulders drew up at the accusation. Didn't he see it was too painful?

"There aren't many of us left, Sarrin." He stepped in close, his voice dropping low. "We're fighting to survive. Fighting something bigger than us. We have to be able to trust each other, otherwise we're not going to be efficient. There's a higher risk of error. You remember."

She closed her eyes. The lessons of Evangecore were good ones, despite the circumstances. Always stick together. Always protect the squadron. They were stronger together.

"We should go," she said, stepping back into the crowd and letting herself be carried away by the current.

"I didn't kill her."

Amelia. Sarrin stopped, the person behind narrowly side-stepping to avoid bumping into her. "I know. I—."

Grant grabbed her elbow, pulling her to the wall. "Get down!"

Grey clad soldiers streamed into the square. The smooth currents of the folk with their little flecks of blue turned frantic.

Mechanical whirring bombarded her ears—surveillance drones. Overhead, the soft whomp-whomps of a hovercraft descended on the square.

Grant grabbed her arm, pulling her to the side of the building where he began to climb. Across the square, she saw Alex and Luca doing the same.

Half-way up, a high pitched scream stopped Sarrin, her foot on a ledge, her fingers dug into the tiniest crack in the facade. She turned to the sound.

The woman from the cafe screamed again, her carefully collected ribbons of colour flashed in the sea of grey as the soldiers surrounded her. She shrieked on the ground as an electrified baton scorched her skin.

"Sarrin." Grant's voice broke her concentration, stopped the monster from drawing its diagram, showing her how to leap down and save the woman. "There's nothing you can do. There's too many of them."

There was always something they could do -- another of Evangecore's idioms -- but as she let the monster play out the scenarios, each of them ended in a swarm and her capture. She was strong and fast, but even if she escaped the square, the surveillance drones or the hovercraft would follow.

Grant was right, they had to get out of the square. She closed her heart to the shrieking, shouting below, swallowing heavily as she turned back to the wall. A glint of silver caught her eye, and a high pitched buzz met her ears, muffled by the hood of her cloak.

She spun quickly, face to face with a grey surveillance drone. Her arm reached out, laser fast, and smashed the machine into the wall, its pieces tumbling to the ground below. But was it fast enough?

"Were you seen?" Grant shouted as he helped her onto the roof.

She didn't answer.

He grabbed her shoulder, sending an electric shock through her. "Were you seen?"

"I don't know," she shouted back, surprising herself with the outburst as much as him.

"Gods." He spun away, tapping his five fingers to his chest absently as he scanned the airspace around him. "They're not following at least. Let's go."

She pumped her arms, accelerating quickly, the building flying by as she jumped from one roof to the next. Somewhere behind her, she knew Grant was doing the same. Hopefully Alex and Luca were somewhere safe, making their way back to Gal's rooftop hideout.

It was a foolish mistake. She'd gotten caught up in the excitement of the crowd, and hadn't been paying attention. She cursed the hood that kept her from hearing the machine. She pressed her five fingers to her chest as she ran, praying she had smashed it before the drone could transmit the last second where it had looked directly into her face.

* * *

Gal stared across the grey skyline, studying the lines traced onto one of the buildings, seemingly at random, seemingly artistic. Seemingly benign. From this angle, he didn't mind the lines. From this angle, they didn't make him feel so doomed. Almost, for a minute, he relaxed, enjoying the purple-grey night of his home world, a place he hadn't seen in years. At least he could thank Cordelia for the small gift of seeing it again, even if he was pretty sure he would die here.

Augments scrambled over the edge of the roof, shouting and panting. The girl, Luca, laid down, gasping for breath. Whatever had happened, they had come back in a hurry, fast enough to tax even their super-human systems.

He groaned. It was after curfew already. Even if they hadn't been Augments, it would be trouble if they were seen.

"They were just doing what they thought was right, Gal," said Aaron.

"I know," he muttered. But it was still cracked for them to go into the city, all of them blue-eyed and marked up the way they were. He squinted, searching the sky, but nothing followed them. Maybe it would be all right.

Grant stood on the parapet, also scanning the sky, and ran a pale hand over his open mouth. "I don't see anything."

Sarrin, on the roof beside him, pushed down her hood. She looked up for a minute before nodding.

"We got lucky," Grant chided, looking down at her from where he still stood on the parapet.

She unwound her grey robe, taking it off, and shook it out stiffly, obviously avoiding Grant's look.

"What happened?" Alex went over to join them.

Grant shook his head, jumping down. He ran a hand through his hair. "There was a surveillance drone when they raided the protest. It got right in Sarrin's face."

"What?" Gal gasped before he could stop himself. Raid? Protest? Gods.

"They're not following us," Grant snapped. He scowled and turned away.

"It doesn't matter," said Gal, walking across the roof to join them. "What if you were seen?"

Grant looked at Alex. "Sarrin smashed it right away. Nothing followed us, I was watching the entire way back. Even if they did see her, they don't know where we are"

"You shouldn't have gone into the city," Gal muttered.

"Did you find anything, at least?" asked Luca. "I saw you talking to someone."

Grant shook his head.

Gal crossed his arms. "Of all the spread things to do."

Aaron glared at him.

"At least we tried!" Grant spun on his heel, suddenly in Gal's face. "What did you do all day?"

Gal gritted his teeth and stepped up to meet Grant. Augment or not, they were being fools. "I didn't nearly get myself and everyone else caught."

A finger poked into his chest, and Grant pushed him away easily. "I liked you better when you were a cracked drunk."

Gal stumbled, his chest smarting as much as his pride.

"You deserve that," said Aaron.

Into the silence that followed, a quiet voice spoke: "What's going to happen to her?" Sarrin stood at the wall, looking out across the city.

"Who?" Alex asked, turning.

"The woman from the cafe.   She was taken by the soldiers."

"I don't know, Sar."

Gal sobered.   They were here arguing, but at least they were here.   If there has been a raid, and a protest, folk would have been taken.   He shared a look with Aaron, remembering there last time he had seen him in the flesh, inside one of the cages at the Speakers' rehabilitation centre.   "It depends on her," he said, "how quickly she repents."

Sarrin nodded to say she understood.   She probably did, the kid had been a living defiance since the day she was infected, only she didn't have a chance to repent the way the woman in the streets did.

Her eyebrows twitched, and she frowned.   "There's something else: I saw an Augment in the city. A baby."

"A baby?" Gal sucked in breath sharply, and Aaron's head snapped around.

"You don't know that it was," said Grant.

Sarrin shook her head.   "I know.   Her eyes were like ours, unnaturally blue."

"Is that possible?" whispered Aaron.

"There hasn't been a case of Red Fever in twenty years," said Grant.   "The virus died out within a year of infecting all of us."

"I know what I saw," said Sarrin.

"How old?" said Luca.

Sarrin shook her head again.   "Three months, maybe less."

"Are you sure?" said Rayne.   "If it was busy, and far away….   Maybe it just looked like the altered Xenoralia iris structure—babies are born with blue eyes that turn brown, perhaps the child was just too young."

Sarrin shook her head.   "She wasn't that far away, and I've been staring into Red Fever eyes as long as I can remember. And…."

"And?" said Alex.

She squirmed, rubbing her arms. "I felt her."

"Felt her?"

"I feel everyone, but her…."

Aaron turned to Gal. "Where did the Augment come from?"

Rayne echoed his question, adding, "Is there another outbreak?"

"The virus isn't active." Alex shook his head. "There are no reports of anyone getting sick. No quarantines in the city."

"Not yet," said Rayne, "but it could be coming. We don't know how it spread last time." She turned to Gal, "We have to warn someone."

Gal felt his heart catch -- he had his suspicions about how the virus had spread. No, not suspicions, he and Aaron had learned the truth when they'd hacked into the Speakers' library: the Augments had been made, plain and simple. "No," he said, clutching Rayne's arm, suddenly terrified she would try to go, shouting about Xenoralia and Augments in the streets, or worse, to her father.

"Gal!" She twisted away, clutching her arm. He'd hurt her again.

"No one leaves this rooftop," he said, heart pounding in his chest.

"Gal," Rayne chided him, "if there's another outbreak, we have to tell someone."

"You don't think…," said Luca, draping to a whisper, "the child was bred."

"Bred?" Grant repeated.

Alex looked between the others. "I don't know of anyone that's had a child. Anyone that could after Evangecore."

"If they experimented…," Luca cut off with a shudder.

Gal shut his eyes.

Sarrin shook her head, "This child had a mother—a

normal, human mother."

"And why would they bring it here?" asked Alex.

"A new Augment." Aaron paced the roof, tugging on his hair. "It's spread. Totally cracked."

Gal bit his lip. "There's nothing we can do about it," he said finally.

"We have to find out more," said Luca, "figure out where it came from."

"This is bad, Gal," agreed Aaron.

Gal shook his head. "No. No one goes back into the city."

Aaron stared at him.

"I'm sure it's fine. It's nothing." Gal waved it off, willing himself to believe it.

"It's not nothing," snapped Alex.

"If this is the virus, people could die," said Rayne.

"There's a vaccine now."

Alex gasped. "Oh my Gods. Halud's broadcasts." He turned to Sarrin. "They're vaccinating children."

She went totally still.

"To protect them," said Gal, feeling stupid even as the words left his mouth. Everything was spiralling out of control. It was happening again. It was all happening again.

"Don't be an idiot, Gal," said Aaron, disgust written plainly on his face. "Hap is making more Augments. You have to stop him."

Gal spun wildly, slamming his hands on the con-plas half wall was he squeezed his eyes shut. He didn't want to. He couldn't. Just couldn't. "Why did Cordelia ever bring us here?"

"We should go check out the hospital," said Luca, ignoring his outburst.

"Agreed," said Alex.

"We'll check it out tomorrow. At first light."

There was a pause. Sarrin's gravelly voice cut across the

roof, and he felt her eyes on him. "You knew, didn't you?"

He pressed his lips together, shaking his head. He refused to turn, to look at her.

"Why would they do it?"

His voice cracked, and he stressed at the faded lines drawn into the buildings. "I honestly don't know."

Grant cleared his throat, and Gal heard him rolling up his grey cloak and dropping it on the floor. "We'll get some sleep and head out at first light."

The others dropped onto the ground, preparing to sleep— but how could anyone sleep? "You can't go out there again," said Gal.

They all frowned at him, Rayne included.

"You nearly got caught today. This is nothing but dangerous and cracked. This place…." He shook his head and pulled his hands in his hair. "We never should have come. All of it is nothing but wishful thinking. You're going to find Halud. You're going to find this Augment baby. And then what?" He wanted to cry, shrieking into the night. "Nothing. Because there's nothing you can do. They'll just keep coming and coming. The more you do, they more they'll come after you." Couldn't they see he was trying to keep them all alive? He'd been here before. It wouldn't do anyone any good. If anything, he'd only ever managed to make it worse.

"There are worse things than soldiers and drones," said Sarrin.

"She's right, Gal," said Aaron. "You have to stop this." He glanced in the direction of the grey-on-grey painted symbol. "You're afraid. I get it. But do you really want the kids to give up? For Hap to win?"

Gal stilled himself. "It's dangerous."

"He's up to something," said Aaron. "Even you don't know how far he could go."

"I'm not going," Gal shouted, "I won't, and you can't force me." Crossing his arms and turning away from Aaron.

"No one asked you to," said Grant, and Gal flinched realizing he'd been arguing aloud with Aaron. "But we're going." Grant pointed at the four Augments and Rayne. "You can sit here and hide if you want to."

"Sometimes the better choice is to hide," he said, still looking out at the grey buildings. "There are some battles you just can't win. Trust me."

They said nothing, and he turned. They didn't spare him a glance as they laid out their goals on the roof, murmuring and signalling to each other.

"We'll go to the outskirts of the city," Gal tried -- couldn't they are how cracked this was? He had to persuade them to stop. "We can hide until Cordelia returns for us. They'll have your friends and we can go from there."

They ignored him, climbing into their makeshift beds. Rayne took a spare cloak from Alex and bedded down beside them.

"You must see how much they need to do this, Gal. Just like we did." Aaron said softly. "You don't think anything you say is going to stop them."

"They all think I'm just being ornery." Gal stepped to the parapet and clenched his hands on the half wall, Aaron leaning on it casually beside him. "But I don't know what will happen if he catches them. I don't know what Hap will do if there are Augments in his Central City. I just don't know. At one time, I thought I knew him, knew what he was capable of, but he's done far worse than I ever imagined."

"Is that what's got you so riled up and scared? I've never seen you like this."

"The problem with Hap is, he thinks he's doing the right thing. He thinks he's a god. He thinks he could never do wrong. And he believes it so much everyone around him believes it too." Gal bit his lip. "They made the Augments for a reason, Aaron. I don't know why they did, but it didn't go as planned. And look at everything Hap has done. God's, the secret facilities, hunting them across the stars…."

Aaron frowned.

"Time has only made it worse. I can't even predict what delusions he's convinced himself of. But there's no way around him and his army. No way anyone survives this."

"You survived," Aaron whispered, staring at Gal, his gaze so full of awe and how.

Fall slammed his eyes shut. Couldn't Aaron understand that that didn't matter? "You didn't!"

"Gal?" said Grant, the others staring at him across the roof. "Who are you talking to?"

SIX

KIERAN RUBBED AT THE SKIN on his forearms. He fought the urge to scratch outright—all he wanted to do was rip it off. The pain hadn't been this bad for a while.

Cordelia frowned at him. "Are you sure you don't want to sit in the tank?" she asked. "Just for a little while."

He shook his head. To emphasize his point, he reached out his crispy hands and held onto some of the more tactile ship controls.

They had left Etar's orbit immediately after the others had gone down. It was risky for Cordelia to get in close like that, especially given what the UEC soldiers had done to her travelling companion, Cornelius. Only a few of the Augments had volunteered to go to the surface in search of Halud. The rest of them milled around the large bridge Cordelia had constructed.

Hoepe glanced at him and shook his head, "Sorry, Kieran, you're maxed out for pain meds."

"I'm fine, really." He needed something to keep him occupied, he was going crazy just sitting in the regen-tank. And they had just arrived at the first planet they thought could house captured Augments. He wasn't about to sleep through that.

But Cordelia built-up a tank around him where he stood, filled with blue gel that would rehydrate his skin and ease some of the pain.

"I'm fine," he sputtered as the tank filled up around his head, only a small oxygen bubble left for him to breathe.

"It's okay, I'll make it so you can hear everything. And if you just think what you want to say, I can tell them anything you want to add."

"Cordelia," he protested.

She sighed. "If you're sure. I don't like seeing you like this." She brought the gel down to the level of his shoulders.

"The arms too," he said. "You know I like to talk with my hands."

She smirked—a human expression she must have picked up somewhere—and brought the tank down again.

"Leave the rest," he said under his breath. The fluid pooled around his waist, but his head and arms were free and dry, even styled if he knew Cordelia.

The shape-shifting alien had taken a liking to him. It was a good thing too, because he had peppered her with questions every minute he was awake. In turn, she'd used him to learn everything she could about engines and FTL drives—she would need it to make the long trip home when this was all over.

Across the room, Rami snapped his gaze to a nearby console, pretending he hadn't been staring at the exchange. The Augment had been on the exploding freightship with him and was still recovering from his own burns, but they weren't nearly as extensive.

At least Rami hadn't once called him a traitor since he woke up from his medically induced coma.

Hoepe peered into the tank, nodding his approval. Most 'common humans' would still be comatose if they hadn't died outright. He credited Cordelia's finely tuned healing gel, but

Kieran had a suspicion he owed Sarrin for his remarkably quick improvement. And for his ongoing discomfort now that she was far away.

He tried not to let himself think about her, or worry too much. After all, she was an Augment, she could take care of herself. But he would have given anything to be on the planet with them.

For the research, he promised himself; it wasn't every day you got to meet a real-life Augment. But it was more than that, she had asked to go home with him when his mission was over. She wanted to spend the rest of her life near the speed of light, recording the story of humanity. And he couldn't wait, somehow a lifetime watching the world spin by seemed a little less daunting with her around.

"Hey, daydreamer." Hoepe's twin brother Leove loomed over the tank, but—the friendlier of the two—he winked. "Remind me why we decided to stop at this planet—C479-alpha?"

What a shock that must have been for Hoepe, to discover a brother you never knew you had. Kieran felt a pang, recalling his sister Lauren whom he would never see again. She had left the Observer ship, chose not to come back after her research mission, and died of old age in natural time.

Cordelia answered Leove's question smoothly: "Galiant thought this would be a likely place for a secret Augment prison."

Hoepe grunted, staring at the rotating, reddish-grey dust ball in the view screen. "It looks pretty bleak. Is it even terraformed?"

"I am reading an atmosphere," said Cordelia. "Not much of one though. Gal indicated it was a prime candidate for terraformation when he explored it four years ago. Excellent soil composition rich in iron and manganese for agrarian pursuits. Pre-existing atmosphere and basic bacteria. And close to Etar 1.   A UEC base was constructed, but colonization was not pursued beyond that point. However, shipping manifests do indicate there is a freight run here fairly regularly."

"I see," answered Leove.

Cordelia smiled and nodded once. "The UEC base is on the far side, southern continent."

"Take us around," Hoepe ordered.

The pilot, Isuma, spun in her chair. But not before Cordelia had already engaged the shape-shifted thrusters and started them on their way. The frustration was evident on the pilot's face. And fair enough, Kieran had been feeling the same. The engines purred too perfectly. There wasn't anything to do to keep a guy from going crazy.

"Can you scan for life signs?" asked Leove.

Cordelia closed her eyes a second. "The sensors aren't picking up anything. But I feel several people there."

"How many?" asked one of the Augments, Thomas. He was already suited up in a type of battle armour. It looked thin and light, Cordelia's design.

Cordelia closed her eyes again. "I can't differentiate. A lot."

Hoepe nodded at Thomas. "Have the teams ready." There was no telling what they would encounter infiltrating the facility. If it was anything like Junk, it might be the entire contingent of elite black ribbon soldiers. But Thomas and the others were genetically enhanced, specially trained, child soldiers. They might be weak from their time in captivity, but they were still stronger, faster, and smarter than most men.

"Okay, Cordelia, time to get this tank off me," Kieran said.

She raised an eyebrow, but the tank didn't budge.

He tried to take a step forward. "Come on. We have to go soon."

The others paused their preparations and turned to look at

him.

"What?" he said, possibly more defensively than he should have.

"You're not going," said Cordelia.

Darn her that she could read his mind at all times.

"Kieran," chided Hoepe, his voice stern like he was lecturing a child. A dumb one.

"I'm not an invalid," said Kieran.

"You can't be out of the tank for more than half an hour," said Hoepe.

"You don't know what's down there. You might need an engineer." There had to be something he could do. Something useful.

"Your skin will dehydrate and then tear and peel off."

"You might need me."

Across the bridge, Rami slowly tugged on his own combat suit. He sent Kieran a look of regret and turned back to his boots.

"Let me out of this thing." He sloshed around again. "Come on." His arm, red and raw like the rest of him, banged on the edge before Cordelia could move it out of the way. "Jesus," he shrieked.

"Kieran, stop." Hoepe came and pressed something into his neck. "You need to rest. You're seriously injured."

"I haven't been doing anything but resting. I want to help!"

The drug hit him and Kieran stumbled back, half sitting against the wall of the tank.

"Sorry," Hoepe said.

He blinked heavily.

Thomas came and patted him on the head—the only part of him still sticking out from the goop. "You're worse than Sarrin."

He caught Rami staring at him again.

"We'll call you if we need anything," said Thomas. "We're

going to go in fast and hard and get them out. Shouldn't be more than an hour"

Kieran nodded. And then Cordelia wrapped him completely in the blue gel, drowning him as he slipped under the heavy sedative.

* * *

Hoepe fiddled with a set of controls, adjusting a view screen he knew nothing about.

"What are you thinking about, Brother?" Leove asked him.

Hoepe grunted. "Just preparing."

Leove's facial expression—easy to read because it was the same as his own—belied that he didn't believe him.

"He's worried about Kieran," whispered Cordelia.

"Ah. Because he's backsliding," Leove surmised. "He has been making incredible progress. Far beyond what we ever anticipated for a non-Augment. We can't be disappointed if his healing has some ups and downs."

"I know that," Hoepe nodded. After all, they had been trained the same way. Almost. Except Hoepe had been alone, his memory somehow wiped of anything before. Leove had remembered. He had been able to see and know their parents up until they too died from the Red Fever. He had even known Hoepe existed, while Hoepe stumbled around looking for some part of him that he didn't even know was missing.

They were identical. But they weren't the same at all.

Leove sighed. "I know you do."

"What does that mean?" he snapped, regretting it instantly.

"It means I know you know healing is never an exact process. I am concerned about Kieran's wellbeing too, but I think this is can't be considered unexpected. Especially now that Sarrin's gone to the planet."

"Sarrin? What does she have to do with it?"

Leove licked his lips, his face serious, like he was deciding how to broach a complicated subject.

The comm system pinged. "*We're on the surface*," came Thomas' voice. "*Preparing to go in. We'll keep the line open.*"

"Understood," said Leove. His jaw clenched tightly.

"Understood," copied Hoepe.

There was a shuffling across the line. The sound of doors slamming open. Feet running.

Leove gripped the back of a chair, until his knuckles turned white.

Thomas' breathing came heavy.

"Relax, Brother," said Hoepe, even though his own teeth were clenched together. No doubt they had both patched up their share of injured Augments in Evangecore and during the war. "They're superior soldiers. They've faced worse than this many times."

"I know that," Leove said through his own tight jaw.

Hoepe raised an eyebrow. "I know you do."

"Isuma's down there." Leove closed his eyes, his shoulders drawing up to his ears, and he blew out a tense breath. "I just wish we had more information about what they're running into."

More running, the squeak of boots on shined UEC compound floors. Hoepe could nearly visualize the path they travelled through the standard design UEC base. Their training in Evangecore mandated they all memorize the schematics for each of the standard building types. They probably never guessed they would use the knowledge like this.

"You don't look well," said Hoepe. "You should let me examine you."

"I'm fine, Hoepe."

"You suffered in Junk the same as the others."

Leove didn't answer.

Across the comm, another door, running, thumping,

thunking.

Then Thomas stopped. "*There's no one here,*" he said under his breath.

Leove shared a skeptical look with Hoepe.

"What do you mean?" Hoepe said.

It took Thomas a minute. "*There's no one here. No soldiers. Anywhere.*"

"What about the others?"

"We're headed to the basement now. We found the secret door, same as Junk."

The sound of boots descending stairs.

"*Oh no.*"

"What is it?" Leove leaned forward, shouting.

There was the ruffle of rapid hand signals, then, "*Cordelia is going to bring them straight up.*"

Hoepe frowned, "What?"

But there wasn't time.

Three bodies arrived in the hospital area around them. They weren't moving. Hoepe had to look closely to see the one breathe. Leove rushed forward. "They're dehydrated."

Hoepe's training exploded into action, cutting off everything else. "Colloids," he ordered. Already he was holding off a vein on the one, trying to place a catheter. Impossible, he was so flat. Still, he pushed the thin plastic into the arm, the dry tissue making it drag.

He fiddled until he felt the needle pop through the vein wall, and then secured the thing. Next he grabbed an IV bag and connected the line, letting it run in as fast as possible.

Leove already had the other two connected.

They glanced at each other knowingly, nervously. Dehydration this bad was almost always accompanied by a host of electrolyte and biochemical imbalances, heart arrhythmias, and organ damage that could be difficult if not impossible to overcome.

Hoepe drew a blood sample from the man's jugular vein in his neck, the only one large enough to access. The blood was nearly black and thick as oil.

Leove said a little prayer, tapping his five fingers to his chest and then his forehead.

The far wall of the infirmary opened, melting away to reveal a newly created room. In it stood all the Augments, those in battle armour holding up the others they had rescued from the facility. They shuffled forward together, angling to the rows of treatments beds that had suddenly sprung up from the floor.

Hoepe gasped, rapidly assessing and triaging, feeling like his body wanted to run in all directions at once. They all stumbled, weak, their eyes sunken. Their bones stuck out, all angles beneath nearly translucent skin and cachexic muscles. All of them on the brink of death.

Leove ran forward into the onslaught, helping one of the rescuers maneuver their charge onto a bed. Isuma pulled off her helmet. Leove touched her cheek tenderly for just a second, then turned his attention downward. His hands flew quickly as he worked. He muttered something and Isuma disappeared.

Hoepe turned to the nearest bed. Female, mid-twenties, severe dehydration and hypovolemic shock. He struggled to push the catheter through the skin. "Plasma-lyte solution," he ordered.

The Augment standing next to him fidgeted once in his combat suit. "Sorry?"

Hoepe pointed to the far cupboards and repeated himself. The Augment left to look, and Hoepe found himself frustratingly paused. He looked across the bay, seeing his brother move from patient to patient, Isuma trailing behind him, connecting IV lines.

The Augment finally returned with a bag of IV fluids—not

the Plasma-lyte he'd requested, but good enough. "Hook up the IV," he ordered, "500-mil bolus."

The Augment gave him a funny look, but Hoepe was already on his way to the next patient.

The blood analyzer dinged softly, letting him know his sample was finished. He bolted over to check the results. "Leove," he called.

His brother joined him, trailed by Isuma. Hoepe fought the urge to tell her to leave, but there wasn't time. "Advanced ketosis, uraemia, hyperglycaemia." A deadly build-up of toxins in the blood stream.

"Hypernatremia, hyperkalemia—his heart could stop at any minute," finished Leove.

Hoepe nodded. "Insulin CRI. Shock-rate fluids. Renoprotective and restorative cocktail."

"Agreed."

"He's seizing," said Isuma, looking into the chaos of beds and Hoepe's patient convulsing wildly on the bed.

The brothers looked at each other, sharing a split second look of terror, and ran. Leove drew up anticonvulsant drugs and injected them through the IV. Hoepe attached a neuro-monitor. Isuma held the man in place, grunting as he shook and writhed on the table.

The seizure stopped as soon as the drugs had a chance to circulate.

"That won't last long," said Leove. "Just the benzodiazepines holding it at bay."

Hoepe nodded. "We need to correct the electrolytes and glucose."

"I've never seen dehydration this severe before, have you?"

Hoepe shook his head. "How did it get so bad?"

"This isn't days," said Leove. "This is weeks."

"There wasn't anyone there," said Isuma. "It was completely empty. Abandoned."

"Abandoned?" said Leove.

"They just left them there, without food or water."

"Why?"

Hoepe shook his head. "We need to get to the other facilities as fast as possible. They may have been abandoned as well."

"Agreed."

"You're forgetting something."   Cordelia suddenly appeared, looking stressed.

"What?"

"The fluids you're using. They're here because you wanted them. But."

"Oh no," said Hoepe.

Leove shot him a questioning look.

Hoepe blinked back the rising panic in his chest. "None of these medicines are real. Cordelia won't let them integrate into the cells. Too hard to keep her self separated."

"You mean?"

"We can't treat them, not with what we have. Or if we do, they'll go back to this way the minute Cordelia pulls back."

Leove turned to Isuma. "Was there a hospital wing?"

She nodded. "There always is." Then, "We'll go down. See if there's anything left."

Leove put a hand on her shoulder and flashed a grim smile. "Thank you. Be careful."

She smiled back. "I always am. They need it. I hope they left something." Then she turned away, calling to others in the crowd as she went. Cordelia followed, sucking them away, back down to the planet's surface.

The strained look returned to Leove's face.

Hoepe reached a hand out.   "We have to keep going, stabilize them the best we can."

Leove recovered, still paler than he should have been. "Of course. It looks like our battle has just begun."

SEVEN

HALUD SAT ON THE SMALL cot, letting his head drop against the wall over and over. Eighteen days of incarceration in the rehabilitation ward, and he'd given up trying to influence the guards. There was no escape. There was no way to warn Sarrin. Hap's torture had been precise, and Halud had nothing but time to brood on the imminent death of his sister.

The door to the anteroom opened, and he leapt to his feet. A familiar, terrifying, grey with black clad figure stomped in briskly. The commandant waved the guard from the room.

"Here to take me to Hap again?" he asked as she opened the thick permaglass door to his cell. The First Speaker had summoned him a handful of times, it seemed for no other purpose than to gloat.

"Hardly." She crossed the distance between them almost too quickly for Halud to see, her hand wrapping around the old pendant around his neck and tugging sharply until the thong broke.

"That was my father's!" he snapped, reaching out futilely.

"Then may you rot with him when this is all over," she said. She spun on her heel, turning to the door.

"What do you want it for?"

She paused, her eyes narrowing as she turned just enough

for him to see the smirk that crossed her features. "005478F has been seen in the city."

005478F—Sarrin. "She's here?" His voice stuck in his throat, coming out no more than a hoarse whisper. She had come for him, just as Hap had predicted. He straightened himself. "What's Hap going to do?"

She turned, her wicked grin continuing. "He doesn't know she's here. He sent me to dispatch a rally in the city—something about folk with blue woven into their uniforms." She glanced at the pendant in her hand and the blue jewel set into it, frowning. "One of the surveillance drones was destroyed, so I took it and examined the last seconds of footage myself. It's her, I'd recognize that face anywhere. I have no interest in menial crowd control, the Augments need to be destroyed. Hap seems to have forgotten that I am his Augment hunter—not that pathetic fool he gave my warship to—and I will serve her to him on a platter."

"You're going to capture her?"

She tensed, fortifying herself as much as her stance. "I failed once, but I will not fail again."

He recalled the first time she had taken him to Hap, the flash of softness and the prayer she had sent up when he told her about Sarrin. "You know what they'll do to her," he said. "It won't be kind."

Her lower jaw jutted out. "She's an Augment. An animal."

"You care about her, about Sarrin. I saw it in your the other day."

She grumbled deep in her throat, her eyes narrowing, predatory and cold, a piercing blue. "You have no idea what you saw." Then she turned, the permaglass door sealing behind her as she strode from his cell.

He pressed against the glass. "Amelia, stop."

Surprisingly, she did, whirling around.

"Why are you here?"

She flashed the pendant at him, all of her viciousness levelled in her gaze. "I am the hunter." And then she was gone.

Halud sat back on the cot with a thump. But the commandant, the Augment hunter, had blue eyes. Not unlike his own. Not unlike Sarrin's. It couldn't be. A hand over his mouth, he sat back, mind racing. But it was no trick of the light, he was sure of what he saw. The commandant had Xenoralia. There was no other explanation.

EIGHT

Sarrin watched as Grant kneeled down and peered around the corner of the tiny alleyway. He turned back and nodded at them. All clear.

She unfurled herself from the wall, drawing the hood up over her face. Beside her, Alex and Luca did the same, tugging grey scarves over the damning barcodes on the backs of their necks. One by one, they stepped into the main street, joining the early morning stream of workers and folk already bustling over the stone walkways.

Luca and Grant crossed to the far side, Sarrin and Alex staying to the near, spreading themselves out so they could hide amongst the folk, avoiding the suspicious eyes of drones and soldiers.

Contrary to what Gal seemed to think, they weren't fools.

And they weren't fool enough to take Rayne with them either.

There was a pang of regret for leaving the XO behind, but her father was General Oleander Nairu, and she seemed determined to go to him. Whatever Rayne's intentions, things couldn't end well.

Sarrin paused to watch a large vid screen on the side of a building.

"You okay?"

Startled, she turned to see Alex. They were supposed to stay apart, but she didn't mind the company. The screen played through the morning cycle as they watched. It hadn't changed that much over the years—there was a new segment added, thanking the Gods for providing this home when their Earth had been destroyed. The other segments were the same as they had been when they had made them watch in Evangecore: the story of the Gods, the history of their descendants, a celebration of the Speakers.

Only Fred Lansford had been replaced by his son, Hap. Other than that nothing had changed.

The cycle finished and started from the top.

"We'll find him," said Alex. "I know it."

She nodded once. They had to find Halud, there wasn't another option.

"We'll find a clue at the hospital. We know he was there, in the research labs, a few times. I'm sure we can find something."

She nodded again, not trusting herself to speak as she stared blankly at the moving images repeating on the screen. Halud had given up everything for her, and while they knew he had made it to Etar alive, there was no telling what had happened after that or what shape he was in. The hospital was the best lead they had.

"What is it?" he asked when she hadn't moved after a minute.

She realized she was frowning. "I didn't see it."

"See what?"

"That he was going to leave."

He smiled, a little confused.

"When he left the ship. I hadn't said a single word to him. I couldn't." She sighed, dropping her gaze to her hands, the hands that were not hers anymore but constructs of the

Central Army. "I can see everything, every permutation of every fight, the way these folk would scatter if a gas bomb landed here or here. But I didn't see that my own brother was going to leave and throw himself into this."

"Ah." Alex rocked back on his heels.

"You all came with me, but you shouldn't have. I don't know where he is, or what's going to happen. I'm not even sure if we'll survive. I'm not what you think I am."

He paused, staring across the crowd until he cleared his throat. "I had a brother in Evangecore. He died—like really died. They took him out of the arena and he never came back."

She searched him.

"I thought the same thing was going to happen to me," he said. "But it didn't. You stopped it. After you tore apart the observation tower, we didn't go into the arena anymore. No one had to kill, or be killed. I don't know what you think about yourself, or why you think we're here, but we knew the risks." He shrugged. "Without you, most of us might not be here—might not have survived the arena.   Might still be trapped in Junk. Might have been blown to the stars by the warship. You saved my life, and now I'm going to help you save Halud."

He smiled free and easy, but she had killed to save him. The memory of tearing through the glassine and into the researchers burned through her. Alex had put his faith in a monster.

He searched her a minute, frowning. "When my brother died, I didn't know it for days.   He was missing, everyone knew logically that he was gone, but it was like I didn't register it, couldn't comprehend it.   The things we saw in Evangecore... well, they didn't leave a lot of room for simple things. It was survival, pure and simple. I still feel guilty about my brother, but don't be like me—don't dwell on what happened or didn't happen. It doesn't matter. What matters is that we can go find him now."

He nudged her on the shoulder, just once, barely—an action she was growing increasingly comfortable with. Following his gaze, she saw Grant and Luca several paces ahead, making their way to the end of the street and the large, open central square where the Speakers' Tower loomed over them. Alex stayed beside her as they followed, the stream of folk taking them nearly to the based of the Central Hospital.

A gargantuan building in itself, seven stories high, the hospital was still dwarfed by the Speakers' Tower. Somewhere, near the top of that tower, was Halud's office. Maybe even Halud himself.

The entrances were guarded. A full tour around the outside of the building revealed soldiers standing guard every twenty metres.

"Is it just me, or is this place pretty locked down?" said Grant.

The others nodded. It had been a long time since any of them had been in a city, but even during the war, there hadn't been this many soldiers in the central square on Earth.

The way the folk veered around the soldiers, it certainly seemed as though it were out of the ordinary.

Flecks of blue continually caught Sarrin's eye as they stood watching.

"We need to ask someone," said Sarrin, searching the moving crowds.

"What?" Grant's eyes flashed, alarmed.

Before he could say more, she spun away. Before she could lose the idea in her head. Before her good senses could talk her out of it. She pushed into someone, blocking out the horrible sensation of their emotions as she got too close.

The person stumbled and tripped.

"Oh Gods, forgive me," she said, forcing her eyebrows top and her mouth narrow in an approximation of surprise.

The man caught his balance and turned, looking at her. A fleck of blue waved from the seam of his jacket.

She cast her gaze down so he couldn't see her eyes. Come at it sideways, Kieran's voice popped into her head. "I'm sorry," she said, making her voice airy and high pitched, "these guards just have me so flustered."

"No worries, love. It has us all on edge." He reached for her, placing a steadying hand on her arm. She forced herself not to flinch. An image of a workplace and a sense of urgency crossed, even through the thin fabric of the cloak.

She tugged on her cloak, revealing the piece of blue yarn that still lay there, woven into the fabric.

He bent his head towards her. "Rumour has it a group of rebels tried to break into the hospital labs."

Sarrin's heart jumped, and she pulled away. "I'm so sorry to have delayed you," she blurted in a dry voice. She whipped around, moving as fast as she dared away from the man.

The others were pressed in the shadow of a building across from the guarded hospital. "How did you do that?" Grant asked, as she returned.

She shrugged. "Rebels tried to break into the hospital."

"Rebels?"

"The same rebels that bombed Evangecore?"

Sarrin shook her head, a real smile creeping onto her features as her mind connected the dots. "I don't know, but they were making the Xenoralia vaccine there that Halud reported on. And I would guess the same 'vaccine' that turned that baby into one of us."

"No," Grant scoffed. "That doesn't make sense. If there's a vaccine, they're anticipating a resurgence of the virus. Maybe it's already started and they don't want to scare the folk."

She was almost sure of it now—the vid she'd seen of Halud in the hospital had shown an infant. Not the same infant, but they had called for all parents to bring their babies for vaccination. Gal had said it: they made the Augments. The question was why.

"We need to find a way in," Grant said, turning their attention back to the hospital.

They could get in, easily, by running through the guards and scaling the wall to the nearest window. But it would draw too much attention. So far it seemed there wasn't an increase in patrols looking for her, but they didn't need to push their luck.

Tracing the building again, Sarrin's eye caught on the loading doors, and the small entrance beside them. Alex nearly ran into her. "The door," she said.

"It doesn't look right."

She nodded. And then pointed to the wall beside it.

"A mark?" he asked. "Someone painted something there a long time ago, but I can't quite make it out, it's so faded."

Indeed, it did look like they'd washed it several times and tried to paint over it, but her genetically enhanced vision picked it out. "A circle," she said, "with two chevrons in the interior."

Grant joined them. "What is it?"

A guard stirred, shifting his laz-rifle twenty paces to their right.

They moved away, finding another shaded, out of the way alcove to stand in.

"Someone forced the lock on that cargo door," Alex said. His gaze shifted to Sarrin and she nodded at him to continue. "There's a symbol on the wall."

"A circle with two chevrons," Sarrin confirmed. "It was pointed that way." The three of them followed her outstretched finger. They'd seen the symbols in different cities during the war.   The chevrons always pointed a different direction, painting a kind of path for them to follow.   In the war, it had led the Augments to caches of food and supplies.

"John P's symbol?" asked Grant.

"Yes," said Sarrin. What would it lead them to here?

* * *

Rayne cowered in her corner on the rooftop, curled up with the blanket drawn up to her face, staring into the cloudless sky.

Gal's heart stabbed his chest with each constrained beat. She had barely moved, shooting laz-beams with her eyes every time he got too close. Better she was alive and hate him than be dead or tortured, he told himself.

He leaned against the grey half-wall, staring blankly until the buildings and paintings in the distance all blurred together.

"Are you really planning to hide here forever?"

Gal grunted at Aaron's sudden reappearance.

"If it weren't for the Augments collecting food and water, you'd have dehydrated yourself to death by now, I think."

"Can't you just leave me alone?"

"Nope."

Gal sighed again, dropping his head.   His eyes caught on the cracked symbol painted on the buildings in front of him.

"This is a terrible plan, staying up here, hoping they don't find us," said Aaron, "and you know that. I know you know it."

"It's not terrible," mumbled Gal.

Aaron shot him a look.   "You used to be a brilliant strategist. This is the worst plan I've ever seen."

"So many people died."

"People die every day."

"I miss you. The real you."

"I'm still here, ish. I'm not really gone. That's what they say." Aaron leaned back against the wall casually, checking something on his hands. "But I wish you'd do something to honour me, you know."

"I think about you every day—when it doesn't hurt too much."

"That's not what I mean. I died thinking I was making a difference. I was happy to do it. We were helping the kids. And we did—help them, I mean." He scrubbed hand over his face, as though trying to collect his thoughts. "I didn't want to die, but I knew the risk. I was okay with it because we succeeded."

"We didn't succeed at anything."

Aaron held up a hand to stop him. "We did. But only part. I thought people would still be there to carry on. I died thinking we were at least a step closer. But you let me down, Gal."

That was the truth, wasn't it?

His friend crossed his arms over his chest. "I wanted us to win. I helped us get close. But I couldn't finish. That was up to you, and you failed."

Gal hung his head, glancing at Rayne. He had failed. At everything.

"I don't mean in the war. I don't mean the cause. You failed me."

He nearly choked. "I'm sorry."

"Don't be sorry. Do something about it. There's still time."

Gal shook his head repeatedly, unable to answer.

"Don't, Gal. Don't make excuses. Don't hide."

"I'm not making excuses."

"You're telling me you honestly don't care anymore. You can just turn your back on everything."

"I still care. But I care more about my life."

"Aren't they the same?"

"No," he shouted. Aaron didn't get it, didn't see the years after he had died. He ran a hand through his hair to calm down. "I can't save them and save myself. It's one or the other."

"I think they're the same."

"The minute Cordelia dropped us on this planet, it signed my death warrant. I have to get off the planet."

"Who cares. It's been signed for years. But, guess what, you're still not dead."

"And I want to keep it that way!"

"You need to go to the rebels, to the symbol. The fact that it's painted there… it means something."

"It doesn't mean anything. It could be something completely different. The people who painted it probably have no idea what it means."

"But you do."

"It means death."

Aaron snapped, "It's a symbol. It means whatever you want it to mean."

"Don't blame this all on me," he shouted. Gal jabbed his finger into Aaron's chest. "You died. You left."

Aaron pulled back. "Not by choice. I would have stayed if I could."

"No, of course it's my fault. My fault. I'm the one that took us there that night. It was my plan." His voice cracked, and he gasped in a shaky breath.

"The plan worked," said Aaron. "I just got caught."

Movement caught the corner of Gal's eye. He turned, heart pounding wildly. He'd forgotten she was there. He'd been yelling at Aaron, at a figment of his cracked mind, out loud.

Rayne stared back, frozen in place. Her eyes were wide, her feet turned towards the descent at the half wall.

"Do. Not. Leave," he commanded. He pointed directly at

her, then motioned for her to sit down, like a child. A wave of confusion took him -- he really was cracked.

Her eyes flared, and she stumbled back, as though from a physical blow.

He shut his eyes, remembering how he had thrown her. Hurt her. What was happening to him?

"I'm going to see my father," she said, her voice steady.

"No."

"You can't tell me what to do. I'm not your prisoner."

"If you go to him, you'll doom us all."

"You're cracked."

"Maybe." Probably.

She took a step towards the wall.

He took two towards her.

"I'm going to go see the general," she said. "Someone needs to get this sorted out." She took another step.

His brain buzzed until the words exploded out, "Hap has standing orders for my death. If I'm caught here, I'll die."

She stood shocked for a minute. "The Gods don't kill people," she said. "They love us all if we let them."

"The Gods don't kill people, but the Speakers do."

"You're cracked," she shouted wildly. "They are the descendants of the Gods, they hear the Will of the Gods!"

"Hap is dangerous," Gal shouted back, letting go of any semblance of sanity. "I don't even know what he's capable of anymore. The things we've seen them do to the Augments…."

"They don't know that the Augments aren't out to hurt us!"

"What," he snarked, "the Gods couldn't tell them?"

She gasped.

"We can't be caught. I don't know what delusions the Speakers have, or that the general has. I don't know what would happen to you."

"My father—"

"Forget it! He's Strength's General. He's—" A voice, his conscience, stopped him. She could at least believe the man she loved wasn't a monster.

"You're delusional, Gal. I've seen you talking to yourself, arguing. There's no one there." She gestured into the empty space, right at Aaron. "Let me help you. You've had a hard time. Hoepe said the JinJiu could have lasting effects for weeks, even months. This isn't you."

"You want to know why I run Freight in the Deep Black— the Speakers promised death would find me if I ever showed my face on a central planet again."

"That's spread." But the gears started turning, he could see it on her face, why one of Hap's favoured captains had been suddenly demoted to the worst haul run in Freight, why he had stayed there for years. "He wouldn't do that. Why would he say that?"

"Don't you get it. I might be delusional sometimes, but it's only because I'm trying to forget. I blew up a UEC ship to protect Cordelia."

"Cordelia?" She shook her head, as if shaking the dangerous thoughts from it. "But Hap was your friend."

"There are no friends here."

"Surely, my dad…."

"Stop, Rayne."

"You blew up a UEC ship? Like you blew up the Ishash'tor."

He stared off into the distance, angry that he'd said too much. Or said too little. "Yes," he said quietly. "I told you, sometimes I am delusional. I drank a lot of JinJiu. I had a lot to forget."

"You need help."

"Maybe. I need you to stay here."

"The First Speaker doesn't want you killed." But there was an edge of doubt in her voice.

"He definitely does."

"You're cracked."

"Are you going to stay on the roof or not?"

"Am I a prisoner."

"Are you going to stay?"

"I hate you."

"I know."

But she turned, stepping back toward the centre of the roof. "I'm going to make you see how wrong you are." And she pressed her five fingers into her chest and prayed.

* * *

Sarrin made her way to the bottom of a building with the symbol high on its wall, following its direction down a long alley. It emerged into a quiet intersection, and the four Augments stood looking for their next clue. A surveillance drone whizzed by, and Sarrin ducked her head.

Luca pointed to a symbol in a window, and they followed it, finding the next symbol on a streetlight. Tucked into shadowed crevices, painted in miniature. They were hard to see, easy to miss if you didn't know to look, but the signs were everywhere. They followed quickly through a warren of small alleys and narrow streets, deep in the residential subdivisions of the city. With each next sign, her heart raced faster and faster, her feet drawing her closer to Halud.

He might not be there—it was a long shot at best, but it didn't stop her heart from hoping.

Another drone buzzed overhead. For a minute it paused, swivelling where it hovered, then whizzed away.

"A lot of drones today," said Alex.

Grant shrugged. "More guards, more drones. The city's on lockdown."

"I don't see another symbol, do you?" said Luca.

Sarrin shook her head, her eyes darting over every surface in the quiet square they now found themselves in. The corners of her vision started to darken and fade. She saw pops of blue everywhere, but when she looked, the folk walking past were all clad in grey on grey, their faces neutral. Where was Halud?

"We'll look around." Grant pushed past, stepping into the middle of the square, out in the open.   Luca followed, moving in an opposite direction, watching carefully even though there was no one else in the square.

The edges of her vision fuzzing, Sarrin moved into one of the streets leading away and searched for the circle with two chevrons.

Another drone paused, its whirring motors taunting, and she ducked down.

The others passed signals back and forth—nothing found. Her eyes met Grant's—there had been nothing in this direction either. The trail had run cold. She lifted her hand to give the signal, but her eyes caught on something far more interesting: a silver chain, tarnished and nearly blending in to the grey on grey, dangled from the step of a rickety side door.

She wouldn't have seen it had she not crouched down to avoid the drone.

Scrambling forward, she pressed on the door, feeling it creak open, and pulled at the chain. It nearly pulsed in her hands, still warm from whoever had held it last. She would have recognized the attached pendant anywhere, with its round shape, and rough silver work, and the blue stone set in the centre.

"What is it?" Grant asked, jogging up behind her. The others were close behind.

"Halud's," she said simply.   "Our..." -- she frowned, a memory assaulting her out of nowhere -- "our Father made it." He'd been a rebel then too, or something like it.

Her clouded vision focussed on the door—unmarked but the right place all the same—and she pushed inside.

"Halud!"

A hand clamped over her mouth mid-shout: Grant.   A flood of his terror bled through her where skin met skin. Of course, she'd been too excited, reckless, foolish to shout out.

Grant stumbled away as though he'd been burnt—she noted it vaguely as she stepped into the small, dark, empty room.

The others shuffled in behind her, the rickety door shutting behind them. Sarrin's vision started to cloud over. The small room was too much like Evangecore, too much like the Uruhu cage. Her mind played sounds: the clicking and whirring of hydraulics, the zap of laz-beams.

"It's just an empty room," Luca said in disbelief, her words both calming and distressing.

"No," Sarrin said, clutching the pendant. She heard them, maybe felt them, behind the wall. They were close, shuffling and positioning.

The panelled ceiling slid back an inch, exposing the blast end of a laz-rifle.

An old one, it looked like. Low-calibre and glitchy.

"Sarrin," Grant hissed, his eyes fixed above them. They all had reflexes fast enough to dodge the old weapon before it could charge, but the room was too small.

Alex stepped forward, his hands held out beside his head. "Please," he said. "We're looking for something. We don't mean you any harm."

The panel slid back just enough to reveal two sets of wide eyes staring back at them.

"You're fools," said the one.

Alex paused. "Please."

Grant stepped forward. "Did you try to break into the Central Hospital? To find a vaccine? We followed your symbols."

The two rebels paused, the grip on their rifles loosening.

The silence was enough. "Halud was here," Sarrin blurted.

Rifles readied above them instantly. Grant stepped back.

"We need to find him," she heard herself, frantic.

"No, you're fools," hissed the rebel. "Go away."

"So he was here," said Grant.

They slid the ceiling panel forward, closing it, but Grant's hand was there first, pushing it open. The rebels clutched their rifles to their chests. They were no more than boys, terrified. "It was a trap," stammered the one. "They're all gone. The UECs knew, they were waiting for them."

"It's just us here, I swear," said the other. "They took them away. Same as they take everyone. They left the pendant here."

"Who left the pendant?" asked Grant, but his voice was too slow.

Sarrin slammed open the rickety door, sunlight streaming in, despite the pooling black clouds of her vision. The monster flared to life, her vision nothing but a pinpoint in the intense black cloud—it had been trying to warn her. She thought it was just the anticipation of finding Halud. But something was wrong here, very, very wrong.

High above, a laz-rifle clicked. Clad in the grey with black uniform of the elite squadron, UEC soldiers surrounded them from all directions. One-hundred-eight, she counted instantly —twenty on the roof, the rest filling the square.

Her body spun instinctively out of the doorway, everything around her slowing. Beams of light shot across and around her body, never touching. The soldiers were too far away, their reflexes too slow.

The boy was right, they were fools. They had been set up. The symbol and the pendant left for them to find. If the boys were to be believed, Halud had been set up, and so had they. She clutched his pendant tighter in her hand.

Alex was shouting, but she couldn't hear over the high

pitched whine in her head. He waved his arms, motioning for her to follow—the three Augments had already started to tear a path through the soldiers, tossing bodies to the side like pillows.

She knew she needed to run, but something kept her there, and she dodged laz-beam after laz-beam. Extreme tactical error.

The monster inside of her growled, begging to be let out, to destroy every soldier in the square. The edges of her vision drowned in dark clouds. But something else fought with her consciousness, a desperate, floating sensation, her mind both in her body and somewhere else.

On top of the building directly opposite her, sat a bio-pulse generator, it's blue orb silent. She couldn't see it, but knew it was there, the same as she knew the hand that was reaching out to trigger its crippling mechanism. Her body tensed in anticipation of the pain that would rip through her.

Of their own volition, her eyes fixed to the figure on the roof of the building, her body stilling. "Amelia," she whispered.

The commandant's hand hovered over the bio-pulse trigger, twitching in anticipation, but it stilled, the same as Sarrin had. Her blue eyes stared down across the square, meeting Sarrin's.

The monster quieted, the fight around them ceasing to exist. The only thing that mattered was Amelia. Her friend wasn't lost, not entirely. Instinctively, she turned her palms out, her breathing steady as she opened herself to the hunter, throwing herself on the mercy of Amelia who had once been her sister.

Amelia's shoulders softened, her hand came away from the blue orb.

Sarrin blew out a breath.

Something pulled her back as a laz-bolt flew in front of her face. Alex had his hand on her cloak. Another bolt burned into the wall beside her.

On the roof, the commandant blinked a few times. She raised her arm, the set of her shoulders as severe as ever.

The moment was lost, but there had been a moment, however foolish it had been. Sarrin ran, her legs pushing against the con-plas hard and fast.

NINE

Amelia pushed out a shaky breath, squaring her shoulders before she thrust open the door to the First Speaker's office and plunged inside.

The First Speaker paced the width of his office, hands flying as he shouted at his general.

Nairu sat in one of the chairs by the desk, rigid as stone. "It is the Path of the Gods, First Speaker. I have Faith," he said in the first moment of silence Hap had offered.

Bulking shoulders heaving, Hap spun on his heel, ready to tear into the general—verbally or otherwise—but he turned to the desk instead, slamming both fists into the thick wood, seething.

Amelia paused in the centre of the room, partway along the mural and opposite a stuffed head that read *Gorilla gorilla*: Great Ape. The glass eyes seemed to follow her in the disturbingly human face. She scuffed her boot on the floor.

General Nairu turned his head at the sound. Her swore as he turned back to Hap. "The commandant is here."

"What?" Hap roared. His beady eyes landed on her, and she braced in a military salute, careful to duck her head and stoop her shoulders. "Oh. Commandant." He gestured to the chairs where Nairu was sitting, calling her forward.

Nairu stood and moved to the side of the desk, Hap on the far side, and Amelia stood between the chairs, refusing to sit.

Hap chewed the inside of his cheek. He leaned forward on the desk. "What do you have to say for yourself?"

"I —," but she didn't know. She had let an Augment go, had her caught out in the open, with an entire platoon of elite soldiers, and just let her run away. And she'd played out the scene in her memory over and over, trying to figure out exactly what had happened, every minute since the girl had escaped until she was standing here.

"You had an open shot. You didn't take it."

She hadn't. She'd just stood there. "The machine malfunctioned. The trigger jammed and failed to activate."

"That isn't how it reads in the report."

No matter how she looked at it, there was no explanation for what happened, for her hesitation. She didn't hesitate. She was the Commandant. The Augment hunter.

She'd caught and killed hundreds.

But this one girl.

"Your assignment is to Security. You were removed from Special Operations."

"I am far more suited to Special Operations. You know this."

"Do not speak over me."

She gulped and bowed her head.

"There was no reason for you to examine the drone footage."

"The drone fell under my purview as Security."

He held up a hand, commanding her to be silent. "Certainly there was no reason to commandeer an elite squadron and utilize classified technologies."

They were her squadron, she had trained them for the hunt. The tech had been partly designed by Guitteriez for her use. But she kept her head bowed, her mouth closed.

She shut her eyes, wishing she could go back into that moment and just pull the trigger. The plan had been perfectly executed, the Augments surrounded. One blast of the pulse-generator would have stilled her enough for any incompetent foot soldier to shoot her and arrest her. But she hadn't been able to do it.

Over and over the moment played. Over and over, her mind knew what it should do, and yet her fingers hesitated.

With no explanation.

Except one word: Sarrin. A name that was becoming too familiar, too everywhere. It filtered through her core, spreading tendrils through her entirety, making her breath constrict and her body warm all at the same time.

"Commandant."

Her head snapped up.

"Did you hear me?"

She was a commandant, she was that. Yes.

"Do you understand that your role is no longer to hunt Augments. It is against the Gods. What you have done is treason. It's blasphemy."

She frowned. "I serve the Gods."

"You have failed in your duty."

No. "The trigger jammed, I—."

"The trigger is in full working order. You have become dangerous. An experiment that has gone too far."

"If I'd succeeded—"

"But you didn't. You failed. You have failed the Gods."

But she hadn't failed Sarrin.

Sarrin?

She'd failed to capture Sarrin.

"What do you mean, 'experiment?'"

But Oleander Nairu stood at her shoulder. He pressed an auto-injector into her neck, its contents penetrating her skin with a loud hiss, and the world faded away.

* * *

Amelia woke, blinking back groggy vision. Her shoulder was cramped, and she grunted, trying to twist into a better position. She was being dragged, she realized, and fought against it, but the drugs were still in her system, making her sluggish and uncoordinated.

Two soldiers gripped her arms. Two of her soldiers, the black insignia running along their grey uniforms identified them as elite squadron. Confused, she glanced up at them, trying to see their faces, to identify them. Harsh white light beat down on her, overhead lamps flickering as she was pulled along the long corridor. It brought a painful pang to her chest, a panicked familiarity that seemed almost overwhelming.

They paused, then hefted her roughly, lifting her up onto a hard surface: a bed.

Another injection pressed into her neck.

Her dull hand reached out, groping along the surface for some purchase on the mattress, but there was none and she slipped into oblivion.

A little girl smiled. She was young, too young. Her foot slid through the rungs as she climbed to the upper bunk in a military barracks.

With a start, Amelia woke, reaching for her pounding chest. But her hand was tied, strapped down. The small space, its blinding white walls and harsh overhead lights, was too familiar. Her heartbeat turned frantic, a wail building up in her chest.

Why had she done it? Why hadn't she just pulled the trigger?

She would have been a hero. Capturing the prize Augment they had been hunting for months and been unable to hold onto. She would have brought her for Hap to kill himself. But Speakers were good, he wouldn't kill. She would have done it in front of him though, as a gift. And he would have reinstated her as the Commandant of the warship, and she would have gone on hunting the most elusive prey under the stars.

It left a bitter taste in her mouth, an unpleasantness in her stomach. A sob escaped her throat.

No one cried, she told herself swallowing back the tears. It made you look weak, and you could never look weak. They would take you away.

Medical monitors beeped at the side of the room, their wires reaching from her limbs, giving the impression that it was a hospital room. But it was a cell, and she was familiar with the construction of cells. A seemingly solid construction, but there was always a seam, always a gap that could be slipped through.

How did she know that?

She curled on the bed as much as the restraints would allow.

She had been stripped of her uniform, laid there now in a hospital wrap. Hopeless.

They liked to crush Hope.

You can't give up, Amy. You just can't, a small voice wailed in the back of her head. *I need you. Please.*

Sarrin.

What was it about the Augment, that one in particular, that defied everything Amelia had lived for?

She examined her wrists: Class 2 restraints. Modified release. Without thinking, her wrist flicked. Back and forth quickly with a half-twist. The restraint popped open.

She looked down in disbelief. Then rolled over, releasing the other wrist, and then the legs.

The monitors beeped along steadily, an increase in pitch and frequency signalling her quick-beating heart.

She forced her heart rate to slow, her breathing to be even. She'd seen enough hospital monitors to know they could be fooled, like any other piece of machinery. They used to....

What did who used to do?

But she had already punched in the commands to start the monitor on a continuous loop. She pulled the sensors from her body, careful to map them so they could be replaced, then rose from the bed.

She quickly identified the seam in the cell, digging her fingers into the small crevice and pulling to separate the wall paneling from the floor. She slipped through the small opening and disappeared into the wall.

The layout of the building, all of its room and its hidden spaces, came into her mind. A schematic she was sure she had never studied, and yet it was there. She had only a rough idea of where she was headed. All she knew was she needed answers.

In the lowest floor of the Speaker's compound, she dropped into the main corridor. She found the door, pushing the control for it to open.

The guard inside startled, then stood rapidly, pressing his hand to his chest in salute. "Commandant," he acknowledged, although his eyes roamed questioningly over her unusual attire.

"Get out," she barked, harsh as she could manage, lest he question why and how she'd come to be here like this in nothing but a hospital gown.

He nodded and bolted from the room.

The Poet laid on the cot on his back, arms crossed over his chest. The pose of the dead.

What was she doing here?

She paced back and forth in front of the permaglass wondering if she should wake him. The hospital gown moved and crinkled awkwardly around her.

An eye creaked open, rolling to the side to watch her without moving his head. So he wasn't asleep at all. She paused her pacing, and he sat up, eyeing her warily.

Her feet took up the swift back and forth movement again, her hands clasped crisply behind her back, the movement the only thing she felt certain of in this moment.

He stood, coming to the glass to watch her more closely. "You don't look well, Commandant."

Three times she paused and tried to ask her question, but she closed her mouth and restarted her pacing. "I need to know," she started, but it wouldn't come. "Tell me," she tried again.

He lifted a single curious eyebrow. "Tell you what?"

She shook her head. What was it she wanted? What was it she needed?

"You don't look well," he said again.

"Quiet," she snapped.

"Where's my pendant?"

Her foot paused mid-air. The last she had seen it was clutched in 005478F's outstretched hand. "I don't care," she said, feet falling back into the comforting rhythm.

He frowned. "Did it get you what you wanted?"

She shook her head, sneering. "Your sister?" She'd wanted it to sound angry, blaming, but it came out a question.

"You didn't catch her. That's what Hap was so mad about it," Halud surmised. "Good. I'm glad. And you never will. She's more than you could ever be."

It was true. Amelia had failed.

She had failed the Speakers, failed the Gods.

Failed Sarrin.

"What is it you want, Commandant?"

"I'm not a commandant," she whispered.

"So what are you?"

"Forget it."

She pulled at the wall panelling in the anteroom, disappeared back into the walls, into the narrow space. She crawled back over the ceiling, to the cell they had put her in and slipped back through the seam, pressing it back into place. She connected the electrodes and erased the looping code. The restraints clicked easily back into place.

She was a prisoner. Nothing less, nothing more.

TEN

SARRIN'S FEET PADDED ACROSS THE cold con-plas floors, passing rows of identical beds. She flopped onto bed 7C, her hands trembling. Sitting there, she fought the unforgiving urge to wail—she'd done that yesterday; it hadn't helped. The other girls had only gotten mad.

Where was Halud?

For that matter, where was she?

"Hey kid, this is my bunk." A tall girl, with a pale face framed by gleaming blonde hair, stood in front of her, her hands on her hips. She wasn't any older than nine or ten, but to Sarrin she was a giant.

"Sorry," she mumbled. Head down, she stood on the bed and wrapped her hands around the ladder that led to the upper bunk. Her foot slipped off the rung and she clung with her hands until she found her footing again.

The girl scowled.

Forcing her shaking body to stand, Sarrin found her footing and leaned back, staring at the daunting distance of only a few feet. She'd climbed higher trees, but that was outside, with Halud, without her whole body trembling as much as it had in the last few days. Without doctors probing her and running tests. Before she had gotten sick.

She shifted, sticking her butt out so she could bring her knee up to her chest, extending to try to reach the next rung. She contacted, and then started to shuffle her hands, to pull herself up, but her stocking foot slid *through and she slammed into the ladder with an oomph, her one foot sticking straight out.*

"Gods," scowled the girl. But she reached her hands up and lifted Sarrin, untangling her. "You're tiny. How old are you anyway?"

Sarrin was still swaddled in the girls arms. She tucked her chin into her chest before holding up a hand with three fingers.

She felt the girl still. "And they sent you here?"

Sarrin rubbed a hand across her nose to keep from crying.

The girl deposited her on the bed. Frowning, she looked around, as though checking no one was listening. "Look, just for now, until you're a bit... taller... I'll sleep on the top bunk, you take the bottom. Make sure it's always made, in case there are inspections. I don't want to get in trouble because I'm helping you out. Understand?"

Sarrin nodded.

"And don't cry," said the girl. "No one cries in Evangecore."

In a flash, Sarrin found herself fumbling with a laz-rifle: *The other girls pulled apart and reassembled the laz-rifles easily, but Sarrin couldn't figure out where to start.*

She fought the urge to cry.

A hand reached down and took the gun. The blonde girl—Amy—scanned the group the group before she bent down to Sarrin's level and pulled the battery pack and then the fuses and ion converters from the rifle, her hands moving slowly so Sarrin could follow.

She handed the weapon back and went back to her own, falling into rhythm with the other girls.

The scene changed again, Sarrin's breath catching in her throat like a physical blow.

Amelia tugged a comb through her hair while Sarrin clutched a pillow to her chest. Amelia's own strawberry blonde hair gleamed in the light having been brushed through thoroughly. Sarrin's was still wet from the shower Amelia had pushed her into, and it hung in dripping clumps around her head. Not the first time, she'd been in Evangecore for nearly a year.

"*Sarrin, listen to me. You have to brush your hair. If it's clumped like this, they'll see. You don't want any reason to be singled out.*"

No, she didn't. A shudder passed through her.

Then, they were in the arena:

An explosion blew up dust on the simulated battlefield twenty metres away. Amelia grabbed her and pushed her behind nearby cover.

Sarrin crouched behind the bush and adjusted her too-large helmet and faceplate. Her laz-rifle stuck out from her lap where it was squished between her legs and chest.

Across the scrub, she saw a boy crawling on his hands and knees. Behind them, infiltrating their front line. He looked at her, then squatted back on his feet and held up his laz-gun.

He aimed at Sarrin.

Amelia threw herself into a defensive position on the ground and let off a series of shots with her laz-gun.

The boy crumpled.

Amelia half-dragged, half-threw her until they had reached another cover of scraggly brush and broken down shuttle parts.

"*He was going to shoot you,*" *she yelled.* "*Gods.*" *She ran both her hands through her hair before she remembered what she was doing and reclutched her laz-rifle. After a minute, she glanced at Sarrin again.* "*You shoot first. Got it.*"

She nodded, because that's what Amelia wanted.

"*You always shoot first. Act, not react. Okay?*"

Sarrin nodded again.

Amelia shook her head once. She was twelve now, taller even than before. "*Gods, Sarrin. If anything happened….*" *She trailed off as she lifted her rifle and let off another series of shots.*

Each zap of the laz-rifle sent a shock through Sarrin.

Zing-zing-zing-zing   Until it started to blend together, repeat on repeat. She shut her eyes against it. Hated the sound. Hated seeing the boy fall over and over and over again.

And the zing became a clang   And then a ding. Ding.   Ding. Ding! DING!

And then a sound that was not a ding. Loud and clear and solid. Like a branch snapping from a tree in a storm. And a sound that was omega.

Time stopped. Her vision was dark.

Targets surrounded her, one close, reaching for her. It moved fast, almost as fast as the holograms in Evangecore. But she was faster, catching it, and throwing it.

The others scrambled away. Someone was shouting. People were on the roof.

She leaped towards the target, grabbing it with her hands. He grappled with her, strong, fast. Her hands fell into place, twisting automatically, snapping his neck. But he dodged, twisting violently out of her grip, and threw himself over the side of the building.

She turned, more target-points behind her. She saw how they moved, watched them circle around, saw their murderous thoughts. Angry. Afraid. Determined.

She leapt at the two that were closest together, grabbing their throats and throwing them to the ground with what should have been fatal force for any guard or UEC soldier. But they rolled away, scrambling.

A heavy whack came across her arm and back.

She leapt backwards, letting herself fall so she could kick out with her feet.

Where was Amelia? She yelled for her, still half in the dream. If this was the battleground, she would be there. The units always trained together. But this wasn't Evangecore.

The target point fell.

She leapt at him, pushing off the rooftop to propel herself. She slammed her knee into the soft abdomen, preparing to make him omega.

Her ears detected the whistling as another wooden staff came down, aiming for the back of her skull, and she flung herself out of the way. He advanced on her again, quickly, and she pulled the spear, taking it from his hands.

Amelia was dead. She died. She fell in combat. In her mind, Sarrin saw the blonde girl collapse beside her.

The target points turned away, they started to run, fast. They leaped into the air, jumping easily to the nearest building.

She hefted the spear and aimed, loosing it with the power of her entire body. But even as it flew through the air, she knew she had missed.

She never missed.

She prepared to give chase. Once she saw them, they would be omega. That was how they trained her. To fail meant more tests, more training, more torture. To win….

A hand grabbed onto her sleeve.

She heard a shout as she threw him to the side. Anguish.

The dark haze cleared only the slightest fraction.

"-Rrin. Stop." The boy climbed to his feet again. Blue eyes. Like hers.

"Where is Amelia?" she roared.

He flinched. "Sarrin," he tried again, his voice shaking.

The name was familiar. She panted, her heart crashing in her chest.

The boy turned behind him, shouting to someone, "I don't know what to do."

In the pause, the targets disappeared across uneven rooftops. She could still catch them, still sense them, if it weren't for his hand on her arm.

She threw him off. A fit of rage took her. "You killed her." She should crush his windpipe—simple, fast, effective.

His blue eyes blinked. No, one eye. The other was covered. Some bizarre part-skin creature.

"Sarrin. It's Grant. Stop. Calm down."

A throaty growl left from somewhere deep inside her, from a monster that was both a part of her and something completely separate.

The boy looked behind him. "I can't stop her. Kieran's the only one who can."

She paused. *Kieran?*

She looked at the boy again, blinking.

Behind him, a girl crouched by the one who was omega.

The darkness began to clear. "Amelia? Where's Amelia?" Her voice held all the longing wail of the eight year old girl whose only friend lay dead on the battlefield beside her. Simulated or not, Amelia had died that day.

Sarrin shook her head.

No, not omega, not the way the Augment hospital in Evangecore worked. Amelia had returned that night, deposited in the dormitory to bed 7C. But she wasn't the same. Sarrin tried to comb through the now tangled strawberry blonde, but Amelia told her no. Told her, "They hurt me because I helped you." Told her, "You have to take care of yourself now. You're special. You can do it."

She blinked.

Her heart rate started to slow. Pain seared across her back and her head. The darkness started to clear.

Standing beside her was Grant, set in a fighting stance, his muscles strung taut. His ugly skin suit with the gaping hole over the eye on full display.

"Where is Amelia?" she whispered, the events of the day rushing up on her. She hesitated to look behind him.

Grant swallowed. "I told you, I didn't kill her. But…."

Sarrin frowned. "I know."

"But Sarrin, She's the UEC Commandant, the hunter. She ambushed us today. She was wearing a UEC uniform." His face had gone ashen. "It's my fault."

Sarrin finally turned her head. Excruciating to hear it aloud.

Luca flinched. Beside her lay Alex, sprawled as though he

were sleeping. But Sarrin knew better, knew the life had passed from him: omega. Blood pooled under his head. A broken spear lay next to him on the ground, a similarly sized hole through the back of his head.

This wasn't Evangecore. There wasn't a team of doctor's waiting to resuscitate him. He was omega, truly.

"What happened?" she heard herself ask.

They stared at her.

Gal, huddled against the wall with Rayne, started, "They came for us. No one heard a thing until you started to…."

She willfully ignored the remainder of his sentence. "Who?" she said.

"The Uruhu."

Her fists clenched. "Why?"

Gal shook his head.

Grant peered over the side of the half wall. "One of them is down there. Moving a little."

"You'll have to bring him up here," said Gal.

Grant frowned.

"They attacked us," spat Luca. He can rot in the Speakers' prisons for all I care."

"If they find him…. They're not supposed to be there, in the forest. Definitely not in the city." Gal let the rest sit unfinished.

The bleak first light of early morning was starting to show. The first sun cracked above the horizon.

Grant ran a covered hand over the head of his ugly suit. He jumped over the ledge. A moment later he returned carrying the unconscious warrior over his shoulder.

He dropped him unceremoniously on the ground, Gal coming to examine him.

Sarrin stared at Alex's body—for it was truly a body and would stay a body. Alex, the boy she had saved in Evangecore. Who had never said anything but thank you.

Who had never once said she needed to do anything more than what she had already done for him. Who had helped her in her search for Halud. Reminded her they all needed someone's help from time to time.

And she hadn't saved him.

She laid a hand on him, met with nothing but cold.

"Hey," said Gal, his voice a pitch higher than usual. "Where's Rayne?"

Sarrin turned. There were only the four of them on the roof.

"Oh no," said Gal. "Oh no, no, no, no, no."

* * *

Rayne dropped the last few feet to the alleyway below, not daring to look back to the rooftop as she took off running. Her heart pounded, feet flailing almost uncontrollably. It was too early to be out, the streets were empty, the city still under curfew, but she ran just the same.

A surveillance drone whirred ahead, crossing an intersection and heading along a different path. It wouldn't be the end of the world if she was caught by a drone—it could only take her picture and move on, but it would be recorded, go on her service. And, most importantly, surveillance drone or not, the Gods would know. The Gods were good, they always provided.

Like they had provided her escape from the roof. That's how she had known it was time to go. In all the confusion, she'd flung herself over the edge, fleeing the madness, and the fighting, and Alex's cold, bleeding body. Fleeing Gal.

The morning air snagged in her throat

She kept her eyes fixed on the Speakers' Tower, a beacon leading her to the central square. Her father's apartments were in the Speakers' Compound at the base of the tower.

It took her a moment to recognize the door, having been there only a few times since the compound was built. She'd spent too much time running freight with Gal. With Captain Idim. The cracked, deranged Captain Idim.

What a fool she had been. She should have been a better servant for the Gods.

She would be.

The Augments were good too. The Gods looked after them too, and they could serve the Gods the same as any of the rest of them. The folk needed to know it.

Breathless, she found the door, and pressed her face into the retinal scanner.

The door opened with a soft click and she pushed it open, slipping inside. She leaned back as the door auto-closed and sealed itself. She hadn't been seen—the Gods were good.

"Hello?" she called out into the dark house. The chronometer on the wall told her it was 0430—the general would be in his bed, nearly ready to rise for the day.

With no answer, she took a step forward, the automatic sensors clicking on the lights in the main floor. "Hello?" she tried again. "Dad?"

Unusual for the general not to come running, especially to an intrusion into his home.

She ran a hand over the neat cut out window between the entry hall and the living space. A grey statue was the only decoration—something new, something from the Artist Laureate. She stared at it a minute, something unsettling in its rigid cut.

The living area was neatly laid out, the furniture plush, befitting her father's rank and his close association with the Speakers.

She went through to the kitchens—another perk in his luxury home, he could have food delivered and eaten at home instead of in the cafes with the folk. The table was made of heavy steel, it's appearance only slightly improved from the tables in the mess hall on the Ishash'tor. She nearly turned away, when a familiar glint caught her eye.

On the table, tucked into the decorative grey bowl, was a book. A long-cherished thing, it's cover worn and browning from age. She smiled, taking it in her hands. The book -- not actually a book -- was a novelty she'd had as a girl. She opened the cover, revealing the diorama within. A scene of the Gods, each of them set in action. Strength stood, pushing on a heavy boulder, Fortitude beside him. Knowledge spoke to a group of folk who gathered at his feet. Prudence watched Strength and Fortitude, her face cast in concentration. Faith stood at the front of it all, her eyes closed, her face deep in thought but serene, as though she could see the outcome, knew it would all be well in the end.

'Day 1' it was called. The previous Artist Laureate had made it for her mother, and her mother had passed it to Rayne on her fifth birthday. Rayne could nearly hear her voice as they stayed up late into the evening, her mother sharing stories of the Gods, of their miracles and their wisdom. The way they worked together. The way they ate and slept and breathed as if they were human, until eventually they forgot what they were, and their stories lived on forever.

A week after her birthday, her mother was found dead. She had been too good. It was the Will of the Gods.

Such pretty things, such things full of vibrant colour were not meant for the hands of a child. The piece belonged in the Speakers' collection, but her father had kept.

She hugged it tight to her chest.

At the far end of the living quarters, the interior door that led into the corridors of the Speakers' Compound opened. The general had been working late, then.

She took a silent step into the sitting room. His back was turned as he shed his shoes and jacket, and she called out to him instinctively. "Daddy?"

He turned, startled.

She hadn't called him Daddy in years. Embarrassed, she dropped her head in acknowledgement. "General," she addressed him by the proper title.

He took three quick strides forward, stopping just in front of her. His face registered an expression she had never seen before—at least not in real life—his eyes lighting up with joy. "Rayne?"

She smiled. "Yes."

He stammered, "You're here? You're alive?"

She nodded.

"I thought…. Your ship, it was overtaken by Augments. Crashed on that moon, and then the warship…. Where is your ship?"

She shook her head, ready to laugh in delight. "The Ishash'tor was destroyed in an explosion." One she had helped cause. But that didn't matter now. "Daddy, I didn't want to be a part of anything that happened. The captain— Gal—he's completely cracked." He didn't even flinch at her calling him Daddy. "But, the Augments, they're not like all the stories say. They're—"

He rested a hand on her shoulder, his brown eyes staring into her. "Where are they?"

He heart leaped—she knew he'd want to help. "They're entrenched on a rooftop. I said I would—"

But his entire body stiffened, the hand on her shoulder suddenly rigid. "They're here? In the city?" His eyes darted to the door and his recently hung uniform jacket.

"Yes. Daddy, I—" She gripped his wrist, but he jerked it away.

"I have to go."

"Wait!"

He pulled the jacket on over his shoulders, reaching for the door. "Rayne, stay here."

She rushed after him, but her toes stopped at the line between his apartment and the corridor. "Where are you going?"

"There's a lot going on right now, Raynie."

"I have to talk to the Speakers."

"Stay here." He lifted his hand, and she responded to the military signal immediately, freezing in place. "Just... don't leave," he said. "Not until I've sorted it." The door shut behind him, closing right in front of her face.

She blew out a shaking breath. But if he said he would sort it out, he would. No doubt, he was letting the Speakers know about her return, clearing her name in front of the Gods.

She found the diorama, sitting with it on the couch, and like Faith, she knew that everything would be okay.

ELEVEN

"YOU SHOULD HAVE TOLD HER everything," said Aaron.

Gal braced against the half-wall, staring at the deserted streets. "I know."

"Now, who knows what she'll say to him."

There was no doubt that Rayne would find the general. But would she tell him everything? Where they were? Would she lead him here, to the roof?

Of course she would.

He hadn't given her a reason to trust him. And he hadn't wanted to give her a reason not to trust the General, breaking her heart in the process.

"She made her choice, Gal," said Aaron.

It was the same thing the Augments had said when he ordered them to chase after her.

Instead, Grant and Luca huddled over Alex's body. They bound him in some of the clothes they had stolen, wrapping him tightly against the elements. They didn't speak, and he hesitated to interrupt them.

Sarrin sat curled in a corner, her face blank as she stared at the wall in front of her. Her mouth twitched subtly. Maybe she was seeing things there that he couldn't. Maybe she had an Aaron.

He shook his head.   Sure, she was cracked, but not as cracked as him.

He turned back to watch Luca and Grant.   There was nowhere to dispose of the body in the middle of the city. They would have to leave it, and hope it decomposed quickly enough to be unrecognizable by the time the UECs found it.

Surveillance drones buzzed along the streets below.   They would find him, sooner or later, that much was certain.

He closed his eyes, imagining the look of horror on Rayne's face as they read his list of treasons and put him to death. Of course, they wouldn't officially put him to death—the Speakers and the Gods didn't believe in such atrocities. They'd send him out to the middle of nowhere and let the elements take care of him.

Ironic.   That's how he had hoped to die.   He had just hoped it would be on his terms, after a long life on a peaceful planet.

Another dark thought crossed his mind: Would Rayne be alive long enough to see it?   Would her father protect her, or would she die for treason before he did?

A soft groan sounded from the last corner of the roof. The one they were avoiding. "Galiant?"

Gal sighed, turning to the noise.   Another complication. "Hello, Urubane."

The warrior sat up slowly, assessing his wounds.   He scowled, then ripped off the make-shift bandages that had been tied across his abdomen and thigh.   He winced as he tugged on the splint that supported part of his broken leg.

"What are you doing?" said Gal.

Urubane shifted to stand, but he crumpled with a muffled shout.

Luca and Grant looked up from their work.   Face set, she stood, brushing off her hands, and slowly made her way to them.   She loomed over the Uruhu who lay crumpled on his side.

Urubane shifted himself towards the wall. He let out another involuntary squawk as he did.

Her face was dark, hard. "You have fractured ribs and internal organ damage. Keep moving like that if you want to bleed to death. I don't mind."

Urubane froze, only his eyes darting, chest rising rapidly with quick, shallow breaths.

Luca's arms darted in, maneuvering him so he sat with his back against the wall. With a jerk, she reset the leg and reapplied the splint. She walked away in a huff.

The colour had gone from his face, and Urubane struggled to catch his breath, but he remained quiet, eyes trained on Luca until she was well on the opposite side of the roof. "You travel with these"—he waved his hand weakly, searching for the word—"abominations."

Gal stared down at him. "Why did you come here?"

"We had to protect the village."

"I told you, these kids aren't going to tell anyone about your secret summer camp."

"The Agada is dead," spat Urubane.

Gal but back his cry, even though he'd seen Ruel fall, he hadn't believed she could be gone. "The kids didn't do that. You left us locked in that cage with that gas everywhere. She came to help us."

"She gave us a warning. The Uruhu will be no more if we stay the current course. We had to act."

"By killing them?" Gal nodded towards the grey-wrapped lump.

"Yes," Urubane's eyes grew dark. "We kill to protect ourselves. But we failed." His head fell back against the wall. "She is just as dangerous as they say."

"Who?"

Urubane jutted his chin across the roof, to the broken girl

staring into the corner.

"Sarrin?"

He nodded. "The others, no. But her."

"What do you mean?"

"The abominations, they were made to destroy the Uruhu. They have not been able to do it yet. We are too strong, we move too fast. The forest is ours and protects us. They've sent their armies and machines, set great fires, sprayed their gas. But that girl, seeing her fight, she could it. She could kill us all. We wouldn't stand a chance."

Gal stared. He had seen her fight. Multiple times. "That's spread."

"Ridiculous? No. You know I'm right, Galiant. We are the last of our kind. We need to protect ourselves. You see why I have no choice but to kill them." He reached down into his fur covering, and pulled out a pointed object. A sharp throwing weapon.

"No!" Gal jumped, putting his hand out in front of Urubane.

Urubane threw it anyway, and it passed far below Gal's outstretched arm.

It curved across the roof, heading for her.

Grant grabbed it out of the air. He stared at Urubane, dark, cold warning in his eyes. Then he snapped the piece in two, and again, until it was fragments falling to the ground.

Urubane gulped. "I don't understand."

"Don't understand what?"

"Why they haven't killed me, like they did the others."

"Check again," said Gal. "Your friends ran. They're still out there somewhere. Your friends left you. It was Grant who brought you up from the street. Luca that tended your wounds. Even after you killed their friend. I thought you were different, I thought you lived a life apart from the Speakers, but you're just as ruthless. We should have left you crumpled on the street for them to find."

Urubane blanched.

"They're not here to kill you. They're kids. They were made. Not by choice. Like you, they just want to be left alone. They don't need you hunting them too." Gal spun in a huff.

As he walked away, Aaron came alongside him. "Nice speech, Johnny."

"Shut up."

* * *

The longer Sarrin stared at the grey con-plas wall, the more the streaks and dots in the mix, the minor imperfections, swirled and blended into an almost colourful pattern.

She remembered every terrible minute, every movement her body made, the power that surged through her muscles. And she had enjoyed it. Enjoyed throwing the target point to his death off the five story building. Relishing in the power of life and death.

And she remembered Grant yelling at her. Grant panicked. Grant shouting, "She won't stop," fear in his voice.

She squeezed her eyes tight against it—no one cried in Evangecore.

She remembered the sound as one became Omega—the end. She'd tried to restart Alex's heart, like she had Kieran, but it was no use. The energy had already left him, seeped out of the bleeding hole in his brain.

So when Urubane threw his weapon, aiming for her, she had waited perfectly still for the sap-sharpened stone to pierce her skull. The blow never came, Grant foolishly stopping it. Urubane was right though, she was a monster. She deserved to die. She was a villain, someone placed to ruin the lives of others.

Like Alex.

The colours swirled in front of her until she couldn't stand their happy dancing anymore and wiped them out with an angry grunt.

Luca sat down beside her—Sarrin hadn't even heard her coming.

Grant kneeled on the rooftop in front of her. "Hey, Sar. You okay?" He reached an arm out, hesitating. She watched it with curiosity, stuck inches above her shoulder, trepidation coming off him in waves. He was afraid. As he should be. Then he resolved it and pressed the hand down, squeezing her shoulder.

She flinched, nearly rolling across the ground to get away. She pulled her knees tight to her chest, wrapping her arms around them.

Luca dragged a finger across the layer of dirt that covered the roof, drawing an idle pattern. "I can't believe he's gone," she said after a minute.

Grant nodded. "Another casualty of the war."

"Don't you think it's funny," said Luca, suddenly brushing out her doodle. "I know he's gone. We bandaged up his body, scrubbed his blood. But I can't help but think he's going to be there, waiting for us in the bunks tonight when we're finished. Patched up and a little worse for wear, sure, but there all the same. He'll crack out a loose smile—a little faded from the morphines—and tell us all about his injuries with a joke."

Grant nodded with a snort. "Hoepe told me once in the war that he'd seen Alex in his Infirmary enough that he knew him by name."

"When was that?" asked Luca.

"After we'd run from the bombings on Corrant. Alex had gone back to save some kids. He ended up getting caught in the blast zone."

"I remember that. He couldn't get out in time. The kids ended up dead all the same, and he was in bad shape."

"Yeah."

They both picked at something unseen on the con-plas floor. "Do you ever think about it?" Luca said quietly.

Grant pressed his lips together. "I try not to."

Luca leaned back against the wall. "I killed a girl, in the arena," she said. "Actually killed her. She never came back."

Grant said nothing.

"You lose yourself. It's easy. They tell you fight, fight, fight. People get hurt and they come back. There aren't consequences. You start to think, if I hurt them, then I won't get hurt." Luca took a shaky breath. "I let a girl go once, saw her and just turned and ran. They put me in isolation for three days, because I needed to know what it would be like to be alone if my weakness—my hesitation—cost the lives of all my friends.

"So you do it. You know. You think, I don't want to get hurt. I'm going to kill this person because it's what they want from me. And the consequences aren't there. You're numb to it, because people always come back, and they're always ready to go back into the arena the next day."

Sarrin threw her gaze down to the floor when Luca looked her way. She had a look of longing, of desperation, that Sarrin couldn't bear.

Grant cleared his throat. "I'm quick. I'm good at fighting. And I don't mind it. They put me in a simulator—old women, pleasant men, children, just a street or a cafe, somewhere normal, bright sunshine. Then they'd turn, all of them, and blast me with laz-rifles. I can't walk down a street without thinking they're all going to attack. Without thinking, I should rip their heads off before they do the same to me."

"Oh," escaped Luca's lips.

"Yeah. It was helpful in the war, I guess, since we couldn't trust anyone anyway. But to walk through these streets here," he waved his hand in the air, letting the rest hang unsaid.

"It's okay," said Luca. "I think—I think we're all a little cracked. I think it would be weird if we weren't."

Grant nodded, but he stared at his hands, refusing to look up.

"I had forgotten myself, " said Luca, "just a violent machine in an arena until… until…."

Sarrin realized she was looking right at her, a strange mix of confusion and hope set deep in her eyes.

Luca smiled then—odd because her eyes looked like they were about to shed forbidden tears. "Until someone reminded me that there was hope out there. Until someone stood up to them. Someone showed me that we could still care about each other, instead of just killing each other in the arena."

Sarrin gulped. Grant reached a hand out to her knee, posting it gently. She nearly yelped as she flinched away. Her heart beat so loudly she couldn't hear Grant or Luca as they turned away, seemingly unfazed by her outburst, and continued their conversation. Slowly, she picked herself up. She darkness swirled inside of her, subconscious images from the stories they shared bombarding her, dredging up her own memories. "They kept me in the simulator for days," she blurted out.

The two turned to face her, and Sarrin suddenly felt small in the silence. She picked at the faint suture lines on her hands. "They wanted to see how fast I could move. For how long. The holograms would burn me if they made contact."

Grant gulped, but he didn't turn away. "How long?"

She blinked, unsure if she should tell the rest. But it tumbled out anyway: "Once for seventy-seven hours, until I passed out from blood loss and exhaustion. Guiterriez left me on the floor to bleed to death, the same as I had left him. But I didn't." Twenty-seven -- the nickname she's earned by scaling the researchers observation tower in Evangecore's arena and killing twenty seven of them -- had given them all hope, but they had tried to destroy her in the years after. Were still trying to destroy her.

Suddenly, not knowing how or why, Sarrin began to talk. She told them about the simulations, the experiments. She told them about the nurse, and the surgeries. She told them about the game she played and the things she felt.

And slowly, somehow, as the words tumbled out, she felt lighter. From the very inside. Her soul felt like it was starting to breathe again. She looked up at Grant. "I miss Amelia," she said. "They took her from me."

"Oh, Sarrin," he said. "We'll get her back. We will."

"And what if Halud is dead?"

He pressed his lips. "Then he's in a better place."

TWELVE

THE GENERAL DIDN'T RETURN UNTIL late in the evening, slipping in the door just before the final curfew alarm. He smiled wearily at Rayne. "Have you had supper?"

She rose from the couch and stood at attention, waiting for him to nod before she relaxed. "I was waiting for you."

"I have beef," he said, and went straight into the kitchen, pulling two meal containers from the vacuum storage.

She smiled. "You'll never find that on a starship."

"Never. This is two-year angus from the farms on Yarna."

"Wow," she hadn't tasted such luxury in years, since her Academy graduation.

He set them in the warmer, then started to clear the table. He tucked the grey, decorative bowl that adorned the small dining table and placed it on a convenient empty shelf. He disappeared into the living room, returning with the diorama tucked under his arm and eased it into the back of a cabinet. From the same cabinet, he pulled out two plates.

Real, ceramic plates. And real, steel cutlery.

Wiping his hands down the legs of his uniform, he surveyed the set table, seemingly satisfied. "I'm glad you're home," he said.

The warmer dinged, signalling the beef had finished

cooking, and he stepped around her to retrieve the meals.

She sat as he transferred the meal onto a plate and then set it in front of her.

"I never thought I'd see you again," she said.

A concerned look passed over his face as he chewed the first bite of his dinner. He pointed to her plate with his fork. "Don't let it get cold."

She glanced at the steaming plate in front of her—a true delicacy—but wasn't hungry. "I need to speak with the Speakers," she said.

The general chewed, swallowing. "What about?"

Her heart raced, palms suddenly clammy. Gal's empty protests rang in her head. But this was her father. If he was anything like the vision she had seen of him when they were on Cordelia—that is, if he was the man she knew—there was nothing to be worried about. "The Ishash'tor... we... we found an Augment, Sarrin. The Poet brought her aboard at Selousa. We didn't know what she was, but then it became obvious."

"Sarrin?" her dad choked, suddenly pale.

"I was terrified"—the words tumbled from her—"certain she would kill us all. But she didn't. I think she was more scared than the rest of us."

"Where is Sarrin now?"

She paused, another moment of uncertainty hitting her as she recalled Gal and the roof. "Here."

"Here?" He stood, dinner forgotten. "Where?"

"It's okay, Daddy. They're not like we think. Sarrin saved my life. Twice. She saved Kieran's and Gal's—she saved us all. We found more Augments too."

"And they're here? In the city?"

She found herself pushing back, leaning away as he leaned over the table. "N-no. Just a few."

"Where?"

She hesitated.

"I want to help them, Rayne. I need to know where they are."

"Gal had a building he knew, we climbed onto the roof. About three kilometres from here. In view of the Speaker's tower."

"I have to make a call."

"What are you going to say? It's only because of them that I made it back to you, alive. They're good, I know they are. We have to protect them. Surely, it is the Will of the Gods."

He paused. "Rayne, my dear Raynie. I want to show you something."

She followed him down the narrow hall, past the spare bedroom and latrine, past his own chambers, and into his office.   His private office she had never been allowed into. She gulped quietly.

He sat at the monitor, quickly typing in a set of commands. "The Augments," he said, "they're very clever."

She kneeled down next to him. "Yes, I know. I've seen some of their engineering repair work. The doctors too." She rubbed the burn mark over her shoulder, now nothing more than a small, faded scar thanks to Hoepe's handiwork.

"No, I mean devious. It may seem hard to believe, but we had them detained for a reason. This is all classified, but I'm showing you because I want you to understand."

She frowned. "You knew they were still alive? Still being held?"

He nodded slowly. "Yes. I'm telling you this because you can't tell the Speakers what you've told me. If they see you've sided with the Augments, then you will be considered just as dangerous as they are. Do you understand?"

She nodded, slowly, not certain that she did understand.

He pointed to the screen. A vid played, kids sitting in a circle, a cluster of mag-blocks in front of them, a complex castle being rapidly assembled.

"This is a video from Evangecore. As you can see, they are very intelligent. They would have moments where they were normal children, playing, laughing. They could function the same as you or I. But then, suddenly." The castle in the video grew, blocks being added rapidly. Without warning, one of the boys dropped a block. Then another of the boys bowled into the castle, knocking it to the floor. The magblocks turned from toys to weapons as the children hurled them across the room. "They're unpredictable. We thought, as their hormones changed, the sudden shifts might abate. But they only got worse."

He changed the video to one of lush plants, a group of adolescents stalking through it. The teenagers turned, surging after another group with laz-rifles and fists. One streaked across the jungle floor, and launched herself up a stone wall, scaling it easily. The Augment punched through the wall, leaping into a group of unarmed scientists, and she tore them apart.

Rayne nearly choked. "Is that Sarrin?"

Her father nodded. "She was one of the worst. Entirely unpredictable."

"She had episodes on the Ishash'tor," Rayne mumbled.

"I know. She still has violent, dangerous outbursts. That's why she was held in solitary on Selousa. They've all been held, as comfortable as we can make them. But there's no telling when they could have an outburst of violence. It's not safe for them to be around the folk. I hope you understand, after the war when they destroyed Earth, it was easier to let the folk believe they had perished. It had caused such a panic, and everything was already in such disarray, we didn't want them to worry."

It all made sense. Rayne had been a fool. She'd seen Sarrin's outbursts—seemingly normal and then suddenly not.

And she'd seen the aggression written on Rami's face.   On
Grant's.   They were dangerous and unpredictable.   Neuro-
chemically imbalanced.

"They're monsters," her father said.   "It's a gift from the
Gods you made it back alive."

She nodded.

"I have to make a call."   He disappeared from the room.

How was it that sweet, terrified Sarrin was the same girl in
the video?   But Rayne had seen her lose control and attack
Kieran and Grant and a hallway full of Augments.   Just as her
father said.   The Gods had taken care of the folk, as always.
But sometimes it meant hiding the truth, a white lie.   A lie she
and Gal had stumbled on and been drawn into.

She clicked on the video, minimizing it in the screen.   A
selection of other videos were available, all in a file noted
005478F.   She picked one at random.

In it, Sarrin sat in a small room on a cot.   Her lips moved,
but there was no sound on the video.   Her matted hair hung
over her face, and a large gash dripped blood on her shoulder.

She picked another vid: Sarrin in a glass box, fighting
nothing, her limbs moving faster than the cameras could
detect.

Rayne suppressed a shudder.

One last video: Sarrin tied to a table, her body arcing with
electric current.   The tetany ended and she lay still, limp,
unconscious.   No—she was blinking, seeing.   Feeling.   But not
fighting.

What were they doing?

Rayne swallowed the growing lump in her throat.

She cleared away the selection of videos.   In its place was a
personnel file, the place for the photograph unusually blank.

Below was a long list of medical entries.

*Experiment protocol Guitteriez178 at 20,000 Volts: Subject did not
respond.   50,000 Volts—subject continues to resist.   Failed to yield*

malleable state.   Subject not suitable for mental manipulation or reprogramming.

No, not treatment notes. Results. From experiments.

She scrolled down.

Experiment protocol Guitteriez154: Speed, agility, accuracy within 99th percentile, maintained over seventy-two hours.   Subject outpaces simulation computer in both speed and endurance. Experiment aborted at 74.3 hours due to equipment malfunction.   Subject exhibits abilities beyond expectations.

What expectations?

Missions and operative training. Level 9. Authorized by: Gen O. N.

O. N. Oleander Nairu.

She continues to scroll through the long list of experiments. They electrocuted her, tortured her, and he had authorized it.

She tapped on the image collection attached to the file. There were none of her face, not even as a child.   Only images that highlighted the way she moved, the way she jumped and flew through the air.   Images of her in a classroom. Images in a combat ring.

There were images of bruises. Then images of a long line of black marks—the procedural marks that they all bore—running down her back, more than she had seen on any other when they'd flaunted them aboard the Ishash'tor. Images of Sarrin tearing apart a group of people. Images of Sarrin in the glass box, fighting something unseen.

And an image of a dead woman. Images of an operating theatre, silver glinting hands, and massive bandages.

Finally images of Halud.   Images of Sarrin on the freightship with all of them.

Rayne stared at a picture, Sarrin in front, Rayne in the background.   How had they gotten these pictures?   The image was high angle, as though coming from above, fixed in the ceiling. The Ishash'tor had tactical security cameras in every corridor, and Rayne knew each of them. These had come from somewhere else, from secret cameras that would have been planted long before Halud had joined them or Sarrin brought on board.

She scrolled back, chasing a terrible realization. The first images, the ones of her aerial acrobatics, they weren't indoors. They weren't in a training facility. They were outside, in an orchard. Before Sarrin had been captured.

Why?

She stood from the chair, heart tittering around in her chest. She had to get out of here. She had to return to the roof. Something was wrong. Something was very wrong.

The quiet murmurs of her father's voice came from his bedroom as he spoke into the secure console there. She crept closer so she could hear the words. "You have full mission authorization. Nairu-*7-6-8-bravo-8*. Keep it quiet. Keep it contained. Any means necessary. Exterminate the rest."

Exterminate.

Gal.

She gasped, pushing back from the doorway. The noise alerted the general, and he stood suddenly, coming towards her. "Rayne?"

His arms were outstretched, but instead of the usual warmth, there was something foreign, dark in his eyes. She stepped back. "You did this to them."

* * *

It was dark, well past curfew, and surveillance drones buzzed through the air. Rayne pushed her legs faster, her muscles screaming just as loud as the warnings in her head. Three drones tailed her, whirring through the narrow alleys ten feet behind.

She reached the familiar building and threw herself up the wall, already shouting out as she started to climb. She had been so desperate to get away, so angry Gal had tried to keep her there. Now, she wished she had never left. She had been a fool.

Gal leaned over the edge as she climbed the last few feet.

"They know where you are," she shouted up. "You have to run."

He didn't question, just pulled her over the edge, his jaw set, eyes giving nothing away. Before, she'd imagined the expression meant he was lost in the JinJiu fog, now, it seemed far more calculating that that.

The three Augments were huddled in the corner, sleeping. They stood abruptly, Luca looking up and rousing the others.

Gal shouted at the man slumped in the corner at the same time as rushed to his side. "Can you walk?"

Urubane nodded, rising. But when he put his foot on the ground, it collapsed, sending him crashing into Gal's arms.

Gal swore, wrapping his arm around the Uruhu.

In the middle of the roof, the Augments stared up at the sky. Suddenly, Sarrin pushed Luca to the side. An instant later, she doubled over, clutching her upper arm. Blood seeped from around her fingers.

An unfamiliar thwap hit the ground beside Rayne, kicking up dust. "Bullets," she realized. "Get down!"

They ducked low by the balustrade, and a wave of nearly silent projectiles tearing up clouds of dust across the rooftop.

Rayne stared wide-eyed at Sarrin, who was tearing cloth to tie around her wounded arm. She hadn't seen a bullet outside of a museum. They were silent. And deadly. More importantly, they could tear a hole through a starship hull in the blink of an eye. They were outlawed outright.

The whump-whump of a hovercraft flew overtop them, it's eerily quiet motors only audible as the machine passed directly above.

"Move," shouted Gal.

Grant's ugly skin-suit sprung from his back, pouring over him. He took Urubane from Gal's arms and threw him over his shoulder. Gal pushed Rayne to follow him over the edge.

This was her fault. Gal had told her, over and over again, not to visit the General. Over and over she'd ignored him.

Quickly, they climbed down the wall. Her exhausted arms protesting as she fought to hold on with shaking fingers.

She made it to the bottom faster than she had made it up. Grant waited. Urubane leaned against the wall, standing on one leg, the other clearly in an improvised splint. A UEC-grey package dropped over the edge of the roof, Grant catching it with a loud grunt.

"What's that?" Rayne asked.

"Alex."

"What?"

Gal scaled down, followed by Sarrin and Luca.

Grant handed the package—the body—to Luca, and hefted Urubane over his shoulders again.

A drone whirred nearby, but Rayne couldn't see any of the three that had followed her.

Sarrin turned, looking behind. At the same time, Rayne heard the pop of bullets raking across the con-plas roof. The hovercraft had turned back and was sending another volley of bullets across their hideout. In a moment, she heard the soft whump-whump again, and then the hovercraft's silhouette blocked out the purple night sky

A surprised grunt sounded in front of Rayne, and she turned to see Luca stumble into the wall.

Gal frowned. "Leave him,"

Luca shook her head. But she glanced at the wound on the back of her leg—just a graze, but deep enough for muscle fibres to show through the wall of blood.

"It's just a body," grunted Gal.

"They'll find him," said Grant.

Gal shook his head. "They already know we're here. It doesn't matter."

Luca looked to Sarrin, but Sarrin shook her head. An alarming amount of blood dripped down her arm and splashed onto her leg.

With a sigh, Luca bent to set the body down against the nearest wall.

"Wait," Gal stopped her. "Give him to me." He took the grey package, staggering once under the weight. With a glance skyward, he nodded to himself, and then waddled forward.

They followed him to the end of the street, to the square where it intersected with a main thoroughfare.

Gal dropped Alex in the middle of the square.

"What are you doing?" hissed Grant.

Gal tore the cloth, pulling it roughly from Alex's body. "Let them find him," he grunted. He tore Alex's shirt, laying him facedown to be sure the barcodes on his neck and arms and the lines of dark procedural marks couldn't be missed. "You want to make sure they're at least slowed down as they try to find us—cause mass hysteria in the folk. An Augment in the centre of the city will do that."

He cast a scowl at a mark on an otherwise empty wall. Then he ran back, pushing through them, back the way they came.

"Where are we going?" Luca wrapped an ark across Rayne shoulders, limping beside her.

Gal shook his head. "Away."

"Wait," Urubane said, his deep guttural voice calm. "Take the alley."

"We're too far from the fence."

"The third door on this alley leads to a basement. There is a tunnel. It is how we came for you."

Rayne looked between the two men, Gal considering Urubane's offer. "You told us not to go back. You would kill us."

"There are many exits. What choice do you have?"

The buzzing of drones caught their attention, and a single drone appeared at the opening of the alley into the street. It paused, its mechanical eye searching. It twitched visibly the moment it recognized there was a group of people, and flew towards them.

Gal swore again. He started running towards it.

"Where are you going, Galiant?" Urubane called after him.

"Can't let it see your tunnel. Go. I'll distract it."

Rayne's heart leapt into her throat as he ran away from them.

The drone jerked to the side, smashing into the wall and shattering.

"Run!" Grant screamed.

Rayne stared at the shattered drone, Gal making a quick turn where he was only halfway to the machine. The drone just smashed itself. The Gods truly were on their side—there was no other explanation.

"Come on," Gal panted as he ran past, grabbing her arm and pulling her. He did the same for Sarrin, who stood alone in the alley staring at the drone. The others ran ahead, but Rayne caught Urubane looking back, frowning at Sarrin.

Luca threw open the door, and they clattered down the stairs to a small apartment.

"Move that," Urubane said.

Grant and Sarrin pushed an old sofa, a bloody handprint left on the plastic. Beneath was a trap door and Urubane quickly swung it open.

Luca tugged on Rayne, pulling and pushing her into the dark hole.

Urubane came down the ladder last, using his hands and one good leg. He swung the trap door shut, casting them into complete darkness.

A hand reached for Rayne, guiding her forward in the pitch

black.

"What are these patterns?" asked Grant.

Urubane's voice rose in surprise. "You can see them?"

Rayne frowned, squinting as she looked around. There were no symbols, just blackness.

"Yeah," said Luca beside her.

"They're symbols," Urubane answered. "Prayers."

"For what?"

"Protection, mostly."

Rayne touched her five fingers to her chest and prayed. For Strength, for Fortitude, Knowledge, Prudence, and above all, Faith.

They walked for what felt like hours.

Slowly, a dim light lit up the blackness ahead. They ran to the end of the tunnel, where the faintest light poured in through a small opening in the ceiling.

Grant and Gal clasped hands, boosting Rayne out of the tunnel, and she scrabbled briefly on the thick dirt and grass before pulling herself out. Fresh air invaded her nostrils, and she looked around to see the thick trunks of trees in the early morning light.

"The forest?" Gal said, turning on Urubane. "I thought you were taking us somewhere else in the city. You told us never to come back here."

Urubane leaned against a tree, all his weight on one leg as he reached for the injured one. He panted slightly, wincing. "The trees already know of your arrival. They will tell the others."

"What?" Gal turned back to the tunnel entrance, preparing to drop inside. "You brought us here so they could kill us."

Urubane slumped down to the ground, shaking his head. "No." He stared blankly at the ground. "I was wrong. You will be protected. Ruel spoke truth, and gave her life for these"—he gestured his hand vaguely at the three Augments. "There is honour in them. And you have protected me from a fate worse than death. For this I owe you all I can give. Besides, I've seen what the skinny one can do. She must speak with the Agada."

THIRTEEN

KIERAN SLOSHED HIS ARM ANGRILY through the blue healing gel. He was confined to the tank, useless. He'd been out for a couple hours earlier and already his skin was cracked and sore.

Hoepe ran a handheld scanner over him. "Try to calm down. I'm going to have enough to worry about without you developing a cardiac arrhythmia."

"Sorry," said Kieran, but it came out like a growl.

Hoepe's hand paused. "This isn't my fault, you know."

"No, I know. I'm sorry." Kieran sighed. "I just—I need to move. I can't sit here doing nothing all day."

Hoepe shrugged. "Your body needs to heal."

Kieran sighed again, forcing himself to sit still and bring his heart rate down while Hoepe completed his scans.

Hoepe nodded at the read out, satisfied, and turned to leave.

"Wait," said Kieran.

"I don't believe more pain medication is the answer."

"No," Kieran shook his head. He didn't need meds, he just needed to feel useful, part of something. "Hey, how are things with you?"

Hoepe glanced around the bridge. It was quiet. Even

though they were about to infiltrate another planet, there were no Augments crowded around, pulling on combat gear and preparing for a major confrontation. No, most of them were probably down in the infirmary, helping the other rescued Augments or preparing for the incoming batch. Only a few would go down to the surface, just enough to load the transport that Cordelia provided and sit with them on the way back to the ship.

"The Augments we have rescued so far are stable. But I don't know how many more we can help. We didn't find enough supplies at either of the outposts, and Cordelia can only make so much. Understandably, she is reluctant to get too intertwined with their bodies, so the treatment is just enough to keep them alive."

It occurred to Kieran that Hoepe might feel as useless as he did having as much trouble as he was. He started to say it, but Hoepe blurted out, "I've been trying to understand Leove better."

"Oh?"

Hoepe glanced around the bridge again and then leaned back against the console, facing Kieran. His face had lost its hard calculation, replaced by something very much like sadness. A console light flashed and a sound pinged across the bridge, followed by the announcement of their arrival at the most recent grey dust ball they were visiting. Hoepe's face hardened again. "I have to go prepare. It will only be a few minutes before they are brought up." He strode away quickly, leaving Kieran behind, trapped in his blue tank.

He sighed, and watched the display Cordelia kept running for him. An empty UEC base, a prison full of weak, emaciated, and sometimes unconscious Augments. Unbeatable, fierce warriors reduced to nothing by the mere absence of food and water.

The team on the surface moved quickly—Kieran watching

through a camera on one of their armoured suits—scooping up the ones who could no longer walk. Then they were on the transport, the rescued Augments' eyes wide as they stared at the magical walls, too weak to question or protest it.

Thomas sat with them, holding, touching as many as he could, while he spoke continuously.

Then they were in the infirmary, and there was a flurry of activity. The healthy Augments ran back and forth, following directions from the two tall doctors, their hawk-like stares seeing everything, every problem.

He should be down there, should be helping. He wasn't a medic, but he was good at fixing things. Cordelia didn't need things to be fixed. But surely he could be a spare set of hands.

He shut his eyes and looked away, splashing in the goo so that some of it spilled out the side. It hovered in mid-air before it was returned to the tank. "Cordelia," he groaned, before submerging himself totally.

When he came up for air, she was standing there.

"Cordelia, run another scan of the surface."

She frowned. "I'm kind of busy right now."

He grunted. "I need to be useful."

"Uh, fine. I don't know what you're expecting to find."

"Maybe a reason. Maybe a clue why they would suddenly abandon a twenty year project and all these people."

Cordelia shrugged, her corporeal form fading away. But the view screen in front of Kieran shifted, readouts from the planet scrolling past. The planet was another dust-bowl, only a few scrubby plants had taken hold.

He turned away from the data, staring instead at the forlorn image of the planet itself, spinning slowly on its axis. Grey grey grey grey grey. He was beginning to understand what Gal had been muttering about all those months in space.

And then—movement, in the northern hemisphere.

He sloshed forward, peering at the image.

"Cordelia!"

She arrived again, looking harried and covered in blood. "What, Kieran?"

"Zoom in," he said. "There."

"This group really isn't doing well, Kieran."

But there was something there. "Zoom in."

The image did.

"Again."

She gasped behind him as the image changed.   "Are those…?"

"People," he said. "Settlers."

"I didn't even sense them."

"Call Hoepe."

The comm system let out a ping.

Silence.

Cordelia tried again.

"Hoepe?" Kieran shouted into the air.

No response.

"I'll go," said Cordelia, already fading.

No, he couldn't just sit in his pathetic tub. He had to get down there.

He stood, his skin aching with the sudden movement. He put his hands on the edge of the tank, and lifted a leg to climb over the side. But his skin, his body after lying still so long, wouldn't move that way. Instead, he half-heaved, half-flopped himself out of the tank like a fish.

He started running. His body screamed at him, but it didn't matter. He made it to the infirmary in under a minute. The doors opened to chaos. He stood, dripping blue gel on the floor, looking for Hoepe in all the confusion.

Finally, the doctor looked up at him from where he was bent over an Augment, a long syringe coming from the man's chest.

Kieran rushed forward. "There's settlers out there."

"This man's heart is failing. His chest is filled with fluid." He turned back, his hands working deftly.

"People. Out there. In the desert."

"Push epi," he shouted at an assistant.

Isuma rushed forward with a syringe, driving it into an IV line.

Kieran did a double take to make sure he was talking to the doctor he thought he was, but it was Hoepe after all.

"They need help."

Finally Cordelia dried him and covered him in clothes.

"I'm a little busy right now. I don't know if I can save him with what I have here." Hoepe frowned and pushed on the man's chest. "It's their choice to be down there."

Kieran stepped back as Leove ran in to help with the patient.

Hoepe drew clear fluid from the man's chest cavity.

"Hypoalbuminemia," said Leove, starting chest compressions. "Pure effusion in the lungs. Starvation."

Kieran blanched. "If they stopped feeding the Augments, they've stopped feeding the settlers."

Hoepe ignored him, looking up to the EKG monitor that had started to pulse again.

"If we leave them, they're all going to be dead."

"They have what they need," shouted Hoepe.

"They don't. For a year, I delivered supplies to colonies in the deep black. We left colonists to their death, dropped them off and never saw them again. The fact that there's people down there still alive is a miracle. You remember how hard it was on Contyna. You told us you had to steal extra supplies to keep the folk there alive."

Hoepe glanced up at him for the first time since he'd arrived.

"He's stable," said Leove, "for now."

Hoepe stepped back from the patient, looking at Kieran down his long, hawkish nose. "So what do you want us to do?"

"Send a team down, bring them back if they want to come."

Glancing warily across the infirmary, Hoepe pressed his lips. But Cordelia had already moved away to prepare. A grim group of Augments wearing the light armour suits started to gather, gritting themselves for the excursion.

Kieran breathed a sigh of relief.

Isuma pulled away to join the others who had started to collect.

"Not you," said Leove, pointing to a nearby stool. "I need your blood."

She gulped and rolled up her sleeve while Leove connected a line from her to the unconscious man.

"You shouldn't be out of your tank," said Hoepe.

Kieran nodded once. The pain had disappeared in all the excitement. "I'm okay."

Hoepe nodded grimly in return. "You'll have to look after the settlers. I have too many unstable patients to deal with."

Kieran smiled. "Happy to help."

* * *

Kieran paced in the shuttle bay. His tight skin pulled as he walked, and he took some joy in the discomfort, knowing that with each tweak, his range of motion stretched.

"You'll wear a hole through my floor," said Cordelia. The woman, in her odd colonial garb, appeared behind him.

"Have things calmed down in the infirmary?"

She nodded once. "A little. Enough I could be here to help you. They might find you —," she gestured at his face, "a little alarming."

He grinned sheepishly. He knew from brief glances in the mirror that the expression would make his face even more gruesome. Hoepe had done a good job, but he still had burns over most of his body.

"It's taking a long time," Kieran said.

Cordelia nodded.

"You know, I don't understand the settlers. I get that they wanted to leave to start a new life, get away from this crazy Speakers and Gods thing they believe in."

"You don't believe it?" Cordelia interrupted.

Kieran caught himself and frowned at the floor.

"It's okay. You know I can read your thoughts. I know you're not from here."

"Then no, I don't." He rubbed his palms on his pants, then fought the urge to scratch everywhere. "So these people leave to start a new life, but on Gal's ship I watched them all die. And it was called the Will of the Gods. And people still wanted to keep going."

"Is that better, do you think? Being free and dying, or living in this falseness—what you think is falseness?"

He opened his mouth, and then closed it again.

Suddenly, Cordelia frowned and stared out across the bay. "Something's wrong," she said. She squeezed her hands together and scrunched her face.

A shuttle crashed into the hangar, tumbling sideways.

"Ugh! It's chaos," Cordelia grunted.

"What?"

The door to the shuttle sprung open. From it leaped a woman, eyes as wild as her untamed hair. She lurched forward. Other savages followed quickly. The look in their eyes wasn't right. The woman fixated on him. With a growl, she started running.

Thomas pulled himself out of the sideways shuttle, blood dripping from a long cut on his forehead.

"Cordelia!" Kieran screamed. He started to run backwards, but his legs weren't used to it and he nearly tripped over his feet.

Cordelia flew backwards. The end of the shuttle bay warped, its physical form wobbling, the wall blanking out so they could see the stars beyond.

"Cordelia!" he shouted again. He turned to run, the settler woman moving fast, metres from him.

Cordelia rolled over on the ground. She reached a hand out as the deranged woman lunged. A clear barrier exploded behind him, the savage woman smashing into it, her head thumping sickeningly against the glass as she bounced back.

Kieran fell, panting. "What's happening?"

Cordelia shook her head. "I've never felt anyone like that."

The other settlers—savages—ran up to the wall, thumping against it, clawing.

Thomas joined them with his small team of Augments, rips and cuts and bruises covering them. "We went down and they just attacked."

"What's wrong with them?"

"I don't know."

The savages beat at the barrier, the window wavering against the pressure. They snarled and shouted, foamy saliva collecting at the corners of their mouths and rolling down their chins.

One turned, frustrated with his current pursuit, and launched at the man nearest him. He latched on to the other's arm with his teeth. He came away with a chunk of flesh in his mouth, and spit it on the ground.

"Jesus," Kieran shouted, covering his mouth. "Can you separate them Cordelia?"

She nodded, waving her hands as though parting the sea, and the savages flew apart. They tried to run back to each other but were stopped by new barriers.

Kieran made the sign of the cross over his chest. "Call Hoepe. Tell him the savages are in worse shape that we thought."

* * *

Kieran rubbed his hand over his mouth but he refused to look away.

Hoepe drew blood from the heavily restrained arm of one of the savages, then injected a dose of antibiotic into the muscle of the same arm. The savage growled continuously, but she was pinned in place, only the flesh of the arm not covered by one of Cordelia's barriers.

Hoepe stepped away, and the barrier reformed.

The savage sprung up, scratching at the translucent wall, trying to make her way to them, spittle frothing wildly.

"What a mess," said Hoepe.

Kieran nodded. He leaned against the wall.

"Your skin okay?"

"Yeah, manageable anyway. I need to move around."

Hoepe nodded. "I'm going to go run this blood, try to figure out what's happened to these people."

"Do you think there's more out there?" said Kieran.

Hoepe frowned. "We're on our way to the next outpost, should be there tomorrow. We'll look. Thomas is going over the scans of the other planets we visited to be sure we didn't miss them. Only three more planets on Gal's list."

Kieran nodded. "No information found on the last outpost either?""

"No. Nothing. The database was wiped clean."

"Darn."

"Yeah." Hoepe leaned against the wall, closing his eyes.

Through the barrier, the savage woman paced, watching them.

"How's Leove?"

Hoepe sighed, then allowed a small smile. "He's my brother, I guess." He pushed off the wall. "I'd better go."

Kieran nodded as the doctor turned and disappeared from

the darkened shuttle bay. He allowed himself a small scratch of his incessantly itchy skin. Immediately he regretted it, the skin welling up with angry red lines, the nerve endings lighting on fire.

At least he had nerve endings. Hoepe had said burns as severe as his usually just burned the nerve right off, leaving the skin senseless.

He frowned, thinking of Sarrin and the stripped nerves in her hands, the silver skeletons inside.

Sarrin, the Augments, the settlers—it truly was a mess. And he had landed smack in the middle of it.

One of the savages stirred in their cell, and the others suddenly arose in a frenzy, throwing themselves at the glass between.

He watched them, uselessly. At least he'd have something to report when he went home to the Observer ship.

Cordelia appeared.

It barely fazed him, so accustomed to her unnatural coming and going, and the tank and the clothing, and everything else just appearing and dissolving as he needed it to.

"What are you thinking about?" She leaned beside him.

"How are the engines running?"

She smiled. "They're just fine, you know that. What are you really thinking about?"

He watched the savages as they started to settle down again. "I just, what would have happened to them?"

She raised an eyebrow.

"Would they have eaten each other? Is that how the settlers die? They starve until they start eating each other, and then the last one starves to death."

"That's an unpleasant thought for you, Kieran."

He shrugged. "Would the Augments have done the same if they weren't locked in their cells? What would I do if I had to survive?"

"They're lucky you found them."

He looked again, at their wild eyes and ruined faces. "Maybe I shouldn't have."

She frowned. "I don't pretend to understand how humans think, but that's not how you think, Kieran." She turned towards him, a smile spreading on her inhuman face. "I think I have something to cheer you up." A data-tablet materialized in her hands.

He took it.

"I picked up a transmission today. It's addressed to you. A strange signal, but I sent it through your scrubbing program, and voila!"

Curiously, he opened the message. It was from his mother.

"She says the ship will be flying through this part of the galaxy soon and they're stopping to pick you up. She sent rendezvous coordinates for a week from now." Cordelia beamed.

"You read my mail?"

"Yep."

"Of course you did."

He had been in Earth-time for nearly five years. His mission was coming to an end, he'd already had one extension. But the Observer ship's course wouldn't take them through this area again for another hundred-and-fifty years.

"Can we even make it there? No one else can know."

Cordelia raised an eyebrow. "Yes, it's surprisingly close to one of the outposts on Gal's list."

"Oh."

"They could be collecting Augments at the rendezvous time. They'd be too busy to notice you leaving."

"But I couldn't get there. We don't have a shuttle."

Cordelia shrugged. "I could extend an arm that far, for a short time. You couldn't take anything with you."

He nodded. "I know that."

He'd always known he would go back. Not for a second had he forgotten it. But it seemed so soon. They hadn't finished rescuing the Augments.

But it was time.

He was an Observer. It was getting harder and harder to remember that. He needed to get back to the safety of the ship before he forget it altogether.

And he needed the time to recuperate. The burns would heal. He just needed rest.

"You don't have to go," Cordelia said quietly.

Kieran frowned. "You know I'm not from here. I don't belong here."

"Those two things aren't the same."

He shut his eyes. It was time to go back. "I wasn't supposed to get involved—don't change the course of events, that's the rule."

"You saved the settlers."

"Did I? Is this saved?"

"Hoepe will help them. And you've saved everyone else—what would have happened if they'd not had your knowledge along. They talk about you, you know. The miracle engineer. Sometimes the Augments wonder if you're a God sent to help them."

Kieran paled. "That's exactly the problem. They're not supposed to have this knowledge, I'm not supposed to share it with them. Observation only. I can't leave a mark." The last time an Observer had over stepped their bounds, it had changed the course of everything, leaving dangerous and unpredictable consequences.

"You've already left a mark."

He grimaced. "That's why I have to go."

"What about Sarrin?"

He stopped. Sarrin. She was supposed to come with him.

She needed to escape, would be hunted the rest of her life. "She's tough," he said, nodding forcefully to himself. "She can take care of herself. She's not as helpless as everyone seems to think."

Cordelia frowned again. "Okay, Kieran. If this is what you want, I'll help you."

FOURTEEN

THE AIR BURNED SARRIN'S THROAT, filling tired lungs. Her bare feet pounded across the warm earth. This running was good, this running was freedom.

She reached her hands down, brushing finger tips against the fluffy, green leaves that fell across the worn pathway outside the Uruhu village. The same leaves left nicks on her bare legs, energizing her, a kind of burning reminder that she was still alive. The pain dripped out of her hands, drop by drop, each step leaving her lighter.

Through the trees, she caught sight of an animal. A large ungulate creature. They ran side by side, Sarrin pushing to keep up with its graceful stride. It was an animal she had never seen before, something she didn't have a name for. Not the creature from her dreams, but close.

She let herself get lost, absorbed entirely in the feeling of matching the powerful creature stride for stride. It seemed to sense her, to race with her, until all at once it veered away. She tried to follow, but it was too fast, even for her.

Her legs felt tired, but she didn't want to stop, couldn't stop. If she did, it would all catch up with her the second she paused; all the thoughts about Alex, and Halud, and Kieran would come crashing down.

Alex was dead.

Halud was lost.

Kieran was…. Her breath caught in her throat and she stumbled. *Kieran was what?* Reflexes caught her, but her shaking muscles only slowed her collapse, and she curled into a ball under the foliage, wrapping her arms tightly around her knees. Kieran was gone too.

This wasn't freedom, not really, not like she'd hoped for.

The Uruhu let her run in their woods, so long as she didn't go south. They let the Augments walk freely in their village because they helped Urubane. But the villagers still kept constant watch, fear written plainly in their eyes. She was a monster, and these people knew it. Urubane had seen it first hand.

An irrational, burning desire to scream and shout seized her, and she wanted to yell at the world and the stars that it was not her choosing, not her fault. But whom would she tell? Who would listen? They all knew she was a monster too.

Maybe Kieran—the idea sprung into her mind along with a memory of his bright eyes, crinkled at the corners. He seemed convinced, more than she was anyway, that she maybe wasn't what they had made her, that maybe there was something still left inside.

It was best not to tell him the truth.

A rustling three feet behind her surprised Sarrin, and she whipped around. Roelle, the Uruhu's new Agada, stood with her hands clasped patiently, as though she had been waiting some time. There were scuff marks in the trail in front of her where she had toed the dirt to get Sarrin's attention.

Sarrin sprang to her feet.

"Don't be worried," Roelle said, her mouth twisted awkwardly over the words, speaking in the deep halting way of the Uruhu.

Sarrin swallowed, her throat dry, and prepared to run. The

edges of her vision started to fog, alarm bells ringing in her mind. There was no way to know what the woman wanted, why she always seemed to be watching Sarrin, or why she was out here this far from the village.

"I've followed you a long way. Your feet are quick. You would be an asset on Goral hunts." Roelle gestured into the woods, and Sarrin somehow knew she was referring to the ungulate creature, a detailed image springing into her head. "But I have a feeling you would not like it. The death I mean. It is a good death. But you have too much death in you already."

Sarrin's legs twitched involuntarily.

Roelle smiled. "Let us walk." She started down the path, but paused and looked over her shoulder after only a few metres, Sarrin still rooted in the same spot. "Ruel, my fore-bearer, sacrificed herself for your life. You know this, yes?"

Sarrin looked away. Even through her own pain, she had glimpsed the old woman's horrific death as the acid mist burned her, felt her painful end, and the even more painful truth that she had done it to release the Augments from their cage.

Roelle sighed. "She was preparing me for my time as Agada, but she left before her time was fully spent. I spent many nights thinking about it. Many nights cursing that she had left me before I was fully ready. And at a time when we needed her wisdom more than ever. I believed the stories as they were told, that you would come to destroy us. But the more time I see you, the more I come to know you, and the more I understand it. We can never control how our lives turn, cannot predict it other than to say it will be unpredictable. But it is life all the same." Roelle waited, tilting her head, studying Sarrin from a different angle. "We are not so different, you and I, your kind and my kind. Perhaps more similar than you know. We are both hidden away. Tasked with something that seems so far beyond us as to be impossible. But it is the same for everyone I think. We all try to do the impossible. Perhaps that is the only way to survive."

There were thirty-nine separate escape routes, each taking her into the forest and the unknown maze of trees. Impossible to calculate the probabilities of each, and yet her mind followed a path that seemed the most likely, knowing each turn as though she had run it before.

"You are plagued, Sarrin DeGazo," Roelle said, disrupting her thoughts. "I see it in you and beyond you. It does not have to be. I see your worry—your friends, many of them have come to peril. You have grief over the ones who have passed out of this life into the next. And envy, I think. Your brother weighs heavily, I can see it. He is lost to you. But he is not really; you have the ability to find him."

Sarrin stuttered, "Gal says he is a traitor. If he's still alive, they'll send him to a colony to die. It will take years to search every planet. He'll be dead long before I reach him."

Roelle smiled and shook her head. "He is not so far, I think. But I am not connected enough to know which of the millions of voices that run through the trees is his. You hear them too, sometimes, I think, though you would like to ignore them. The calls of every living being resound through the universe, connecting us into one infinite whole. It takes time, skill, and willingness to learn to listen. This is how Ruel trained me and how, I think now, I will train you."

Sarrin took a step back.

Roelle shrugged. "I make the offer freely."

Turning, Sarrin made to run, but her feet kept her rooted as she stared down the path. Some invisible force held her still, kept her feet from pushing off.

"This ability is a gift of the Uruhu passed to you. I can show you to control it, to use it. I have seen everything that transpired on the rooftop from Urubane who passed the memory to me." Roelle touched Sarrin on the shoulder, and images, memories not her own, assaulted her: The dark rooftop, lit by purple night. Uruhu warriors climbing, springing silently over the edge of the wall.

Sarrin gasped, watching the boy die and the monster spring to life—a memory not from her own mind, but from Urubane's. The monster attacked viciously and without abandon, moving faster than any natural person could.

She reeled back, away from Roelle's touch, panting.

"I have looked into your soul, and this is not who you are." Roelle reached out again, gripping her shoulder.

Another memory played out, this one Grant's or maybe Luca's: Sarrin bent over Alex's bleeding body, her hands pressing on his cold chest, head bent in utter defeat.

She came back to herself, shaking and cold. Somehow she had fallen to the ground, curled on the forest floor. She wiped the moisture from her eyes so Roelle couldn't see her cry. No one cried in Evangecore.

"The ways of the Uruhu are strong in you. I am here when you decide you want the teachings." The young woman looked away finally, tilting her head, listening to something unheard. "Their machines are coming. Best to return to the village before the gas falls."

Slowly, Sarrin stood. Her legs were heavy, her heart moreso—fitting for a monster such as herself—but she picked them up and followed the Agada back to her hut.

* * *

Gal pulled his knees to his chest, trying to make just a little more room in the cramped hut. The villagers left a large berth between themselves and Gal, but he didn't want to take up any more space than he had to.

Roelle poured water she had boiled over her small fire into wooden bowls and passed them around. Gal tucked into his meal, the picked greens and boiled grain mash much worse looking but remarkably more tasty than UEC rations, making it one of the most delicious things he had eaten in years.

A young boy, no more than two years-standard, toddled in his direction. He reached Gal quickly, a grin planted across his face, and smacked the captain on the thigh with both of his little fists. Gal stared down at the child, completely naked except for a twine with a few beads that hung around his neck.

The boy blurted nonsense before hitting his leg again.

Gal raised and eyebrow. "Do you want to sit with me?"

Eagerly, the boy gripped his pants and started to climb, perching on Gal's knee, only to be removed an instant later. His mother held him to her chest, admonishing the child in a language Gal could not understand.

He sighed and returned to his grain mash.

"Do you really blame her, Johnny?" Aaron sat next to him, shoulder to shoulder.

"Not really," Gal whispered. "And stop calling me that." He glanced at the people sitting around him, but no one seemed to notice.

"These people deserve to be happy, Gal."

Gal nodded. Then, "So?"

"'So,' Gal?" Aaron laughed. "These people deserve to be happy. You don't disagree. The UECs are trying to get rid of them."

"The gas?" He shook his head. "It's for the trees. It's not harmful, just to the Augments."

Aaron raised a single eyebrow. "You watched Ruel die the same as I did. And stop eating their food, it doesn't look like they have much."

The warm mash he had just shovelled into his mouth suddenly turned unappetizing, and he worked it back and forth until he could stand to swallow, putting the half-eaten bowl down in front of him. As he looked around the over-crowded hut again, he realized the Uruhu were thin, not dangerously so but the babies weren't fat, and the mothers weren't curved the way they should be.

"Maybe they need help, Gal."

"Go away."

"Gal?" came a soft voice.

Startled, he looked up to see Rayne staring at him.

"Are you all right, Gal?"

Voice deserting him, Gal nodded. His heart pounded in his chest. It was the first time she had willingly spoken to him since the Ishash'tor had exploded nearly a month before. Had she heard him talking to Aaron? Was she aware that he was well and truly cracked?

He meant to apologize to her for … everything… to explain it all, but he still couldn't quite figure out how.

"I shouldn't have gone to the general," she said quietly. "You were right. I didn't see it; I didn't want to see it. And I'm sorry."

He stared, frozen.

"You knew, didn't you?"

What could he say? He nodded, watching her face fall. "I didn't want you to find out. I knew how much you loved him."

She picked at a frayed thread hanging from her uniform. "I found all these files on his computer. I saw… I saw what they did to them." She glanced across the room to where Sarrin sat with her back turned to them. "Horrible things, tortures, experiments. And they had my father's authorization all over them."

"I'm sorry I didn't tell you."

"I just wish I didn't feel so stupid." The grey thread pulled away, and she twisted it in her hands. "But I understand why you didn't. And I understand why you wouldn't let me go to see him. I'm sorry I didn't listen. I'm sorry I told them where you were." She took a shaky breath. "I thought... I thought the Speakers were good, that they wouldn't hurt the Augments, that they'd been helping them as much as they could. But we found the facility on Junk. And still, I thought, 'yes, but the Augments were dangerous to the rest of us, they needed to keep them locked away.' But they weren't dangerous. And so then I thought, 'the Speakers, they don't know. Somehow they think one thing, but it's not true anymore.' I thought telling them about the Augments would be good news. I thought I was helping."

"I know," said Gal, quietly.

She reached across the space between him, taking his hand. He stared at where they intertwined. "I don't know what to do anymore."

"It'll be okay," he promised. "We'll go away, far away. Into the Deep, Deep Black if we have to."

She nodded silently. She understood—after everything that happened, she understood, and she agreed. They weren't safe here, not on Etar, not anywhere under the Speakers' control.

"Huh," Aaron said.

Gal sent him a baleful glare. Why did he always have to show up at the worst times?

"It looks like there's *something* you're still willing to fight for, Galiant. You'd do anything to keep her safe, wouldn't you?"

Gal grunted.

"What about the rest? It wouldn't be that hard to bring them too. The Augments, the Uruhu. Indaer is dead, and Etar is dying."

He frowned at Aaron. It would be easier though, to set up a real colony in the Deep Black if there were more of them. He could bring Rayne, and the rebels, anyone who wanted to go, and find a planet somewhere for them to live on. He could see it now: golden fields of crops, little, curly haired children running, shrieking with laughter.

Maybe there was still a chance for him.

* * *

Sarrin kept her back to the small treatment table in the crowded hut, desperately trying to keep her legs and elbows from brushing anyone. It wouldn't be safe. Not with how edgy she had felt since her meeting with Roelle. Not with the way the Uruhu passed memories back and forth with a simple touch.

A scout sat on top of the table, a compress held to his face and bandages tied to his arms and one leg. He had been caught out in the gas as the Central Army's hovercraft made another misting run, barely managing to return to the shelter of the village before it scalded him. The wounds were superficial, Roelle had told him, and would heal in a few days, but the sight of the ugly red skin made Sarrin's own skin crawl. And think of Kieran.

"I don't think you should stay here anymore," Gal said suddenly. "We need to find another place."

Urubane growled. "You are a fool, Galiant Idim."

Gal bit his lip. "So I'm told."

"This is our home. We will not leave."

"They're not going to stop this bombing." Rayne gestured vaguely at the little window build into the hut. The bombing had stopped, but acid mist still hung in the air. "They don't care about you."

"They care that we are long dead." The warrior pounded his fist into the floor.

A nervous shake had started in Sarrin's leg as Urubane's anger rolled over her. Roelle laid a hand there, and Sarrin jumped, but the touch was peaceful, calming, and the tremor stopped. The Agada sent her a faint smile.

"Come with us," Gal tried again. "We'll find a new home, away from the Speakers."

"You will go to find *your* home," spat Urubane. "This is ours."

Gal sighed, rolling his eyes to the ceiling.

"The gas comes more and more often," said Roelle.

Urubane's fist clenched. "The Others think they will wage war with us this way—the cowards way—but we are too strong and they are fools."

Roelle shook her head. "We have made our homes safe from the toxins. Those that travel outside the village carry with them coverings and know the safe places. We survive. But I believe those that seek to destroy us know this. And they know that which we cannot be without. Our forests have shrunk, there is less space for us to hide. Less space for the food which we grow. The gas affects not only us, but animals too, like the Goral. Soon their population will not be sustainable, soon it will not be able to regenerate itself. If this happens, the balance will be off, the forest will suffer. And we will starve."

"Let us help you," Gal implored. "We can find another planet. There are dozens out there."

With a sharp snap of her fingers, Roelle cut off anything else Gal might say. "Death is not something to be feared, Galiant, merely a continuation of this life once all that we need to achieve is done. Perhaps that is why it has eluded you."

"It's eluded me because I know when to run."

Ignoring him, Roelle crossed the hut to the single, small window. It was made of glassine—the only hint of UEC technology or materials Sarrin had seen in the village. "This is our home and we will not go." Light shone through the little window, and Roelle let out a sigh of relief. "The gas has settled."

"Finally," huffed Urubane, jumping to his feet. He bolted for the little door, undoing the tight clasps which sealed it shut.

Light streamed in, and Sarrin rose with the rest. A hand caught her on the arm—the same peaceful, calming touch— and Roelle stared back at her. "Wait for me a moment."

A loud chime sounded, and Sarrin heard dozens of hut doors creaking open and villagers re-emerging into the light. The open door called to her, her legs jittering to escape the closed-in space and run free in the woods once more, but Roelle had asked her to wait, and something in Sarrin told her she should.

The Agada tended the injured warrior, the two of them communicating silently as Roelle moved her hands in waves around his body. The burns had already started to heal in the hour they had been locked in the hut—faster than an Augment.

Roelle finished, and the scout jumped down from the table. Stepping past Sarrin, Roelle left the hut with him. She stretched her arms up to the suns and filled her lungs with air, then, without even glancing at Sarrin. took off running.

Hadn't she wanted to talk? Sarrin stared after her rapidly disappearing form.

Come, I have something to show you. The voice, unmistakably Roelle's, jarred in her head, and Sarrin instantly moved to follow.

Roelle was quick, and the trails she led them on old and long overgrown. Only glimpses of Roelle flashed between the trees far ahead, but Sarrin's feet seemed to know the way, the path as obvious in her mind as though she'd followed it every day of her life. She pushed hard to keep the Agada in sight. They were heading south, the one direction the Uruhu had asked her not to go. She rounded a bend, nearly crashing into Roelle standing on a ledge, overlooking a wide-open valley below.

Ahead of them, everything Sarrin could see was charred.

Once massive tree trunks were the only things that stood, black gnarled skeletons that reeked of death. Everything else was gone, pale and deserted.

Roelle spoke without looking at her: "The United Earth has a single minded determination to destroy us. This is what remains of their war."

Sarrin gulped, surveying the destruction. A deep keening started in her heart, her legs suddenly weak and she fought to stay standing.

"You feel this despair too, yes?"

"Why?" Sarrin whispered, unable to pull her eyes away.

"Everything is connected," Roelle answered, hoping down from the grassy ledge and picking her way down the ashy hillside.

Sarrin followed even though every instinct in her told her to run.

"You see we have differences, and yet we are the same?" Roelle asked. "You see this, yes?"

"I don't know."

"You do. You are too smart not to know."

Sarrin frowned.

"You are different from your captain." Roelle turned back to face her. "He seeks to help us by removing us, but you see we are connected here. The birds and the goral and the trees speak in our bones. The death of this forest is, in a way, our death. But if we leave, we will lose our connection to the world itself, and we will die. Perhaps more slowly than if we are hunted down, but we will die all the same. It is as the humans do, now that their home is lost."

"What?"

Roelle stared into the sky, her young face hardened with determination. Her skin picked up the greyness of death from the ruined forest around them, contrasting with her wild eyes, the vivid blue and white shining like a beacon in the dead landscape.

"I don't underst—."

The Agada snapped her fingers, and Sarrin stared at her hand, confused, until she noted the hovering cloud of ash and debris behind her. The cloud swirled, clumping itself into a sphere. And then into the shape of a goral. And finally to a person walking between the burned trees.

Roelle let the fragments go, and they fell, the shapes dissolving into nothing.

Sarrin stared until the last clot of ash had floated to the ground.

"You can do this too, yes."

Her heart thrummed, muscles twitching, but she was rooted in place. "Uh."

"It is not a question. Urubane saw you smash a drone in their city. I made the offer to train you, but I see now with the attacks on our village that it can no longer be optional. Galiant and Urubane are right, our time is running out here. I will teach you now. The knowledge is yours, to do with as you wish, if that makes a difference for you. Come." Roelle started again down the slope.

"When did this happen?" Sarrin said. "The war, I mean."

"Before my time," said Roelle. She judged Sarrin. "Before your time too, I suspect. Forty-nine of our cycles."

Sarrin did the math. "That's one-hundred-sixty years-standard."

Roelle nodded.

"It hasn't grown at all?"

"Only on the very edges. The trees are afraid of this place. Such destruction terrifies life, sends it into hiding. Two hundred of your years ago, the Humans came to this planet to colonize it. It was warm, well oxygenated, and the soil was fertile. It was ready to support life. Only life was already here when the first settlers came." She said 'human' like it was something else, something other.

"I still don't understand," said Sarrin.

"But you do. We are not Human. We are Uruhu."

Sarrin stumbled.

"There were many more tribes, many more villages then. When the Humans came, all the Agada went to meet the settlers. It seemed a peaceful agreement was made—all life is connected, we are all the same, even when we are different; we were not opposed to sharing our home. The Humans went away, back to Earth. We thought all was well. We thought they had lost interest and gone elsewhere, so we continued with our existence. The Human need for exploration is not ours. But the Humans did return, nearly a full cycle later. And with them they brought war." Roelle looked to Sarrin. "Yes?"

Soundlessly, Sarrin nodded, her mind reeling.

"Their army attacked, but our warriors were stronger, faster. We fought them off, sent them running for their starships. They returned again, bringing with them firepower and machinery that was more than we could hope to match. The forest burned. Our warriors were strong, but the singular mind of the Humans was bent on our destruction, and that carried them. We lost hundreds of villages, thousands of our population. We thought surely it was over, surely that was it."

Roelle stopped, staring into the black skeleton forest that now towered around them. After a moment, she turned to Sarrin. "And yet we knew they had not killed all the warriors that we lost. Some of them were captured, taken for experiments. We didn't understand why. This is not our way, to prolong the killing. It should be swift, precise, merciful." Her hooded eyes stared at Sarrin, waiting to see if she understood the implication.

She nodded in response, though it was truly too overwhelming to say whether she understood or not.

"We did not understand it until the day that you arrived and the guard read your memories. We knew then that you had been made to destroy the Uruhu. You are part Uruhu and part Human, yes. You have our strength and speed—Urubane has seen it in you. Through some trickery, our blood flows in your veins. Human and Uruhu. Our strength. Their destruction. You, Sarrin, have the ability to destroy us all, to be rid of the Uruhu forever. Yes?"

Sarrin's blood—Uruhu or Human—ran cold. No, no, no, she wanted to scream. But she could see that she could destroy them, the same as she could see the picture of war Roelle painted for her, the same as she could see that what Roelle spoke was truth: their blood, her veins; the same and yet different. Connected.

The edges of her vision grew dark. She was a monster. Well and truly. Designed of destruction, born of destruction, and ripe to wreak destruction. Hours spent in training simulators, Guitteriez's maniacal push to understand, to see how far her abilities extended, it all started to come together. Her Path.

The Central Army and its Speakers had a problem: an alien race—professed to never have existed at all—slept on their doorstep. The stories of the Gods would all be found false. And the Army would crumble.

A growl started deep in Sarrin's chest, a deep seated reflex to make Omega all of her target points. She had been made for destruction.

She saw herself in the city. Watched as the monster destroyed the Uruhu on the rooftop, throwing Urubane's lifeless corpse to the ground. But the monster didn't stop there, it killed the folk in the central square, their flashes of blue marred by red. Even the colourful woman from the cafe died by her hands, eyes wide with fear. She saw herself climb the tall Speakers' Tower, saw herself leap inside it, a rabid, snarling monster.

She was both Human and Uruhu, and at the same time, neither. She would destroy them both.

People don't always need to become what they are told to be, Roelle's crystal clear voice cut through the violent machinations of her mind.

The darkness cleared. Roelle's hand pressed against her forehead, soothing. "You are powerful, yes, but these thoughts are not yours. Your gifts are untrained, and this is dangerous to you moreso than it is to anyone else. You lack the control even our young children are capable of, and you get swept away in the slightest current. There is much work to do."

Before Sarrin could object, Roelle took her hand, filling her with warm images and a sensation she hadn't felt in years: hope. "You are still Human. You are still Uruhu. Let yourself take the best of both. You have the power to destroy, but also the power to save. Yes?"

Sarrin stared, speechless.

With a reassuring squeeze, Roelle led her by the hand to a nearby boulder, making her sit, and began to show her how to control all the gifts of her mind.

FIFTEEN

KIERAN RUBBED THE DRY, CRACKED skin on his arm gingerly, buying himself a minute of relief. According to the message he'd received from the Observer ship, the return pod that would give him his ride home would appear in three hours. Three hours to break his dependence on the gel tank.

It wouldn't be pleasant, but if he missed the pod, it would be another hundred-and-fifty years, Earth-time, before they came back through the system. He needed to find some kind of painkiller he could take with him.

The doors to the Infirmary opened, and he found the tall doctor hunched in the corner, head bent over a series of lab samples. "Hey, Hoepe."

Hoepe glanced grimly at the timepiece built into the display without looking at Kieran. "You're early."

"By a few minutes."

Hoepe grunted again. "Find a bed. I have to finish this."

"Bedside manner's improvin', hey?" Kieran flashed a grin, though the doctor didn't turn back.

Kieran picked his way through the maze of occupied hospital beds. They had rescued over two hundred Augments, but nearly half of them were still unconscious. A dark shudder rolled across his shoulders, the dry skin pinching.   Three of the Augments had died, despite the doctors and Cordelia doing all they could.

The Central Army had just left them to die, tortured and trapped and abandoned them to rot.   Thrown away like garbage.

It could have been Sarrin.

He swung himself onto an empty cot, his too dry skin stinging as he stretched and shifted, and he let out an involuntary gasp.

One of the rescued settlers—looking much more sane now that Hoepe's vitamin and mineral cocktail had started to take effect—looked up from the bed opposite his, acknowledging him with a quick, close-lipped smile to hide the gaps where some of her teeth had fallen out.   The settlers too had been tossed onto barely habitable planets, like the scrap that littered Junk, no longer useful and hidden away.

His heart pounded as he recalled the savage woman lunging at him across the shuttle bay, but he forced a smile, just like his mama always told him to do.   "You're lookin' better."

She dropped her gaze to the floor, and ran a hand through her patchy hair.

He should ask her more, question her about her experience, gather data for the Observers, but it seemed so much harder now.   When he'd first arrived, he'd hoped for something interesting to happen, eager for adventure and to have an exciting report when he returned to the Observer ship. But now… God, it was just all too real.

Leove arrived, flashing Kieran a quick smile before turning his attention to the woman.   The air around her shimmered as an invisible barrier was dropped and he stepped inside. Apparently Cordelia still felt it prudent to fix a wall around them in case of violent outbursts.   He checked her reflexes and drew a sample of blood from the crook of her elbow, disappearing to the lab at the far end of the room. The invisible barrier sealed once more with an audible pop, and she sighed, dropping her head into her hands.

"Hey," he said, "Leove's a good doc, he'll have you fixed up in no time."

Her eyes lifted for the briefest moment, her mouth open ready to speak, before her gaze fell to the floor once more.

Hoepe appeared at Kieran's side, his expression dour as always. "Your skin looks dry. When was the last time you were in the regen-tank?"

Kieran shook his head. "Cordelia is busy," he lied. "I'm fine."

Hoepe frowned at him, raising a single, displeased eyebrow.

"I can't sit in that tank all day. I'm goin' cray-cray."

Hoepe quirked an eyebrow at his choice of words, but otherwise silently ran a handheld scanner over his torso. "Avoiding the regen-tank is delaying your healing."

"Cordelia won't be here forever." Kieran squirmed, more like he wasn't going to be here forever. "I won't always have access to the tank whenever I need it. I have to build up my tolerance to the real world again." In the next three hours.

The perpetual frown on Hoepe's face seemed to lighten as he gauged Kieran. "I concur." He typed something into his data tablet. "Your cardiovascular and musculoskeletal systems are looking improved. It is time to start weaning yourself from medical supports."

"Really?"

"You expected me to say something different?"

"No, but…. Well, yeah, I did, Doc."

A hint of a smile softened Hoepe's features, and he reached a hand out to Kieran's shoulder. "We anticipate returning to Etar within a week. I expect you will demand to go to the surface."

Etar. Right.

Kieran swallowed heavily.   "We're still on our way to Hation 6, right?"

"Yes. And Selousa. However, we don't have any leads on additional facilities or any way to know if these are the only ones." The doctor sighed, his massive shoulders caving in. "I fear we may leave some behind."

"Me too." He felt a pang of guilt for not knowing. But in three hours, he'd be leaving. There was nothing he could do about the rest. He'd have to find out what happened through newsfeeds and broken up communiques. Maybe Cordelia could send him a message to let him know how it all turned out.

"I need to test a sample of your dermis," Hoepe said.

"My what!" Kieran yelped as Hoepe pressed a tool into his shoulder, taking a bite of his fragile skin.

"A skin sample." Hoepe held up a chunk of tissue. "I wish to determine how fragile your skin is."

"Well it sure hurts," Kieran said, reaching up to hold the gauze. *Jesus.* The biopsy site hurt, but it left a cascade of pain shooting across his skin, the nerve endings buzzing like they were still on fire.   "Can you give me some meds or something?" Something he could take with him, hopefully.

"An analgesic?   I thought you wished to wean yourself completely from the medical supports."

"You just took a chunk out of me!" Kieran started, but he noticed the faint smirk in Hoepe's eyes and the doctor lifted an auto-injector to his neck and pressed, the warm sensation of the drug soothing his pain all at once. "Your sense of humour isn't getting any better, Doc."

Hoepe flashed an actual smile. "Wait here while I examine the sample."

"Sure thing."

But Hoepe paused, the muscles in his broad back clenching as he stared at the lab bench. "On second thought, I'll wait here a moment."

"Why?" Kieran leaned over to peer around the doctor. He caught sight of the problem immediately: Leove had his arms wrapped around Isuma, both of them smiling as he murmured something into her ear. "Oh."

"I fail to understand the purpose of their closeness," Hoepe said. His back was still turned to him, but Kieran saw the droop in his shoulders.

He sighed in sympathy. "Beats me, Doc. People don't do that where I come from."

Together, they watched Hoepe and Isuma. "I will admit she has proven to be a helpful assistant for him, their communication concise and efficient—she had been an excellent asset in our recent medical crises."

"Ah," agreed Kieran. There was something about their intimacy, the happy glint in Leove's eyes, that stirred something in him, and made him think, inexplicably, of Sarrin. "I saw a couple'a older kids do something like that once, on the shi— the place where I'm from. Mom told me no to worry 'bout it, it could only complicate matters."

"Agreed." Hoepe grunted. "I have occasionally found Leove distracted. Primarily when her safety status is unknown."

"Yeah." But Kieran found it difficult to take his eyes away. Sarrin's safety status was unknown.

Leove turned, pressing his lips to Isuma's hairline, and started towards them. Hoepe jerked his scanner up, pretending to run it down Kieran's arm, as Leove rejoined the settler-woman. He spoke quietly with her, showing her rest results on his data-tablet.

Kieran watched him curiously. What was it Leove knew that he and Hoepe didn't? Despite their identical features, Leove always seemed lighter, happier than his twin.

"Kieran?" Leove interrupted his thoughts, and he was

surprised the doctor was standing in front of him. Hoepe had retreated to the lab.

"Yeah, doc?"

"Are there still high density protein rations?"

"Yep. We picked up some new stores from the last planet."

"Would you mind taking Adeina to retrieve some for her and the other settlers? I believe their digestive systems are ready to handle something more substantial."

"Is she okay?" Kieran asked the doctor, the woman's gaze dancing between him and the floor. He couldn't shake the memory of the woman lunging at him in the shuttle hangar, banging against the barrier Cordelia hastily constructed between them.

Leove shrugged. "She is much improved. And Cordelia seems to have perfected the protective barriers, should the need arise."

He plastered a grin on his face, jumping down from the bed. "Sure thing, Doc." He was still on a mission of observation, for the next few days anyway.

"Thanks, Kieran."

Leove turned to the girl, tapping her on the arm. "Adeina, this is Kieran, he's going to take you for some food."

She folded her hands in close and nodded—a gesture that reminded him terribly of Sarrin and made something in his chest ache.

Leove flashed him a thankful smile before moving to another patient on another bed.

"Hi," said Kieran, turning on his friendliest smile. The barrier shimmered away between them. "Well, come on. Leove wants you to have some protein rations."

Keeping her gaze cast down, she shuffled off the bed and followed him from the infirmary.

"Are you going to tell me the story?" she asked.

Surprised to hear her speak, he looked back. She gestured

at his skin, and he grimaced. "Our last ship exploded. We were trying to get it far away enough from everyone, and I stayed too long." In hindsight, it had been a terribly stupid thing to do. A good Observer wouldn't have interfered, would have let the rest of the crew deal with it, but in the moment, it hadn't even crossed his mind.

She was quiet a moment, nodding and running her tongue over the gaps in her teeth. "I know a thing or two about sacrifice."

Reaching the storage room where they kept the rations and medicine they had raided from the abandoned facilities, Kieran pressed the control to open the doors. He waited for Adeina to follow him through the open door before letting it shut.

He opened a small crate and pulled out the standard-issue ration bars. "What do you like? Lychee or Strawberry? Frankly, none of them taste like the real thing. Or there's something called Landenfruit—I don't even know what that is."

When she didn't answer, he picked one at random and peeled the seal-pack open for her.

She stared at it in her hands for a minute, before slumping down to sit on a nearby container. Carefully, she cracked the bar into small pieces, putting one in her mouth. "All my teeth are loose," she admitted when she caught him staring.

"Oh." Kieran suddenly felt very foolish. "I bet Cordelia could make a blender and we could soften it with some water. Make it easier to eat."

She looked up, smiling sadly, and nodded her head.

"I don't think any of us are going to get out of this unscathed. How did you end up out there, anyway?"

Her gaze dropped back to the bar. "You're nice."

"My mama always said you'd catch more flies with honey. Frankly, I don't want you to try to eat me again."

To his surprise, she laughed, and popped another piece of ration bar into her mouth. "Tell me something, is it true that you and the other doctor don't know what love is? I heard you complaining about Leove and Isuma, the kissing and cuddling."

"What? N-no...." He had a feeling this was something very basic, something he should try to pretend he knew about so she didn't realize he was from somewhere else, but he was curious.

"I feel bad for you," she shrugged. "You've never... you don't have anyone?"

He shook his head, confused.

"I just like to think at least someone found some good in all this mess."

He stared at her, perplexed.

"Here. I'll show you." She moved faster than he'd anticipated, suddenly beside him. Kieran braced, squeezing his eyes shut in anticipation of the horrible sound of flesh thunking into an invisible barrier. But it didn't come. Cordelia's barrier didn't rise between them. And the woman wasn't attacking. Her mouth was pressed into his.

It wasn't unpleasant, per se.

She stepped back, staring up at him.

"What was that?" It was the same as he had seen Leove and Isuma do when they thought no one was watching.

"A kiss. Romance. A sign of affection." She squinted at him. "You really don't know what that is. Didn't your parents...?"

His parents had been matched by a geneticist's algorithm to participate in his procreation and produce genetic diversity. Sperm mixed with egg and then deposited in his mother's womb. He was pretty sure they had never pressed mouths together.

"Well, I wanted to say thanks. For being so nice. That's

all."

"You're welcome?"

She pushed the last of the ration bar into her mouth, leaving the small storage room with an armful of different flavours for the other settlers.

As she left, Kieran lifted a hand to his lips. They tingled oddly. The entire experience had been strange and unexpected. But not unpleasant, definitely not unpleasant. Maybe, he thought, with someone you cared about. Maybe it could be something different. Something sweet. His mind flashed a picture of Sarrin. Maybe it would be something to look forward to.

* * *

"Ready, Kieran?" The colonial woman stood in front of him, her hands clasped neatly in front.

He nodded once, glancing down at his bare, mutilated chest. "Are you sure you have time, Cordelia? They'll be bringin' the new batch of Augments up any minute."

She nodded. "I can do two things at once, you know." She sent him a grin and a wink.

He pressed a smile on his face, but it was hard, the muscles seeming to have forgotten how.

"Are you sure you want to go?"

He looked up at the peculiar alien woman. "Yes. It's time for me to go home. Just, can I wear something more than underpants?"

Cordelia shook her head. "You know anything I make can't go with you. All your clothes burned up. You're lucky I found these for you. At least you'll have something to go home in besides your birthday suit."

"Where did you get them?" On second thought, he put up his hands. "No, I don't wanna know."

She smirked.

A corridor opened, stretching out of the seemingly solid

wall in front of him, and with an encouraging gesture from Cordelia, he took a step forward. "You'll be okay, won't you? It's just sometimes these FTL engines have a—"

She stopped him with a shake of her head and a knowing smile. "Yes, thank you, Kieran. With all the jumps these last few days, I've got a good understanding of the gravimetrics involved. Once all of this is over, I can take myself home. Thanks to you."

"Okay."

They walked in silence, Cordelia following him as he walked the seemingly endless corridor. He didn't want to ask about the physics of it, how they could possibly walk the 38 lightyears from the ship to the rendezvous point.

"Will you be all right?" she asked.

He nodded. "Yeah. Hoepe says I'm doing better, I just need time."

"That's not what I meant."

"This is my home, Cordelia," he said, gesturing in front. "You know that."

She turned her head to watch the stars go by through viewports that suddenly appeared in the walls of the corridor. "You see things so beautifully, Kieran." She said it almost sadly. "Of everyone, I like to look at things through your eyes the most."

He frowned.

"I'm going to miss you, I think."

"Cordelia, I'll miss ya too."

"We're here," she announced, her face suddenly cheery once more.

And so they were. He looked up with a start. The Observer ship's retrieval pod hovered in front of them. A unique design, it was tethered to the ship and could be shot out ahead, decelerating to the point a shuttle could dock, and then reeled back into the ship, accelerating until it matched the speed of the ship. It saved the massive amounts of energy required to bring a ship in or out of near-luminal speeds.

Cordelia fashioned a shuttle around them, flying it close to the pod and connecting with the airlock. "After you," she said.

Kieran knocked on the shuttle hatch. Knock-knock-kn-knock-knock.

Two knocks came as the response before he heard the airlock being released on the other side and the hiss of pressure normalizing between the two vessels.

The door in front of him opened, and on the other side stood his mother. She was unchanged in her favourite rainbow sweater, dark leggings, and huge smile, only a few months older than she had been when he'd left five years ago. "Kieran!"

"Mom!" He threw himself into her outstretched arms. It hadn't been a lie, she really did give the best hugs, and he nearly melted into this one except his jagged skin caught on her sweater, and he let out a yelp.

She stepped back, holding him at arms length, eyes trailing quickly over what he knew was a gruesome sight. "Oh my."

"I had an accident," he said. "Just a month ago. Sorry I didn't have time to tell you. But I'm okay."

Her lower lip quivered. "Well, you're here now." She pressed into him again, gentler this time. Hug complete, she pulled him into the pod. "And this," she pulled Cordelia in behind him, "must be Sarrin."

Kieran rubbed his arms. "Ah, no. Sarrin couldn't make it. Cordelia is my ride."

"I thought you were bringing Sarrin back with you. You know the rules about telling folk who are going to remain in standard-time."

"Not to worry." Cordelia curtseyed before them. "I won't tell a soul. I'm not even human." She made a show of removing both her arms and then transforming herself into a fuzzy purple ball before turning back into the ostentatious colonial woman he had grown accustomed to.

"Oh my." His mother looked at Cordelia, then turned back to him for an explanation. "What is she?"

"I'm an explorer, like you," answered Cordelia. "But I was strand—."

Kieran stared at the floor, rubbing his arms. "Mom," he interrupted. "I never told you I was planning to bring Sarrin."

"I suppose I just assumed. The way you went on and on about her in your reports."

He rubbed his chest, feeling the pain there more acutely than anywhere else. "A living Augment, Mom. A massive conspiracy. Cordelia is an alien, and we've thought for centuries they didn't exist."

"I'm very much looking forward to your full debrief."

"I wish you could have met her."

His mother folded her hands in front of her and waited.

Sarrin. He slumped against the doorframe. Blue eyes, steel hands, matted hair, procedural marks covering the entirety of her back, and a body so skinny it looked like she might crumple under her own weight. And yet she was strong. She could crush a man's larynx with her bare hand—his hand went to his throat, remembering the time she had confused him for an enemy.

Only once.

Sarrin, and the pain in her eyes when she came back to herself and saw what she did. The pain when she had to tell him about each of her gifts… curses. But she had told him. And she had learned to recognize him even in the throes of a deadly trance.

The pain in his chest wasn't his skin at all.

This—his mother standing patiently—was home.

But so was that.

"Kieran," Cordelia prompted him. "I have to go." She glanced at the countdown clock on the wall of the transport pod, as if to illustrate her point.

"Wait," he said, catching her arm. Then he looked at his mother. "I can't come with you."

She tilted her head to the side, her facial expression changing only the slightest. "I know."

"What?"

She gave him a sad smile. "A mother knows these things. Lord knows I saw it with your sister, and I see it with you."

"Lauren?"

"She wasn't made for this life, the life of an Observer. She was made for adventure. Like you. She was made for love. She fell in love Kieran, and she decided to stay."

"Love?" He thought suddenly of Leove and Isuma, and the rescued savage woman's garbled voice saying, 'At least someone found some good in all this mess.'

"I suppose maybe I had hoped it wouldn't happen for you," his mom said. "But you and Lauren were so close, so much the same, you both loved each other so fiercely. This Sarrin, she makes you happy, I think."

He remembered the joy he had whenever he was with Lauren, the pain when he knew he would never see her again. His heart cracked in his chest. If he went, he would never see Sarrin again. If he stayed he'd never see his mom and brother again. He swallowed heavily, his eyes burning. "Mom?"

"I love you, Kieran. I'm glad I got to see you one last time before you go to live your life." She hugged him again.

His life. So many times he had risked his life, overstepped his bounds, completely disregarded the Observer rules. Why hadn't he seen it before? He wasn't an Observer anymore. He was a participant. "Thank you."

She pulled away from him, wiping at the sides of her eyes. "Besides, you never would have made a very good Observer, you can't sit still for more than five minutes."

He laughed, and she laughed too.

"You have to go now." She glanced back at the timer, still holding his shoulders.

"I love you, Mom. And tell Dad and Andy... I wish I could say goodbye to them too."

"I'll tell them," she said. "Don't forget to send your debrief." And then she gently pushed him back, beyond the hatch of the little pod, and released him. The airlock shut with a clang of finality.

Cordelia stood beside him, holding his hand. They were standing on a thin platform, open to space around them. He watched as the transporter pod accelerated away from them and then disappeared.

"Come on." Cordelia turned and took three steps. "The others are having a time. There are more Augments in this compound than any of the others. Worse shape too."

Suddenly, their little platform was beside the ship and the wall opened and swallowed them inside.

Kieran looked around at the bustle of the Infirmary.

"Kieran?" Hoepe looked up at him, turning away from the delicate work he was bent over. "What are you doing in your underwear?"

Kieran grinned. "I'm here to help." He wrapped an arm around one of the rescued Augments and helped them to a bed. He was home.

SIXTEEN

KIERAN TOSSED IN HIS BUNK. Every fibre of the sheets seemed to be made of needles, poking and pricking his tender skin, no matter how he laid. He suspected the sleeplessness had more to do with his ever-churning thoughts. He had been so close to home. He'd actually hugged his mother. And then watched as she sped away at nearly the speed of light.

It felt like a bad dream.

Mostly, his thoughts revolved around Lauren: she had died some two-hundred years prior. He'd mourned, feeling the gutting loss of someone who had been so young, who had died before their time. From his perspective at least. He was forced to watch over the course of months on the Observer ship until news of her death reached their data fragment collector.

But now, his mother's words echoed in his head: *She fell in love Kieran, and she decided to stay.*

His sister had been in love. Was she happy? Did she have friends? A family? Children? Had she stayed happy? Or had she wandered in Earth-time until her death, wishing she had made a different choice?

His breath caught in his chest, and he bolted upright in

bed, unable to breathe.

The lights came on around him. Cordelia appeared, and he found himself splashing down into the blue gel of the regen-tank.

Sputtering, he clawed to the surface, gasping for air.

"I felt you were in pain," Cordelia said innocently, looking at him over the rim of the tank, her head tilted sideways in curiosity.

"I'm fine." He splashed once—wholly unsatisfying in the dense goo—and laid back, his lungs filling normally with air once again. "My skin's fine."

Cordelia sat, the corner of a bed materializing underneath her.

"I'm never going to see them again. Not Dad or Andy...."

Her eyes perked up. "I could—"

"No, don't make 'em appear. It's not the same." He sighed. "And for what? This isn't my fight, it's not my world. They're gonna need someone to look after the engines—a sub-luminal ship doesn't just run itself. And there's so much data to go through. It never stops. I was supposed to bring someone back to help, not leave myself."

She held her arm out, grasping his hand and pulling him as the tank and rest of the furniture disappeared. She smiled to stop his spiralling thoughts, they weren't helping anything anyway. "We've arrived at Etar. Hoepe wants you on the bridge."

He was dry, dressed, and styled in an instant. The wall melted away, the edge of his quarters unbelievably opening into the busy command centre. "You know sometimes we like ta do things for ourselves."

Hoepe greeted him with a tense nod. A great green and purple ball rotated on the view screen: Etar. It was stunning, and yet it stirred an uneasiness in the pit of his stomach. He supposed many of the others looked on it as home, but it wasn't. He'd spent some time there when he went to the Academy, but it was some strange and foreign land, alien, not his home at all. Not yet, anyway.

"It's so beautiful to see it like this, isn't it?" Adeina, the recovering savage woman, stood beside him, staring at the screen.

He answered with a non-committal grunt.

"Hoepe says anyone who's strong enough has to go down. Cordelia is getting tired." Adeina too sounded tired, and he looked at her, surprised she didn't look as excited as the Augments around them.

"You're from Etar, aren't you? That's your home."

Her lips pressed together in a thin line. "It was home. I don't know what they'll do to me if I'm found there."

He eyed her stooped frame. "What do you mean?"

"Going to that colony was the only way to please the Gods. That's what they said."

"Yeah, but the colony was dying. You nearly died there."

She bit her lip. "You don't understand. I was caught questioning the words of the Gods. My family thinks I chose to go, the ultimate act of devotion. I was supposed to die there."

He gulped. That's what he had just committed himself to, right, instead o going home, he committed himself to die here in standard-Earth-time. "You're lucky you didn't."

"This planet, it's horrible. I would go as far away as I could, as fast as I could."

Her frank words surprised him. But everything he knew about the Speakers and about the folk, about the horrible legacy of the Gods, agreed. He closed his eyes, picturing the transport pod, wondering if he could somehow go back and stay there. But it was a foolish thought, and one he didn't really mean. Because as terrible a place as it might be, it still had the one thing he would, and did, give up everything for.

"Everybody ready?" a cheery voice sung across the deck. Cordelia skipped across the front of the room, waving her arms as person after person disappeared. She stopped in front of Kieran, holding his face in both her hands. "Tell Gal he can't come back."

"Wha—?" The floor opened underneath him, and he was swallowed, speeding down a semi-transparent tube through the clouds and to the rapidly approaching forest below.

* * *

The cloud of ash swirled around Sarrin.

"Good," shouted Roelle, "Now shape it. Control it."

Sarrin squinted—not that it helped—and focussed on the image of the goral she held in her mind. The cloud shifted, the pieces wavering as they changed direction. The beast began to take shape—first the thick body, the head, and the bizarre horns.

All at once, the creature exploded in a cloud, raining down around them.

Roelle crossed her arms and sighed. "This is a simple exercise. You must only use the full potential of your mind. Try it again."

Sarrin took a shaking breath, staring at the small mountains of ash piled at her feet.

"You've done this before, yes? I saw it in you."

She pressed her lips together and nodded. But it hadn't been like this. She'd been running, afraid, fighting for her life when she'd smashed the drone in the city. Once, she'd directed a view screen to fly into Guitteriez and kill him, another time she'd made data tablets and loose papers fly around Kieran's room, completely unaware she was doing it.

Roelle was waiting, and Sarrin grunted, trying to ready her mind. Roelle said this was an exercise they taught children, the ash light and easy to shape. She'd passed harder tests in Evangecore. It should not have been difficult.

The monster whispered to her: it was because she was a killer. Playing with ash in a burnt valley held no promise of destruction. It was already dead, she would need to find something alive and breathing.

Her gaze caught on Roelle, going dark around the edges.

Quickly, she pushed it away, and focussed on the scattered debris. She reached her mind out to it, attempting to grasp it, to connect with it. But it was true, it was already dead, there was nothing there.

A black tendril crawled across her vision, and she shoved it down, redoubling her efforts on the ash pile.

"Don't focus only on the ash. It is not alone, everything is connected. Cast your gaze wide."

Sarrin looked up at the Agada woman, and Roelle spread her arms. The trees shimmered in the wind, their branches flipping almost in unison. At the same time, the ash, as far as Sarrin could see, stirred and then lit into the sky like a flock of birds. As if they were alive, ash birds swooped and called, dancing in the sky above them for a full minute until they landed on the ground and melted into nothing.

How could she breathe life into something so dead?

The Agada only smiled, gesturing to the pile of ash she had neatly placed in front of Sarrin once more. But, her ear turned suddenly to the side, expression far away. "The trees speak. Do you hear?"

It was not the first time it had happened, and Sarrin shrugged the same as every time before. Roelle claimed the trees brought her messages of what was happening in the forest, that once they had told the Uruhu the goings on of the entire planet, every tribe and scouting party, even the goral they hunted for meat, known to each other.

This time, a familiar pang tickled Sarrin, surprising and disconcerting. But not unfamiliar. She had no idea how she knew it, only that she did: Kieran was here.

"More of your kind are arriving," Roelle said.

Sarrin was already running, climbing the slippery ash slope to the path above, oblivious to the Agada woman calling out behind her; oblivious to anything in her surroundings. Her legs only knew to pound the dirt as fast as they could as she cut through the trees, sprinting through the maze of woods.

* * *

Kieran landed, his arms instinctively shooting out to balance himself. Around him, Augments appeared out of nowhere. Adeina stumbled and fell, and he reached out to grab her arm.

He let her go just as quickly, hissing as she clutched onto his arm and the still mostly-raw flesh.

"Thanks," she said quickly, frowning at his sudden pain.

He waved her off, and tried to take a step forward to get out of the landing-zone. It was chaos, and he bumped straight into an Augment as he appeared.

Hoepe landed, staring at a data tablet in his hand that quickly vanished. He grunted, meeting Kieran's gaze. "She said the others were in a village not far from here."

"A village?" Kieran raised his eyebrow. "This is Etar's forest preserve." It had to be, taller trees than he'd ever seen before surrounded him. Not even the fruit trees that grew in the hydroponic gardens could compare. If the landing of over a hundred people hadn't been so chaotic, and if his skin hadn't smarted so much, he would have been in awe.

Hoepe shrugged, seemingly unfazed as he alternated between scanning his tablet and the forest in front of them.

"How d'you suppose we find them?" Kieran asked. But he didn't need to.

Fast moving footsteps, lots of them, shook the forest floor. The warriors appeared all at once, dark skinned and clad in animal hides and bones. The nearest hefted a spear, pointing it at Kieran's throat. Beside him, Hoepe faced the same treatment.

"Who are you? Why are you here?" the first shouted in a deep guttural tone, his mouth moving around the words as though they were foreign.

Hoepe slowly lifted his hands, and Kieran did the same. "Easy fellas."

"Are you here with the captain?" shouted the second warrior.

Out of the corner of his eye, Kieran met Hoepe's gaze, noting the slight nod the doctor gave him. He answered the warrior, "Yeah. That's right."

"He said he would bring no more." The warrior glanced at the others behind them, his mouth dropping. "You are all two-blooded?"

Kieran frowned at Hoepe in confusion.

"Like the two women and the man with his strange skin?" the warrior clarified.

"Strange skin?" Kieran muttered, looking down at his own rippled arms.

"Grant," said Hoepe, his arms still up in surrender. "Yes, yes. We know Grant. Most of us are Augments, like him."

The warrior turned away, gesturing and speaking to another in a language Kieran didn't understand before the other sprinted into the forest.

"You are not meant to be here," the warrior announced, but he eased the spear off of Kieran's neck. His strange, pale eyes scanned Kieran up and down. "What happened to you?"

"Uh." Kieran's heart raced. "It's a long story."

"You're uglier than a goral's insides."

"What?"

"Kieran!" a voice shouted across the clearing. He knew the voice, even before he saw her sprinting through the trees. Sarrin.

She slipped through the guards, startling them as she knocked their spears away without a second glance.

His heart thrashed around in his chest, crashing against his ribs with joy. A smile spread on his face, and he instinctively braced and opened his arms in anticipation.

She skidded to a halt a step away from him. Near enough to touch.

His heart still crashed around, his eyes drinking in all of her —the crystalline blue of her wide eyes, the smudge of dirt on her cheek, the pale skin stretched across her cheek bones.

It took all that he had not to step forward and wrap her in his arms. But this was still Sarrin, half-wild, her eyes unreadable. As the seconds ticked by, he realized he had no idea how she felt. He'd stayed for her. He'd given up everything, he knew, for her. What if it had been a mistake?

Her hand came up, touching the rippled skin of his face, radiating soothing warmth. He sighed, pressing into her palm, savouring the touch.

He smiled.

She smiled back.

He was home.

* * *

In the Agada's hut, Gal leaned over the rough map Urubane had provided. It had been drawn in white ink on dried leaves fortified with the dark sap they used for everything. More leaves had been added as they mapped additional sectors of the city, and he had to admit it was incredibly accurate, marking the streets and city squares, and the extensive network of tunnels they had dug under the city.

Beside him, Rayne traced the line of one of the tunnels. "I think that's the one Urubane took us down when we left the city."

Gal nodded, but he had his eye on another tunnel. "This one takes us nearly to the Armoury."

"We can't fight our way off the planet."

"No, but if we can find uniforms, disguise ourselves, it will be easier to sneak aboard the orbital stations and commandeer a ship."

It sounded cracked even as it left his mouth, and frustration spread across Rayne's face. She rubbed her temples. It had been her idea to steal a UEC ship and disappear into the Deep, Deep Black, but even Gal, in all his years with the rebels, had never considered something as spread as trying to steal a ship. Certainly not one big enough for all of them. Besides, where would they go?

"Maybe we should try to get hold of Cordelia again," Rayne suggested.

Gal shook his head. "There no telling when she's coming back."

"There has to be some way to get ahold of her, to tell her what it's like here."

"She can turn into a planet that looks perfect on the sensors from lightyears away, I don't know what her range is exactly, but I'd guess she already knows."

The creak of the hut door interrupted Rayne. Urubane pushed inside, leaning on the doorframe to take the weight off his injured leg and glaring ferociously. "More have arrived."

"What?"

"Yes. Nearly one hundred. They say they are well enough now to come to the planet."

"Where are they?"

"They enter the village was we speak. The Agada brings them." He shook his head, the tone of his voice saying he didn't approve, but said no more.

Gal glanced at Rayne. If more were arriving, that meant Cordelia was here. He pushed past Urubane. "Where are they?"

Urubane hobbled after them. "They bring them to the

fires. How many are there? The village cannot hold more."

Gal took a sharp turn, heading for the communal eating area at the edge of the village. He heard them before he saw them. The Uruhu warriors arrived first, a stream of Augments pouring from between the trees behind them.

They quickly filled the small clearing, the weakest—those supported by others—took space on the benches, while the others stood or sat on the ground, packed around each other.

"It is too many," Urubane huffed beside him.

Gal clenched his jaw. Urubane was right. They had nearly run the food stores dry, and with this many, they would be camping in the woods. If there was a gas attack, they would be squeezing over and under each other in every hut to try to fit everyone in.

Hoepe emerged from the woods, Kieran beside him, clutching Sarrin's hand, and Gal felt the breath rush out of him. "Thank the Gods," he muttered.

The doctor and Kieran made their way to him immediately, pushing through the crowd.

"How many?" Gal blurted. He couldn't believe he was seeing so many Augments, still streaming out of the woods.

"Geez," said Kieran. "How 'bout nice to see ya?"

Gal stared at the engineer's ruined skin. It was good to see him, alive, off the ship, smiling.

"Two-hundred-seventeen," Hoepe answered crisply. "Half remain on board where Cordelia can support their intense medical needs."

"And settlers?" He knew he was snapping, the words falling out faster and harsher than he meant, but he needed to know. "Did you find any still alive?"

Hoepe nodded crisply. "Nearly two dozen."

"That's all?"

"Their conditions were harsh."

"And what about Selousa?" he interrupted. "Did you go to

Selousa? Was there a settler named Minerva?"

Hoepe glanced down at his tablet.

He needed to know. He knew he was being ridiculous, nearly crawling out of his own skin. The fact there so many still alive should have been good news, it was good news. But he needed to know.

He thought of Aaron, and he thought of Minerva. Her and her friends on the Ishash'tor, on his ship, hauled to Selousa like cargo. Minerva's face as she stood at the wall and plunged herself into that hostile, barren landscape.

If she was dead…. He should have…. He should have taken them all away. Turned the ship and run, taken them all into the Deep, Deep Black when he'd had the chance. But he'd been too afraid of the Speakers. Too concerned about his own life, his own comfort.

If she was dead.

Hoepe must have see the agony on his face, because he glanced up from his notes, his voice trying to be comforting. "I don't know. They were all far gone, Gal. Many remain on board where Cordelia is supporting their intense medical needs.   However, they cannot leave her ship without her pulling back all of her influence which is currently keeping them alive."

His eyes flicked to the edge of the woods, the stream of Augments slowing now. At the very last, one of the Augments came into the clearing, carrying a frail woman, skin hanging off her bones. He did a double take; it was her. Gal pushed his way through the crowd, reaching them as the Augment lowered her, and Minerva half-sat, half-fell onto the nearest log.

He heard Rayne behind him: "Tell Cordelia we need her to pick us up. It isn't safe here."

"Minerva," he breathed, uncertain.

She glanced up. She looked nothing like she used to, skin

grey and hanging off her—he would have mistaken her for one of the little grey demons that plagued him, had it not been for her flame of auburn hair and the same familiar determination in her eyes. "Gal," she wheezed.

He glanced worriedly from her angled cheekbones to her pointed elbows, knock-knees poked through tattered and brown-with-dust clothes. She adjusted herself so she could face him more easily, and saluted.

Rayne, behind him, said again, "Call Cordelia."

"Cordelia told me to tell you specifically you can't come back," Kieran said.

He couldn't take his eyes off of Minerva. What she had become. Because of him.

"Thank you," she said.

"Thank you? I'm so sorry." He crouched down, taking her hands.

Behind him, Urubane said, "There are too many."

"We need to find medical supplies," said Hoepe. "Cordelia is only able to support the wounded to a certain extent. Without proper supplies we cannot treat the injured permanently."

"No, trust me, our priority is to get off this planet as fast as we can," said Rayne, frantic. "If Cordelia is in orbit, she can pick us up."

Minerva gripped his hands with what strength she had. She had been so fierce once. What had he done? She smiled gently, and whispered. "The rations—I know you sent them. We held on just long enough for the rescue to come."

Behind him, the others bickered.

"If your ship is here, you must go," said Urubane.

"We can't," said Kieran.

"It's too dangerous here," cried Rayne. "We need a ship to take us to the Deep, Deep Black, it's the only way!"

"Rayne." Gal half turned, not daring taking his eyes off

Minerva. Arguing would get them nowhere. There were a lot of people, a lot of very sick people. But Minerva was here, she was alive. That had to give them a little bit of hope, right?

"Cordelia is here, Gal!" Rayne cried.

Hoepe put his hand up. "She has graciously agreed to wait in orbit until such time as we can treat the others and they are capable of leaving the ship without dying. We need to go into the city to find medical supplies. Cordelia is tired. We have asked a lot of her already."

Gal gave Minerva's hand a squeeze.

"The city's too dangerous. It will be crawling with surveillance drones and foot soldiers." Rayne glanced at him. "They know the Augments are here, everyone will know after we left Alex's body in the central square."

"Alex is dead?" Kieran gasped.

Minerva squeezed Gal's hand back, her eyes locked on his.

Hoepe's back had gone completely stiff, an immutable board. "How did Alex die?"

"UECs!" cried Rayne. "Tell her it isn't safe here. We need to get all these people to safety."

"Rayne," he said, finally turning, "calm down." Minerva was here. She was alive. Not all was lost.

"Never give up the fight," said Minerva. "We only survived because of the rations you left us."

Behind, Rayne gasped, "Rations?" but Gal ignored it. He'd admit later how he snuck the extra container of supplies and weapons to the settlers as they departed the Ishash'tor, right under her meticulously watchful eye.

Minerva continued, "There were no other colonists on Selousa when we went through the wall, just bony corpses and mad-men. I regret we had to use the rifles.... They were wild, cannibalistic, they would have killed every last one of us. By rationing, all twelve of us survived." She lifted her bone-thin arms. "Mostly."

Gal returned her smile.

"I'm glad you're here." She clamped his arm with bony fingers. "We all thought you'd died. What other reason would there be for you to abandon us, to give up the fight. We've tried to carry on, but there are so few of us, and they caught us meeting in the cellar of a cafe and sent us to the planet—no questions, no rehabilitation, nothing. They sent us to die. But, Gal, now that you're here…."

He cut her off with a shake of his head, pulling his hand back as he stood. The warm joy of seeing Minerva alive and the fit of nostalgia it brought was starting to fade, the harsh reality of the last four years digging into him again. "I don't do that anymore. John P is dead."

She stared up at him from bagged eyes, her mouth hanging slightly agape. "You've lost the fight."

The words hung in the air, stinging. But he took a deep breath. "It's too dangerous, you know that." He pressed his lips together, half-expecting Aaron to show up beside him, but Minerva was reminder enough. His fist clenched. It was too dangerous. It really was. "You saw what happened to everyone. To Aaron. To you."

"Too dangerous?" She stood on shaky legs, pressing an accusing finger to his chest. "When has that ever stopped you? When has that ever mattered? You were—."

He stopped her with a sharp glance before she said, glancing warily at Rayne.

All eyes were suddenly on him. "What's she talking about?" asked Rayne.

Minerva stumbled, falling back to her seat with a huff, and he realized just how weak she was. And if she was on the 'healthy' ones who were able to come down to the planet, he didn't want to see the others. "Whoever you are now," she said between heavy breaths, "whoever you were then, it doesn't matter. You know what they're capable of, you've seen it. Don't tell me you can just walk away. Not when we have a chance to do something."

"There is no chance, Minerva. They're too powerful. They always win. The Will of the Gods is too strong. Rayne's right, we have to leave. Cordelia is our best chance."

Minerva shook her head. "They killed Aaron—not sent him to die, not subjected him to the Will or whims of the Gods, but actively chose to end his life. How many others? I have a son, eight—will you tell him his mother's death—or his death—is the Will of the Gods?"

Gal stared at the dirt.

"Don't give up the fight," she begged him.

Rayne put a hand on his arm. "I've heard you talk about Aaron before. Did he… did they send him somewhere to die?" She looked at Minerva. "Is that what they did to you?"

Minerva nodded.

Rayne's bony fingers clamped on Gal's arm. "What do we do?"

He knew all eyes were on him. They were all always on him. But John P was dead. He'd died years ago. Gal was just a cracked, old freightship captain in over his head. "There's nothing we can do. The Speakers are too powerful. This is simply the way it is, but we can get ourselves to safety."

A heavy pause hung in the air.

"I've seen the files on the general's computer," said Rayne, glancing at Sarrin. "They did unspeakable things to those kids, and we, every UEC soldier, supported it. And if what she says is true—that they send people to the colonies to die—then I couldn't live with myself. Gods, Gal! We ferried them there. We might as well have killed them ourselves."

"Rayne…."

She crossed her arms over her chest, eyebrows furrowing as she worked it through. "The Gods we Serve, the Gods we

Trust."

"Rayne...."

"It doesn't mean the Speakers, Gal. It means us. It means the good in this world. We have to trust that there is good. You've always said I'm one of the best Tactical officers you know. Well, maybe there is something we can do to help the folk, maybe this is my Path to Serve. Disappearing into the Deep, Deep Black is tempting, but I can't imagine it now, not with what we know. I couldn't live with myself."

He opened his mouth. They were doomed, he wanted to say, but he knew full well the pain of walking away, of making oneself forget. He was willing to do it to himself again for her, but he couldn't make Rayne life with that pain.

"Okay," he said quietly.

Rayne turned to Minerva. "Do you know where the rebels are now?"

Minerva nodded. "I think so."

"Then we'll help them," said Rayne. "Never give up the fight, right?" She smiled down at him, and then to his shock, quoted the great John P with as much reverence as she had once done with the Speakers: "These eyes cannot unsee. This heart cannot unfeel. I am human, and so human I must be."

A grin spread on Minerva's haggard face. "Sounds a lot like someone I used to know."

Gal licked his lips. That's what he was most afraid of.

Alarms rang in his head—this was getting more and more dangerous—but there was a determined glint in Rayne's eyes, and he would do anything for Rayne. Anything. He echoed the old litany: "Human are we, human we will be."

SEVENTEEN

HALUD WOKE AS THE DOOR to the anteroom slid open and immediately braced himself. He expected the commandant to sweep into the room, cape billowing, her eyes filled all at once with stony ferocity and terrible fear, so he was surprised to see a young man, tall and wiry, and decorated as a lieutenant. The lieutenant had none of the commandant's blatant ferocity, instead his movements were clipped and harsh. He conferred with Halud's guard, and then ordered the door to the cell released.

"Where is the commandant?" Halud demanded, sitting up on his cot.

The lieutenant barely spared him a distasteful glare before turning back to the guard, a smug smile passing between them.

"Where is the commandant?" Halud repeated himself. "What's she done with my pendant? It is a symbol from the Gods, it is not to be taken from me."

With the same quick, precise movements, the lieutenant slipped into the cell, towering over Halud. "Commandant Mallor has been relieved of duty. I am here to escort you."

"There's not a chance in the Deep that I'll go with you. The First Speaker has said what he wanted to say. And I've heard all I want to hear."

The lieutenant reached down quickly, snapping Halud to his feet in one fluid, precise movement. "My orders come directly from the First Speaker himself. It seems he still has some use for you."

"You're still listening to that cracked fool?" Halud forced himself to huff out a laugh. "I thought he had suffered a mental break."

The soldier twisted Halud's arm behind his back, stressing the shoulder joint until Halud cried out. He wasn't as strong as the commandant, but was just as mean, and not quite so even tempered. Half bent, Halud was forced out of the cell and down the hall.

"Let go of me," Halud wheezed through he pain. "Hap won't want me injured, I'm still the Poet Laureate. And I'm already coming with you."

The grip eased, but the lieutenant still pressed his arm into his back.

Halud climbed the stairway, a sticky sense of distaste burning the back of his throat. So many times now Hap had called him to his office to do nothing more than gloat. This would be more of the same.

At the top of the stairs, Joyce smiled at him, seeming not to notice the lieutenant or the forceful grip he had on Halud's right arm. A silly grin spread across her face that made her look half cracked.

Halud rolled his eyes and returned some of the smile. She was sweet at least. Idiot. But harmless.

Her manic smile relaxed. "The First Speaker is expecting you, Master Poet." She reached up to rub her chest, and the fabric of her grey dress bent back, revealing a colourful lining. The blue caught her pale skin tone and made her look almost pretty. Except there should be no colour on her at all—it was a thing for the Gods, such beauty for them alone.

He stared, wide eyed, and just for a moment her face slipped out of its silly facade. The smile became serious, the look became hard. Just for a flash.

The lieutenant pushed Halud forward, up the great twisting staircase and into the office of Hap Lansford, dumping him inside the door.

Halud aimed for his usual chair at Hap's desk, but the office's layout was not the same. A chair had been set in front of the long wall of unsettling exotic and extinct animal heads. Before it was a camera with its cinematographer. A producer stood nearby, and she grabbed Halud and thrust him into the chair. A type of restraint was fastened over his lap, his wrists bound to the chair behind him.

"What is this?" he snapped, looking to the desk and Hap Lansford's silhouette turning from the window. "If you think I'm going to do an address for you, you're cracked."

Hap only grinned.

The cinematographer went through his usual checks, touching Halud's face, adjusting the lighting, adjusting him.

"What are you doing?" he demanded again as the huge Speaker strode towards them.

"You know what I need from you."

"I told you I wouldn't do it. I won't say your words."

Hap shook his head. "That's not what I need. I need your face."

"What?"

The Speaker thrust a tablet at him, a vid already playing. "Things have moved... differently than anticipated. Your sister walks freely in the city, and I cannot have it."

"Sarrin." He glimpsed her on the screen, just a flash before she scaled a building and disappeared. Then he looked to Hap, realization soaring in his core. "You don't know where she is."

Hap ground his teeth.

The video continued to roll, a busy city square, but there was something about the folk: they all wore colour. They all wore hints of blue.

A protest.

His mind flashed a picture of Joyce and the strange slip with her dress.

The realization hit him: "You're losing control of them, Hap."

The Speaker pressed his lips together. His eyes looked almost wild, desperate.

The brief flash of hope he'd felt at the realization fell away to dread; there was no telling how far he would go, what he would do as the folk slipped away from him. "Let my sister go, and I can help you contain them." Halud lurched against his restraint. "You know I'm the only one who can. You need me." He licked his lips. "You want me here so that Sarrin sees me and comes for me, but if you put me on that screen, I will stir up a riot the likes of which you have never seen. The Poet Laureate, in chains! What will the folk think? What will they do?" He could see it now, the confusion, the outrage. What he said was true, he felt the power rise in his chest. "I know how to talk to folk. You can keep me in the dungeons until I'm grey and dead, for all I care, but let her go. She's one girl, it's no matter to you. I can tell you how to stir the folk, how to bend the entire world to your will. I'm the one they listen to, Hap, you know that."

"Blasphemy."

"The Gods don't speak to you anymore. It's me the folk trust."

Hap's face turned red, and for a moment, Halud thought he had him, but he turned back to the cinematographer. "Is your machine set?"

He nodded, "Yes sir, set to broadcast live."

"Good. Leave."

The cinematographer nodded, spinning on his heel. The producer followed.

"Don't do this," Halud tried again, straining against his restraints. His heart raced wildly. Because Hap was right; if Sarrin saw his face, she would come here, and Halud needed to not let that happen. Not after everything, not after what he'd sacrificed. "It's a mistake. Let her go."

A row of people watched from the opposite wall: all the Speakers and their Generals. Joyce and her scribble pad. And her flash of blue.

"All of you too," snapped Hap.

The Speakers and their generals paused, uncertain. Angela Ashbury, speaker of Knowledge opened her mouth, but seemed to think better of it. They filed from the room silently. Joyce waited idly, checking a note on her pad, the last to leave. She sent him a subtle shake of her head completely devoid of her characteristic smile—a warning—then turned, skipping out of the room, notepad clutched to her chest.

The wooden door closed with a heavy thump.

Everything was moving too fast.

Halud looked back to Hap, and was met with his fist. The blow sent him sprawling across the floor, still tied into his chair. Such violence was against the Gods, but here they were. The Speaker lifted him up, stool and all, setting him back in front of the camera.

"You're a fool, Hap," he growled.

Hap moved out of the frame, pressing a control on the camera so that its little recording light began to flash. "Now tell the folk what you've done," he growled. "Tell them your defiances against the Gods, you sick, pathetic creature."

Halud spit out a mouthful of blood. "Do what you will to me, Hap. The Gods protect the folk, not the cracked Speakers." He took a deep breath, staring Hap defiantly in the face. "The Gods protect the folk!"

The light on the camera blinked off, Hap's facing burning a deep red.

Halud glared. "The Gods will never smile on you again."

* * *

Amelia wiped the sleeve of her shirt across her forehead, careful not to lose her grip on the laz-rifle in her hands. The jungle heat was oppressive, and she took a moment to rest under the cover of the broad leaves of a Colocasia bush.

Colocasia: broad leaves that provide rain and sun shelter, root edible only after soaking.

Under the thick cover, she was entirely non-visible. She could rest.

Except.

Except.

Her heightened hearing picked up the clunk of a boot, then the sharp snap of a laz-rifle being reassembled quietly and quickly.

They were out there.

Who?

It didn't matter.

Amelia threw herself out from under the elephant ear, sprinting over the terrain. She launched herself just in time. The laz-bolt seared across her abdomen.

The commandant bolted awake on the narrow medical cot. The monitors started to alarm, and she strained against the bonds that held her wrists and ankles.

The singular door to the cell cracked open, a smooth panel on the wall moving out and to the side. She forced her heart rate to slow, as the doctor stomped forward, peering down at her. She held her eyes shut, forcing her body to mimic the deep relaxation and unpredictable twitch of a REM cycle.

He prodded her a few times, pressed the silencer on the alarm, and left, satisfied that she was still asleep and that the alarm had been nothing more than a bad dream.

Amelia recited prime numbers to one thousand.

When enough time had passed, she unclipped herself from

the restraints, programmed the monitors, and slipped from the hospital cell into the spaces between the walls. Her legs and arms moved of their own volition through the maze of support beams, and almost by surprise, she found herself looking down on the guard outside of Halud's cell.

Lazy, the man had fallen asleep, snoring gently as his laz-rifle sagged in his grip.

Silently, she dropped down behind him, twisted the trigger points to push him into a deep sedation, and let him slump to the floor.

Halud watched her from where he laid on the bed. They stared at each other a long time. Silently, he rose, coming to the edge of the glassine wall. His face was bruised and swollen, blood seeping from a crack on his lip. He pointed to the control panel.

She flicked on the two-way communication between the anteroom and the cell.

"Why are you here?" he asked, his speech slurred by the fat face.

"What happened to you?" she asked. But she already knew.

He looked away. "Do you know where my friends are? The rebels I was with when you captured me. I need to get a message out."

She shook her head. "Gone."

"Gone? Where?"

"One of the colonies," she said quietly. "They were dispatched almost immediately."

"What?" His hands banged on the glassine.

She stepped back, startled. The words, 'I'm sorry,' caught on the tip of her tongue. Then a surge of anger coursed through her—like he was the only one who had lost someone. The Augments had kil— ... the Augments had what?

"Hap's lost his mind," he said, pacing, agitated, across his cell.

The anger swirled again. "The First Speaker is descended from the Gods," she snapped, her mouth answering automatically before her mind could comprehend what she was saying. "You will show him the proper respect." But she finished the sentence, the words trailing off, and a sinking sense of something forgotten causing her breath to catch. She brought her hands to her chest, bracing for the pain that she inexplicably expected to come next.

Halud stopped his pacing directly across from her. He looked on with weak eyes—doleful, pathetic. Strong and intelligent. "It looks like they've captured you too, Commandant."

Her crumpled hospital gown swayed around her shins, her legs embarrassingly bare. She held her chin high, growling, "I am in medical treatment."

"For what?"

"For—." She didn't know. But it must have been something. It felt like a war was playing out in her head. Voices and sensations jumbled around, none of it making any sense. She started to pace.

The Poet watched. "What are you doing here, Amelia?"

She glanced at him, her foot paused in midair as she contemplated answering him. He was the traitorous Poet, there was no reason for her to be here. The sight of him made her sick.

But he was the only one, wasn't he?

The only one who what?

Who understood.

She drove her hands into the side of her head to stop it from spinning. "My mind is breaking. It's like a thousand glassine shards shattering over everything."

His brow knitted together.

"I'm not cracked," she said. But she was thinking and

talking like she was.

His voice was calm and steady as he watched her interest. "Yes, you are. We all are."

The anger flared again, and she rushed the glassine, slamming into it so hard that it shook with a a low vibration.

To his credit, he didn't back away. The pathetic fool knew he was protected. It took an incredible force in just the right place to shatter a window and leap through to the other side. Not that it couldn't be done. She'd seen it done.

Where? When?

"Do you know what they call you?" he asked. Of course she did, but he answered anyway: "The Augment Hunter. You hunt children—helpless children who've never done a thing wrong—and you destroy them. Destroy their lives, their families, their hope."

Her hands smacked the glassine. "Why would I destroy them?" she shouted. But the emotion wasn't anger. "I—." Her limbs shook, voice quavering as the air rushed from her chest, leaving her empty and gasping against the glass, like a gravity trap had been set to high and was near to crushing her. "You've got it all wrong." But she was the one who was wrong.

She fell to the ground, her legs crumpling under her. She was the thing that he said: she lived to destroy the abominations, the Augments, and their sick, twisted hatred for the Gods. That was her purpose. The Gods she Served. The Gods she Trusted.

"Commandant," Halud said quietly, squatting down in front of her. "Why do you keep coming here?"

She stared at him, trembling on all fours on the ground.

Because he understood. He understood what?

"Your eyes are blue. Crystalline and pale."

She knew her own appearance well enough. "So?"

"You of all people should know, *Xenoralia nervosa* pulls the pigment from the eyes."

Her heart slammed into her throat. "You're cracked." The Poet was insane.

"I watched a child's eyes change instantly as he was injected with the virus. Only an Augment would have blue irises like yours."

"Don't be ridiculous. Your eyes are blue too."

He shrugged. "Yes, they are."

A familiar fury caused her fist to clench at her side, some unnamed killer instinct welling up inside her. "You're an Augment?" She was the Augment hunter. Augments were an abomination. She would seek and destroy them all.

"Yes." He peered out from his cell. "And so, it seems, are you."

It wasn't true. The Gods she served. A raw memory of searing pain opened up across her flesh. She leapt to her feet. "I don't believe you."

She slipped into the space between the walls, ignoring the niggling memory of the girl who had first showed her how.

EIGHTEEN

SARRIN TUGGED AT HER HOOD, scanning up and down the street to be sure they weren't being followed. After the decision had been made, they'd wasted little time before coming into the city.

It was only a small group—any more and it would be impossible to sneak through the city in the descending dusk. Minerva led the way, leaning heavily on Gal. They'd already turned the corner out of sight. Grant paused at the same corner, several paces behind. In the narrow alley she had just come from, Kieran followed behind her, and Rayne and Luca spaced out behind him.

Her heart did a strange flip flop as she thought of Kieran. She could hear his tight breathing from here, and the shortened, ginger stride. He hadn't recovered enough for this, not really, but he'd protested when Hoepe suggested he stay behind with the others, and she had done very little to help the doctor dissuade Kieran.

After all the weeks apart, somehow she just wasn't ready to walk away again. In Evangecore, she would have been shot— just like Amelia had been for looking after her. But this wasn't Evangecore, was it?

Roelle's warning flashed in her memory:

"The line between friend and foe can blur. All we can do is decide who we will be."

She'd gripped Sarrin's arm, then, fixing her with a deep stare. *"You are still untrained, your abilities unpredictable. I worry there is too much of the Other in you. Do not lose yourself."*

The person walking behind her let out a surprised yelp, stopping short, and Sarrin realized she had stopped walking in the middle of the road.

Kieran's hand was suddenly on her back, pushing her forward.

"Stay close to your sha-fa-na," Roelle had said, pointing to Kieran. *"He is good for you, yes."*

She forced her feet to move, chancing a glance at his scarred face. The corner of his green eye crinkled, and he pushed her ahead. Two people walking together would draw too much attention, but she still ached when his hand left her. She shook off the memory of how it had felt to touch his face, walking hand in hand through the woods, so close to the dream she had of the two of them running and laughing and falling into each other.

She turned the corner, her eyes finding Grant as he picked his way through the crowd. They had come onto one of the main thoroughfares, this street busy, the lines of people flowing in defined paths, and she fell into line with the traffic.

She reached out, the way Roelle had taught her. There were a lot of people, but she needed to know where Kieran was, and if Rayne and Luca were safe behind him. The weight of so many folk nearby it made her head spin, but she felt him there, not three paces behind.

A desperate keening wail cut through the din, slicing into her mind. Her head whipped around to look for the source even as her thrumming heart told her it was something she didn't want to see.

"You okay?" Kieran was suddenly by her elbow, his sleeve

brushing the back of her cloak. He scanned her face, eyes now tight with worry. "I saw you stumble. Is it too many people?"

They were stopped in the middle of the square, folk streaming around them. They needed to move, keep following Gal, but the wail demanded attention, shaking her to her bones.

Her eyes flicked immediately across the square to a flustered woman reaching into a pram. The mother lifted a crying baby into her arms.

With a start, Sarrin realized it was the baby's little voice that was screaming. It was like nothing she had ever felt before. Pale blue eyes, nearly white, flashed like a beacon. An Augment baby. Almost as much Uruhu as Human.

"What is it?" Kieran asked, suddenly at her shoulder.

She hadn't even had time to tell him about the baby she had seen and the *Xenoralia* vaccine, so she answered him with a shake of her head and started to push through the crowd. She would draw too much attention, but the voice demanded attention.

Reaching the woman and her baby, she reached into the carry bag underneath the pram and pulled out the grey child's toy shaped like a hydrocarbon molecule that she knew she would find there, the babe projecting an image of it into her mind as clear as shouting.

She handed the toy to the infant who ceased its wailing immediately, pushing a hydrogen atom into its tiny mouth, its pale eyes closing contentedly.

Sarrin stared. What would this child be? So much more Uruhu than even her. What gifts would it have? Another thought struck her, and she frowned. The Speakers and their researchers had chased her across the stars to see what she could do; what would they do to this child?

She looked into the eyes of the mother, the woman

scanning Sarrin curiously. She should say something, some warning, but what was there to say?

The mother looked down at her child, at its unnatural crystalline-blue eyes, and back to Sarrin, her eyebrows slowly knitting together as realization dawned.

Sarrin pressed her lips into a tight line and nodded, confirming the woman's worst fears. The child was an Augment. It was just like her. No, Sarrin had been three when she was infected. This child would be stronger, faster, more powerful in every way. With training, the most dangerous weapon in existence.

But still human.

As fast as she'd come, Sarrin spun away.

Behind her, the woman screamed.

That would certainly draw attention, and Sarrin angled quickly across the square to where Kieran waited, watching. She kept her head down, expecting a drone or even a guard to come for her. But even as she ran, folk around her shifted. Shouts sounded around her. The organized lines of folk walking by dissolved into chaos.

She pushed her way to Kieran through the churning sea. "What's going on?"

UEC soldiers flooded the square. A man ran past and was tackled to the ground.

"Look." She followed his arm to one of the large viewscreens.

On it, a bloodiest Halud, tied to a chair, stared defiantly into the camera. "The Gods protect the folk, not the cracked Speakers."

Black clouds wrapped around her vision.

Kieran's hands were on her in a second, pulling her backwards.

A man leapt up, shouting. "The Speakers are cracked. The Gods protect the folk!"

Suddenly, there were swirls of blue everywhere, mixing with the grey and black tendrils. A group of folk knocked over an elite guard. A hovercraft thumped overhead.

"Get down," Kieran shouted, pushing her as her vision descended into blackness.

* * *

Gal clenched his arm around Minerva's waist, dragging her faster, as a riot broke out into the square.

"Gal." She patted his arm weakly.

"It's not far," he said. With every turn they'd taken, he'd been more and more dreadfully certain they were walking right back to the old lair, right where it had all started. He never should have agreed to this, but he knew the way, knew they just needed to turn into the alley ten paces ahead.

"Gal!" she said more forcefully, pulling away. "We have to help."

"Minerva," he tried, but it was too late. She'd already stumbled away and into the crowd.

Beside him, ten folk took down an elite guard. Gal sidestepped to avoid getting caught in the fray. Where was Minerva?

What was Hap thinking? To show a vid like that, of the fallen Poet denouncing the Speakers. But then Hap had always underestimated the folk. That's how John P had been able to rally so many, to cause so much trouble for so many years. He understood the power wasn't in the Gods or the Speakers, it was in the folk.

Cries of, "The Gods protect the folk!" echoed around him.

He spotted Minerva, her hands on a young boy. A black-clad soldier lifted his laz-rifle, and Gal froze. But the boiling crowd rolled into him, knocking the guard and Minerva and the boy all over at once.

The boy scrambled away as the folk beat the soldier, tearing him apart.

Minerva still laid on the ground, when the crowd had passed, and Gal ran to her. Her head was bleeding, her eyes closed. He shook her shoulder gently. "Min? Minerva?" Demons. He pressed a hand to her neck. At least she wasn't dead.

Scooping her into his arms, he ran for the alley. His feet following the old path easily.

Aaron jogged up beside him. "Wasn't that great, Gal?"

He glared back. If Aaron was here, it couldn't be good.

"Remember when we used to do that? Hijack the feeds, drive the folk into a frenzy. There's nothing like a good crowd mentality. When they drive each other into a frenzy, all those years of barely surpassed frustration and indoctrination erupting to the surface."

"Hap's a fool," Gal panted.

"Yeah, but what a rush! Don't you miss this?"

"No," said Gal. "We were all fools. You died. And look at Minerva. How can that be good?"

Aaron glanced at her, her too-thin body hanging limply in Gal's arms. "At least she tried, Gal. Is trying. You could have helped her."

"I don't do that anymore."

"Don't give me that line. You're running away, the same as you have been. Trying to save yourself. How is that going by the way? How do you feel now that you know what your indifference has cost?"

Gal swallowed, his eyes on the alley as he kept running. Wasn't this enough? He was doing something now, getting Minerva to safety. Right?

The old door looked exactly the same as he remembered it, down to the painted circle with two chevrons in the corner. His hand banged on the metal before he knew what he was doing.

His whole body shook. This wasn't a good idea. He could

just leave her here, drop her and run. They would find her and bring her in.

"Look, Gal, the old symbol still lives," said Aaron.

He shook his head, refusing to look at it. "It was drawn by a stupid kid," he muttered.

"Maybe so."

The peek-flap on the door opened, a set of eyes and a laz-rifle looking out.

He shuffled Minerva in his arms, bringing his hand up to form a chevron over his chest.

It had been a long time, with no way to know if the password had changed, but the door creaked open.

Aaron nudged him, so that he stumbled forward into the dark, waiting den of a dozen armed rebels.

"Looks like all these people still believe in what that stupid kid started," Aaron said, as Gal slowly eased Minerva down and brought his hands above his head.

* * *

Kieran dragged her backwards as the dark clouds swirled across her vision. Flashes of folk fighting in the square shone through.

"Sarrin," he called, his voice laced with panic. "Stay with me. Focus."

A man cried out, "The Gods protect the folk!" and her mind painted the picture of Halud, tied to the Speaker's chair.

She pulled out of Kieran's grasp. "I have to find him."

"No." He grabbed her hand, the shock of it stopping her. "Look at me."

She did, his green eyes cutting through the trance as the monster whispered instructions to tear the square apart. And the Speaker's building, and the whole city until she got to Halud.

"There's too many," Kieran said. "Everyone's already gone

this way. Come on."

She let him drag her away from the square, into an alleyway. Kieran's fear thrummed in her veins where his hand held hers. Without the crowd, the chaos was less, but the monster still pushed, its voice louder now. It was too close.

Kieran squeezed her arm. "Just take a deep breath." It dawned on her that he was afraid of her, afraid she might lose control, and she pushed the monster down.

He kept pulling her, right to a little grey door, the rebel symbol painted in the corner. "This is where they went in." He rapped once, but there was no answer.

The monster strained against her hold, clashing thoughts and emotions spinning around her head until she was ready to drop from dizziness. She lifted her hand to force the rickety old door, but it exploded outwards before she reached it, forcing her and Kieran to duck as it ripped off its hinges and crashed beside them.

"Whoa," Kieran said. But he didn't let go as they stepped into the dark room.

A dozen laz-rifles swivelled in their direction. Twelve target points, untrained. A growl escaped her lips. It would be easy to make them omega.

Kieran nudged her.

"No, no, they're with us!" Rayne cried out. She knelt on the floor in front of them, her hands on her head. "I told you, we're here to help."

An old woman, rounds of ammunition slung across both shoulders, barked a single laugh. "You're wearing a UEC uniform. Why would we trust you? You can't even help but stand like a soldier. At least try for me, sweetheart."

One of the rebel guards moved, his fingers twitching on the trigger of his rifle. "Just give the order, Morana. What do you want me to do?"

There wasn't time for the leader to answer. The monster

pulled out of Kieran's grip, lunging across the room in a flash. When the darkness receded, an old laz-rifle sat in her hands, the bio-sensor reprogrammed. The rebels were on the ground, a smoking scorch mark on the wall behind where they had been.

Kieran's hands were on her arm, his eyes wide. He must have reached her in time to jar the shot. None of these rebels were omega after all.

Across the room, Grant stood in his ugly grey skin suit, a laz-rifle similarly in his hands. Paranoid glances flitted across the room from both sides.

No, not sides, she corrected herself. They weren't at war with each other. She didn't want to be at war with anybody. She let the rifle drop from her hands, and it clattered on the floor. Across the room, Grant set his gently down.

"We aren't here to harm you," Kieran said. "Let's all put our rifles down."

"She just tried to shoot us!" The rebels climbed to their feet, rifles still in hand.

Kieran grimaced, putting his body between Sarrin and the others. "Things got a little outta hand, is all."

"You're right," said Rayne, still on the floor. "I used to be a UEC soldier. A few weeks ago, if I'd found this base, I would have arrested every one of you. But the things I've seen in the last month, what I've learned…. I'm here to help. And I am the General's daughter and one of the foremost tactical officers in the Central Army. I can be helpful."

The rebel leader frowned, her scrutinizing gaze falling to Sarrin. Even if she believed Rayne, it was clear Sarrin was the one she didn't trust. Sarrin shut her eyes; just one moment of lost control was all it had taken. Roelle's reminder echoed in her head, but it was already too late.

"Look, please," Gal said from where he still kneeled on the floor, Minerva's body in front of him. "She needs medical attention. She's the one that brought us here, but she was knocked out in the riot in the square."

"Minerva defected. She went to a colony. Why should we trust her?"

"She was one of your lieutenants, right? She'd been with the rebels for years," said Gal. "She didn't defect, she was sentenced to die. We found her and brought her back. But she needs help."

The rebel leader paused, considering, then nodded at one of the guards He and another ran forward, lifting Minerva's body between them and disappearing deeper into the building.

Another of the rebels glanced at Grant. "What are you?"

Grant growled.

"He's an Augment," answered Rayne.

"Augments," the leader barked a laugh again. "They're supposed to be dead."

"Supposed to be, maybe," said Sarrin. She pushed her hood back so the leader could see her unnaturally crystalline blue eyes shining even in the dark bunker. She lifted the sleeves to expose the barcodes on her arms, trying not to flinch as the rebels gasped.

"There are dozens more," said Rayne. "We came to help you. And because we need your help. The Speakers are corrupt. They no longer speak the words of the Gods."

The leader frowned. "If there are dozens of Augments, why do you need our help?"

"Manpower," said Kieran, his hand still resting comfortably on Sarrin's arm. "We need your network. All of your rebels."

The leader scoffed. "You're cracked, then. You and your plan. There's barely any of us left. Our numbers have fallen ever since John P died. And what few there were, we lost in that spread business with the Poet and the hospital."

Sarrin's heart skipped a beat. "Halud?" She closed the

distance to the woman before she knew what she was doing.
"We have to help him."

The rebel leader stepped back. "He's on his own. It was a
set up. We wasted more than a few good rebels, all because
he believed they were making new Augments."

"They are."

Kieran was at her side again, a grip on her arm. "What?"

She turned to him, nodding. "The baby in the square, it
was an Augment."

The leader crossed her arms, but her expression softened.
"How do you know?"

Sarrin shrugged; it was too much to explain. She waved
vaguely at her eyes and the marks on her skin. "I just do."

"But why would they?" asked one of the other rebels.
"The Augments started a war."

She shrugged again. "To start their own war and destroy
the Uruhu."

Behind her, one of the rebels laughed nervously. "The
virus was unintentional. You're asking us to believe someone
made it."

"It *was* engineered," said Rayne. "Someone did make it.
They made the Augments." She cast a sorry gaze at Sarrin.
"And I have proof."

The leader looked back and forth between them. "If what
you're saying is true…."

"It is," said Rayne.

She looked long and hard at Sarrin, but the monster had
receded, for now, and Sarrin spread her empty hands in front
of her. With a long sigh, the leader nodded. "No weapons."

She spun away, and the others followed her through the
same dark doorway they had taken Minerva through. Sarrin
paused, pulling Uruhu knives from hidden pockets, letting
them clatter to the ground.

"Jesus," Kieran laughed, waiting as she started unwinding a

narrow vine. "I missed you."

* * *

Gal tried not to let his frustration show as the rebel's chief technician peered at an old 2D monitor, and slowly pounded out a command on the analog keyboard. He glanced at Rayne, not sure what he was expecting, but if Aaron were here, they would have rolled their eyes at the rebels' so-called best hacker.

"I need to try to break through the firewall," the tech said, as though sensing Gal's restlessness. "Obviously, it's some of the best defensive programming under the stars, so it's going to take some time."

"Through?" Gal moaned, rubbing his face. "No, you don't go through."

The tech turned to glare at him, his wide eyes shining in the dark. Gal stepped back, and the tech returned to work, but after a few more painstaking keystrokes, Gal yelped, no longer able to contain himself. "We've been here an hour. You don't go through the Speakers' firewall, you go around it. You've got the General's daughter right here, you fool." He pushed the tech out of the way, reaching for the antique computer. "Here. Let me."

He had promised himself he wouldn't. He'd left that life behind. And John P was dead. There was no use in going to the past. This was now, and these were the rebels they had today. But the tech was just so slow.

His fingers floated over the keys, the harsh clacking fading into the background as he focussed on the lines of code scrolling in front of him.

Rayne leaned down beside him. "What are you doing?" Her voice was warm and a surge of joy flooded through him, immediately followed by fear and the horrible incongruity of what he was doing deep in this old rebel compound, so like the hackers lair he and Aaron had first fallen into a lifetime ago.

But he was almost there. He looked up at her guiltily. "I went through your communications log. Did you know your dad keeps all of your messages?"

"He does?" She straightened, suddenly distant.

"There." Gal hit the last key with a flourish. "We're in."

"Really?" She leaned over him again. "How did you learn to do that?"

He stared at the screen so he wouldn't have to meet her gaze. "Just here and there. You said you had the password for his computer, right?"

She nodded, and he shifted out of the chair so she could sit. A moment later, General Nairu's private interface appeared on the screen. A few taps later, and they were staring at lines and lines of Augment files. She opened the folder marked 005478F. Sarrin's file.

Gal stared at the pictures. "Dear Gods," he murmured. "That's why they hunted us across the stars."

Rayne nodded. "Her file was the most extensive I saw. But there are hundreds of files, thousands of experiments." She opened another file, and another. Hundreds of notes, images of bruises and suture lines, vids, too much to take in, flashed by on the screen. The dates told him some of it was old, some of it was recent. The experiments had never stopped.

A sudden pit opened in Gal's belly, and he grabbed the back of the chair for support. He shouldn't have gone. He shouldn't have pretended to be dead all those years. The kids; they'd known it was bad, but he never would have guessed as bad as all that. He thought it had ended with the war.

"Gal, are you all right?" Rayne peered up at him. "You're moaning."

"I didn't think it would get that bad," he croaked.

She smiled sadly. "None of us knew."

No, he wanted to tell her, *he had known*. Maybe not all of it.

But he'd been the one, the guy who should have stopped it all. He'd known where the virus came from. Why the kids had gotten sick. And he'd made a promise to Aaron. He'd made a promise to himself. "Rayne, I—."

"This is incredible!" The tech pushed in, leaning over Rayne as he stared at the little 2D screen. "Is this everything?"

Rayne shrugged. "Everything on the general's computer."

"I have to take this to Morana. With this type of intel, we can't fail. The folk are already spread, but if they see these pictures of children—children!—they'll tear the Speakers to pieces. Their reign will be over by suns-down tomorrow."

Gal sat back as the tech pressed a quick command, the data downloading onto a chip he held in his hand. Then they followed him down the dingy hallway, into a room cramped with people. In the centre of the room, the leader, Morana, gestured through a 3D holographic display.

She paused as the tech pushed through the rebels to hand her the chip. Taking it in her hand, she thanked him and slipped it into a pocket on her coat.

Gal glanced at Rayne. Surely the rebel leader would look at the files. Even the idiot tech had known how powerful that information was. He clenched his fist to steady himself.

Morana returned to the holographic display. Her voice fading to the rush of blood in Gal's ears as he watched her gesture through a simulation of the city.

"Are you going to look at the files?" he shouted suddenly. He realized he was shaking.

Morana paused, the entire room turning to stare at him, and he took an involuntary step back. Across the room, Kieran peered at him. Sarrin, by his side, raised a single eyebrow as she watched. "We're discussing our extraction plan for the Poet," Morana said bluntly, dismissing him.

"Sorry." Gal held up his hands, trying to fade into the

background. What was he doing? Seeing the pictures of Evangecore, remembering it, it had unsettled him. That was all. He was no longer the rebel leader. That was someone else's job; Morana's job. He was just a pawn, just a soldier like the rest of them. Morana was the leader. He should let her lead.

"What's on those files will change everything," he found himself saying instead. "Proof we need to shut the Speakers down for good."

Morana glared, folding her hands neatly in front of her. "Thank you, Mister Idim." She turned away from him, and back to her display, now showing the Speakers' compound. "As I was saying, our informant on the inside…."

"You know it's not enough." Aaron was suddenly beside him, bending down to whisper in his ear. "An informant? Gods, Gal, how easy were they to kill? You saw what happened in the street. The Speakers… Hap is out of control, with what happened in the square, you know he's unhinged." His wide eyes penetrated Gal, right down to his rapidly beating heart.

"He still controls the Central Army, Gal, a force that's bigger than the people it polices. If this isn't done right… who knows how far he can be pushed before his temper gets the best of him. It's worse than his fathers, you know that. A blow like extracting the Poet from his compound, if they can pull it off, will send him into madness. And if he still controls the Army after his compound is breached, he will decimate the city. He'd rather no folk than lose control of the folk. You know this as well as I do."

Gal's entire body shook. He was aware of Rayne murmuring something beside him, but couldn't make out what she said.

"It has to be one fell swoop, Gal. All of it at once. This is the big showdown we've been waiting for. We have everything we need: irrefutable proof, and her." He pointed to Sarrin, who was still watching Gal with open curiosity.

Gal shook his head. "No. I can't."

"You are the *only one* who can," Aaron shouted at him in exasperation. "You have to unite the folk, ignite them, everyone at once. Folk, Central Army, everyone. John P can do that. You can do that."

"No," he gasped.

"What happens if you don't?"

Around him, the rebels turned into ugly grey demons, hair falling from their rotting flesh. One by one, they started to fall. A cascade of bodies drew their last breath and fell to the floor, rushing in a wave around the circle.

His eyes caught on the demon-Rayne standing beside him. Her honey-brown eyes flicked to meet his as the wave of dying demons raced up to her. "Stop!" He held out his hand before she could fall, saving her. He had to save her.

Aaron was right. The rebels plan would see the planet dead by sunsdown tomorrow. He'd spent too much time with Hap not to know it.

"It's now or never, Johnny." Aaron pushed his shoulder, sending Gal stumbling into the middle of the room.

Sarrin watched him curiously, tilting her head, one corner of her mouth quirking up as she nodded. Heart pounding, an image, a memory, superimposed itself over where she stood. He'd seen her before, in the burning wreckage, a teenage girl pulling herself from the rubble, her eyes meeting his across the battlefield with the same knowing stare.

The realization forced him to take a breath, and he started: "My name is Captain Galiant John Peroneus Idim. John P." He looked around the room at the group of very real, very human rebels, suddenly watching on his every word. "I'm sorry I've been away so long. The world got very hard for me, for a very long time. But we have a chance now that have never had before, and we will never have again." His eyes caught on Rayne. "John P never died, much as I wanted him to, because this, this moment, and what happens tomorrow is what I lived my life for, and what I could never forget. In our day, the rebels nearly unseated the Speakers. We hacked the newsfeeds, we infiltrated the compounds, and we bombed Evangecore." He watched Rayne press her lips together, but she didn't turn away. Not like she should. But it didn't matter anymore, this was important, this was bigger than him and the woman he would sacrifice almost anything more. "And, if you'll let me, I think I have a plan that will end it all."

Truthfully, it had come to him while he was speaking, his brain working out the details as though he had never left and spent all those years running freight.

He glanced at Morana, guiltily expecting her to kick him out of the room for interrupting a third time. Instead she stared him directly in the eye for a long minute. "I did think you borebore an uncanny resemblance to the rebel." To his surprise, she stepped aside, inviting him to take over the 3D display. "Let's see what you've got."

He flicked across the hologram of the city, taking a deep breath. Across the room Aaron caught his eye. He smiled once, and faded into the background, leaving for the last time.

NINETEEN

SARRIN STARED ACROSS THE SEA of buildings, dark now with only the deep purple of full night behind them. With her legs pulled up to her chest, she only half listened to the buzz of security drones, currently far away, and contemplated the tall tower in front of her.

"Thought I might find ya up here."

She turned at the sudden intrusion. Her heart did a strange flip flop as she turned to watch Kieran climb the last rungs of the ladder behind her.

"It was too close in the lair," she said as he sat beside her, turning back to the cityscape. She still felt the compressed, sticky heat on her skin of the cramped bunker and heard the click-clack of laz-rifles being disassembled and serviced. It had been nearly enough to send her into a trance until she'd found her way out here.

He sat close, heat radiating off his skin. Normally the proximity would have set alarms off in her mind, the monster flexing it's outcome power, but not with Kieran. Never with Kieran.

He had been growing redder in the last few hours, and even in the near-dark she could see—or maybe feel—the tension lines creasing his face. "You're in pain."

He nodded, hanging his head, seeming, almost, to deflate. "Yeah. All this running around, and it's dry here."

She closed the distance, wrapping a hand around his arm and pushing soothing energy through the connection, the same as she had done in gel tank when he was healing on Cordelia. The tension in his face instantly eased. "Thank you," he breathed.

She said nothing. She shouldn't be touching him at all, but it was a small comfort she allowed herself. If a monster could have comfort.

Gal's words echoed in her head: "We need to send a message. Show them that we'll fight back. Which is why Sarrin will be the one to destroy the Speakers." Gal was no fool. He had seen her file, knew exactly how she had been trained and what she was capable of. He knew she was a monster, and had found the perfect plan to showcase it. For good. For the death of the Speakers who had caused such irreparable harm. If she could destroy them and buy freedom in the process, then so be it.

Kieran wrapped his hand around her wrist, high enough that would could feel him where the nerves hadn't been stripped from her flesh. He smiled at her, a smile she didn't deserve, but she smiled back all the same. "Halud will be okay," he said.

She blinked. She hadn't even thought about Halud. But it was his freedom she was buying, wasn't it? He was always the good one, the Poet Laureate who spoke the words of the Gods.

"Morana says their operative on the inside is good, has been there for years, and shouldn't have any trouble getting him out once the fighting starts."

Sarrin nodded.

He squeezed her arm. "I was worried, I thought you might have gone to find him by yourself."

She blinked. Going after Halud herself had only been a fleeting thought. But—that's what she was doing on the roof, wasn't it? Surveying the Speakers' Tower, keeping an eye on Halud, looking for weaknesses, for opportunity.

The monster flared, whispering a calculated set of instructions. "I could, you know," she told Kieran, interrupting the monster. "I've completed more complex missions. I could infiltrate the tower and Halud and I could be far away before suns-rise."

Maybe that would be better.

But Kieran sighed. "I don't doubt it," he said. "I'm sure you could do it; go in and rescue Halud, mow down an entire platoon of soldiers, raze the entire building, whatever you had to do."

The monster set about a familiar thrumming in her core, a rush of adrenalin as the violent image of it flooded her.

"But it would still be a trap. Gal's right, I think, the First Speaker is trying to lure you in. You'd be playing right into his hands, and I don't like that idea at all."

Sarrin pressed her lips together. He was right. Hap Lansford had set a trap, the same as he -- through Guitteriez-- had set a trap for Halud and hunted her across the stars. Only the last few weeks, she was fairly certain, had been her own. Hap Lansford wouldn't have planned on them finding Cordelia or meeting the Uruhu. That part of her life, at least, must have been hers.

Tomorrow would be hers too, as she destroyed the Speakers. That would be something they would never have planned, surely. And her freedom would be just on the other side of it.

Beside her, Kieran shifted. "The baby in the square, was it really an Augment?"

She jerked her head. She'd nearly forgotten with everything else. "Yes," she answered. "The Speakers are making more."

She felt an emotion surge through the spot where his hand wrapped around hers: anger.

"What right do they have?" Kieran spat. "The Speakers don't have a clue what they're dealing with." He rubbed a hand across his mouth, his agitation pouring over her.

The sensation shocked her, the monster flaring to life. An image of her ripping the meaty head from Hap Lansford's body filled her mind. She shook off his hand and grabbed the rooftop to steady herself.

"What I don't understand is why," said Kieran.

As the black clouds cleared from her vision, she looked at him. He was usually so quick, but then he had been on the ship while she was with the Uruhu. "They want to destroy the Uruhu, the same as they destroyed Cornelius and tried to destroy Cordelia."

"That's why they trained the Augments?"

She shook her head. "That's why they made the Augments. Roelle told me, we're part Uruhu. The Red Fever, the retrovirus, carried Uruhu genes so that we would be as strong as they are. The humans weren't strong enough to do it on their own."

"Huh." Kieran clasped his hands under his chin. "I can't..." He frowned, training off.

She scratched her arm in the silence that followed. "There's something I don't understand. The Gods, they protect the Humans, but not the others? I was made to destroy the Uruhu, that was my Path. But why wouldn't the Gods protect the Uruhu and Cordelia and Cornelius?"

He leaned forward, one eyebrow raised as he stared directly into her face. "You're joking."

"What?" she gasped, startled.

"I thought you had figured it out. The Speakers aren't Gods."

She squirmed. It was true the Augments didn't believe in the Speakers, but they still believed in Strength, Fortitude, Knowledge, Prudence, and Faith. They still believed the stories. "The Gods descended and helped humanity in the beginning. They were good to us. Do they know something more than we do? What if it is my Path to destroy the Uruhu?"

"No god would tell you to destroy something." He shook his head, letting out a long breath. "I shouldn't tell you this. The 'Gods,' the ones that saved humanity in the beginning, were just people. They were Observers."

A cold sweat broke out on her back.

"Humanity lost its planet—the one before the last one. Actually, mankind has managed to destroy several planets over the millennia. The Observers left from Earth once its climate became uninhabitable, and we've been watching ever since.

"This time was worse than the others. For three generations humanity lived in starships that failed to travel even close to the speed of light before they reached a planet that was even remotely habitable. In that time a lot of knowledge was lost—basic things like how to seed crops, build shelters, even how to move and travel on foot. A group of Observers came down to help, for fear humanity would be lost all together.

"They were just people. People who could be strong, who could be leaders in dire times. But they underestimated how much the people would lean on them, and how much they would come to lean on the people. They stayed. They had families. Eventually the truth was lost and the legends took over. 'Gods descended from the heavens to lead humanity.' And the myth was fed and fed over the years, until thousands of years later, there is no real connection with the Observers and the Speakers are just men. The same as everyone else."

He frowned again. "Do you understand?"

She nodded, not sure if she did, but the words at least she could comprehend.

"These Speakers are men. Men with a power that has not been earned. They don't commune with the heavens. They do as they see fit, they probably feel they are right. But it doesn't mean they are. It doesn't mean they have any right to tell you your Path, Sarrin.

"Faith, and Knowledge, and Fortitude, and Prudence, and even Strength are important. They are things to believe in, things to pray for. But they don't come from a God or a Speaker. They come from inside." He tapped his five fingers to his chest, in the spot over his heart. He did it emphatically, the first time she had ever known him to pray, but then it wasn't really prayer, was it? "It comes from here."

And then he pressed his five fingers into the space over her heart. "Your Path is here."

She stared down at his hand.

"Sorry," he said, taking it away.

The space over her heart suddenly felt cold.

"I'm afraid," he admitted, staring down at his hands. "I'm afraid of what tomorrow will look like. I'm afraid of what the Speakers are capable of. I'm afraid of what you're capable of, afraid that you might lose yourself. I don't even really like Gal's plan. It's not you." He whispered, "I'm afraid I'll lose you."

She stared. No one had ever really been afraid for her before. "I'll be all right," she told him.

"I know." He patted her leg gently, but she felt his uncertainty through the touch.

"Hoepe says you might be a God, sent here to help us."

He snorted. "Pretty far from, I think."

But she didn't. Not with what she knew about the Gods now. "I won't tell anyone," she said, "about the Gods."

He nodded. "It's a pretty big secret. The first rule, the one that's drilled into us before we leave for our sojourn, is to not interfere. There's no telling what could happen if the folk find out, what repercussions there might be thousands of years from now."

"Like the Augments." She grimaced.

He leaned back, saying nothing, but it was clear: thousands of years ago, the Observers had come to help, imbued some of them with a special status, and the Speakers had washed war and created the Augments.

"We've uncovered a lot that isn't what we're told," she said finally. "I suppose that's what you came here to do, to check on the real status of things. We'll write about it when we go back."

He straightened. "Go back?"

"To the Observer ship. It should be recorded, right? That's what you, what we, do, right?"

"Sarrin,"—a strange look came over his face—"I'm not going back."

She sat up straight. "What?"

"I thought you realized it when I came with the others to Etar."

"But that was the plan, our plan." She wanted to go with Kieran to the Observer ship, escape all of this, live a quiet life in the stars where the Speakers would never find her. Where she could pretend none of this had ever happened. Where there would be no need for the monster to ever show itself again. "We would go after we rescue Halud."

He shook his head. "Halud, the Augment children, the Uruhu, the Settlers. You. There's too much here, too many people that need help. I couldn't go, I couldn't leave. The Observer ship came when we were rescuing Augments. My mother stopped, but I didn't go. Now they're of on the long run around the seventh sun. They won't be back for a hundred -and-fifty years."

"You missed them?"

"No." He laughed, warm and gentle, not mad like he should have been. "I decided I couldn't go. I said goodbye. I stayed for you."

She shook her head. She'd begged to go with him once, that was true. But if he'd given it all up for her, for a monster... she was worse than she thought. "You had a chance to leave and escape all this. Why didn't you go?"

He smiled again. "Because observing, running away, not being involved, its no way to live. The things I care about are here." He leaned forward, emotions shooting off him like sparks of fire. "Don't you see, Sar? That wasn't my home anymore. It might have been safer, it might have been easier, but I couldn't observe. Not when everything I cared about was here. I couldn't wait idly, hoping everything turned out okay. Much as this, right here and now, is hard, much as its difficult, I want to be a participant. I want to be with you, wherever you are, whatever you're facing." His mouth pressed into hers.

The shock sent her spine rigid, her heart racing, but it was like they were locked together, fire searing them, sealing their flesh together.

A kiss. A Gods-honest kiss.

The monster careened around her head uselessly, trying in vain to make sense of it.

She blinked as Kieran separated, resting his forehead against hers. "You see, I would risk every pain for even a chance to do that again. Just promise me you won't lose yourself tomorrow."

She nodded, numbly.

The light of the first sun broke over the horizon, casting long shadows through the city. Tomorrow was already here, they would go soon, start getting into position for Gal's plan.

She wouldn't lose herself. The only problem was she had no idea who herself was.

* * *

"Are you ready, Gal?" Rayne asked him quietly.

He hadn't even noticed her come into the room. It was only them and a handful of guards in the bunker. The others had already left, moving into position to wait for the rising of the third sun, and the inevitable chaos that would rain down.

He hadn't planned an operation this big in, well, never. This was it, this was the one.

"Yeah," he answered Rayne, but his voice came out flatter and less confident than he had hoped.

Unfazed, she came to him, adjusting the lapels of the old coat he had found over the painted shirt he had made. It had been important to dress like the old John P, and cast aside his UEC uniform; it was time to stop hiding.

"Do you know what you're going to say?"

"Yes." He nodded. That he did know. He was going to tell everyone the truth. The big, capital-T Truth. About him, about the Speakers, about the horrors they wrought in Evangecore.

"Are you're worried?"

"Of course." He sighed. "I've been away a long time. A lot longer than I should have been. Will they remember me? Will they even care?" He looked away. "Will anyone even survive?" He'd stopped being John P because so many people had died, because he didn't want any of it to be his fault anymore. It turned out people were still getting hurt. And he was about to step right back into the fire, in a big way. In a really big, very intractable and forever way. "What happens today will change everything, for better or worse."

"And I've never been prouder to stand beside you."

He glanced at her quickly, at her radiant smile. "Really?"

"Yes, Gal."

"You're not upset?"

It was her turn to sigh and look away, but she brought her honey-brown eyes back to meet his. "No. I thought a long time about it. I think, if we hadn't met the Augments, or Cordelia, or the Uruhu… I think if we hadn't seen everything we've seen, I wouldn't have ever believed it. But now, it's easier for me to see what John P was about. I've only ever wanted to do what was right, I just had my information wrong. My trust in the wrong place. I mean, my dad, he…."

He wrapped a hand around her arm to stop her. "He was your dad. You loved him. Like you were supposed to."

"Yes, but I still think I should have saw, should have questioned something. Like you did."

He wrapped her in his arms. "We're all doing the best we can with the information we have. I'm just glad you're here now." He kissed the top of her head.

She pushed away gently, laughing. "I guess he never would have signed off on us getting married anyway." She wiped one tear from her gorgeous face.

Gal froze. "You still want to marry me?"

"What?"

"After everything I did, all the lies, the bombs, everything? I was cracked Rayne, well and truly cracked. I saw things that weren't there. And I hurt you. Badly. In ways I can never make up to you for."

"Of course, Gal. I still love you. I always have." Pressing her warm body against his, she kissed him, the most wonderful sensation Gal had ever experienced. "But if you could tell me everything from now on, that would be very much appreciated."

He laughed. "You got it. Now, let's check this equipment. Kieran will be half-way up the tower by now."

She nodded and pulled away. "I'll grab the last of the cameras from the other room."

He grabbed her hand, spinning her back towards him just as she reached the door. "I love you."

She smiled, her look full of confidence. "I love you too. And Gal, it's going to work. I might not have been a supporter at the time, but I still knew John P. All you need to do is say the words and the folk will see."

"Okay." He watched as she left the room, and then turned to the videography equipment. Hap would not see the setting of the third sun.

Sharp pain cracked across the back of his head, and his vision went dark.

*   *   *

"Be careful." Kieran looked deep into her crystalline blue eyes and ran his hand under her cheek.

Sarrin nodded, but she didn't smile. Her eyes had already started to go far away, no doubt calculating and preparing for what she was about to do. What Gal had asked her to do.

He pushed down his frustration, watching her skirt through the growing crowd, a tiny figure in a grey cloak in a sea of grey.

She would work her way into the Speakers' Complex, right to the top of the tower, and wait for the moment when the chaos in the city had reached its peak, and all eyes would fall to her as she smashed into the offices and killed the Speakers, their prize weapon turned against them, and putting an end to a war that never should have been in the first place.

The dramatic irony was not lost on him, and yet he wished it could be anyone but her.

First though, Gal would address the folk and soldiers as John P. Tell them the story, the truth, about what they had allowed to happen right under their noses.

Subtle flashes of blue kept catching his eye, and he hefted the pack of cables onto his back.

Gal had requested physical connections to be made, instead

of just wireless signals—they were more secure, less prone to glitches and delays, and unable to be blocked by signal jammers. The Speakers would try to stop the broadcast as soon as they saw it, but Gal was determined that nothing would get in his way.

It made Kieran think back to the day he submitted his duty request to the least desired ship in the fleet. But Gal's ship went to the most remote and desolate colonies, the places where the most history could be made and go unnoticed. He'd never expected anything out of the broken man or his old ship, but he had gone to do his duty as an Observer. And yet, as he'd watched the drunk and addicted captain stumble around, he'd had a feeling that he was something more; that Gal might be the most interesting thing he would see in his time in Earth-time.

Double-checking the cables, the ends dangling out of the large pack so that he could extend them as he climbed, he started to work his way up the outside of the tower to the signal generator. His skin burned, but Hoepe had given him an injection to relieve the worst of it.

He caught sight of Sarrin, her grey cloak blending into the grey roof of the building below him. And in the square between them, Grant led a team of Augments, silently taking out the guards, while rebels and folk with their flecks of blue twirled in a chaotic dance of distraction. A laz-rifle went off. Grant's ugly grey skin suit burst out of his back and wrapped him in its protective layer. More soldiers rushed into the square, and screams echoed up the walls.

Closing his eyes, he focussed on climbing. It was part of the plan, all part of the plan. He needed to make his way to the signal room so Gal could make his broadcast.

Pain exploded through his shoulder, a laz-bolt searing the wall beside him. He swore as his grip slipped, smoke pouring from his cloak. Not part of the plan.

He hung from one hand, trembling. The smell of burning flesh stung his nose, as memories of the explosion aboard the Ishash'tor that had nearly taken his life played out in his mind.

He took several calmed deep breaths. He'd been shot was all. Just shot. Not lit on fire.

What had his life become that being shot was a better alternative? Oh well, he was here now, like he told Sarrin, a participant. He didn't let himself think about the fact that he wouldn't be being shot at aboard the Observer ship; he'd made his choice.

Another laz-bolt cracked across the grey stone in front of him, narrowly missing his face. He jerked back reflexively, his left hand slipping.

Suddenly he was falling. Fully aware that he was four stories up without a place to land. He clenched his teeth and prepared for the inevitable.

But the splat he'd anticipated didn't come.

He let his tightly shut eyes open just a crack. Just enough to see the tower in front of him. He was falling up.

He scrambled onto the second story ledge as he was deposited there, panting as he pressed himself into the solid surface.

On the roof opposite and now level to him, he caught sight of Sarrin's face, eyes wide, skin white with fear.

Another laz-bolt sparked across the ledge, and Kieran threw himself down, pressing into the tower.

Sarrin's razor gaze snapped to the ground, her expression suddenly cold. The UEC soldier below flew backwards, his rifle landing squarely in Sarrin's hands, and she rapidly disassembled it and reprogrammed the biosensor. She took two steps across the roof and leapt over the square to the Speakers' Complex. One more bound and she was on the ledge next to him.

The soldier slumped against the wall, unmoving.

Kieran swallowed heavily. Her vision swimming, more monster than girl, she roughly pulled his hand away from the throbbing wound on his shoulder to examine it.

"Sarrin?"

She grunted once. The wound was less than a finger depth, the laser already cauterizing the wound. It just hurt like crazy.

"I'm okay," he said, as much for her as for himself. She'd grabbed him right out of the air.

She stood, grunting again and hefted the laz-rifle, pointing it at the guard slumped in the square below.

"Wait," he reached out, but pulled back as pain from the laz-wound flashed fresh from his shoulder. "What are you doing?"

"He is not omega," she growled, her finger squeezing the trigger.

"No!" Ignoring the pain, he lunged, grabbing her sleeve as the shot fired.

The laz-bolt went wide.

Sarrin glared, the rifle turning on him, and he put his hands up. "It's me," he said.

Her eyes swam, and she blinked several times.

"This is what I was afraid of," he said, watching her come back. "Don't lose yourself."

She shook her head, her eyes refocussing. She stared at the slumped guard on the ground. "I'll come with you," she said. "I—. It's better when you're here."

"Okay." He would prefer she was close too, for lots of reasons. He pointed up the tower. "We have to connect the broadcast."

She nodded, refusing to meet his gaze, even when he laid his hands on her shoulder. "You saved my life, Sarrin. It's good."

"There is too much," she said. "Too many. I don't know if

I can…." She gestured vaguely to her head.

"I know."

She lifted her palm, a laz-bolt redirecting like it had come up against some kind of invisible shield.

He gulped. "We'll stay together."

"This is important," she said. "A chance to be free. But I have to fight for it; I have to walk the Path. The monster has a purpose, I have to believe that. I'll turn everything they've done to me against them. But I don't…."

He nodded once. "It's okay to fight for what is important to you. But it has to be you fighting. I'll be with you the whole time, okay?"

She nodded.

He looked up at the tower, at the daunting four floors between them and the transmission room. "Come on."

* * *

Halud laid on the uncomfortable cot, half-awake half-asleep. The guard snoring in his chair shifted, stretching his neck.

It had been a full day since Hap had brought him to his office and beaten him for all the folk to see. He forced his mind to be still, to stare up and study the blank ceiling above. It was no use thinking about Sarrin, or Gal, or the entire cracked situation that had already unfolded. He just had to pray she wouldn't come for him.

The door to the anteroom opened, and he sat up. To his relief, it wasn't Sarrin. It wasn't a smartly dressed officer either. It was a run-down, bedraggled, half-wild commandant who took one quick stride to the guard and struck him across the throat, so he fell unceremoniously to the floor.

Her eyes were bloodshot and her hair was soaked with the sweat that beaded across her forehead. Her blue eyes were wild, Augment eyes. She slammed both fists against the glassine. "I don't believe what you say." She hit the glassine once more for good measure and paced across the floor.

Halud sat with his hands on his thighs on the cot and watched. There was nothing to say. And the comm wasn't on anyway.

She pulled a crumpled paper from somewhere in her crumpled hospital gown and thrust it at the glassine. "What is this?" she yelled.

Mildly interested in the unravelling of the commandant, Halud stood on his aching legs. Served her right for hunting Augments across the stars that she should be one too.

On the old napkin, drawn in hand in the way only the Artist Laureate ever practiced, was a picture of a girl. A young girl. With dark features, and a haunted look in her bright eyes. A girl he had last seen falling from an orchard tree.

He looked up at the commandant, any mirth he might have felt at her torture instantly replaced by a gaping fear in his chest. "It's Sarrin."

The commandant stared, scowling at him, and he realized she hadn't heard him across the soundproof glassine. But somehow she had, because she flicked the picture over, brushing over it with her thumb.

"I knew her," she said finally.

Halud's eyebrows rose, his heart thumping wildly in his chest.

Then, against all odds, the fierce commandant started to cry. "What have I done?" She rested her head against the glassine, staring at the picture. "I loved her. I looked after her. She was so little, and I…."

Halud looked from the picture to the commandant. Was it possible? The commandant had known Sarrin? Even… been her friend?

It struck him, in the weirdest of ways, that this might be an actual sign from the Gods. The strange coincidences and coming togethers that Hap and the other Speakers had valued so much, often manufacturing as proof of their power to the folk, this was one and Half was witnessing it right in front of him.

She looked up at him again. "I killed so many Augments. I hunted them. I…I…."

Halud put his hand against the glassine, opposite hers. He couldn't say anything. There was nothing to say.

Suddenly, her head twitched to the side, and a hand came up to wipe the tears. "Someone's coming." She looked back to him, her eyes intense. "You have to get out of there."

He pointed at the door.

She reached for the console, punching in a command. But the door stayed closed. "They must have deactivated my access codes." Fear flashed across her features, and he realized it was not for her but for him. In a flash, she had disappeared, pulling the panelling and slipping into the wall.

He thought maybe he was wrong, and she might leave him, but in another instant, an invisible seam in the back corner of the cell opened and she pulled herself through.

He took a step back. Bedraggled as she was, she still loomed over him, and still looked strong enough to snap his neck.

"We have to go." She waved towards the open panel.

He knew it. This was the escape he had been looking for, but the commandant looked entirely cracked. Sign from the Gods or not, there was a completely unhinged gleam in her blue eyes. He shook his head, taking another step back. "I'll take my chances. They brainwashed you, you're remembering now, but I don't know how long it will last. You could forget at any time."

"Please,"—she reached for him—"let me make it right."

The door to the anteroom opened. The commandant pushed him behind her, coiling to spring the way he had seen

Sarrin do countless times. He felt a deep pit of fear open within him. Death was coming, either from the guard coming in the door, or from the commandant.

But, at the door stood a short, slightly plump, pleasant looking girl. "Oh, this is convenient," she said in her usual sing-song voice.

Halls stepped forward in shock. "Joyce?"

She puttered across the room, barely casting a glance at the guard slumped at the ground. She held a laz-gun casually in her one hand, the other pressing a plastic chip against the console. The door popped open, and her eyes lit up with glee.

"What's going on?" Halud sputtered.

Joyce waved at them. "Well, come on. Both of you."

Halud glanced at the commandant, who looked possibly more perplexed than he felt.

"What's going on?" he tried again.

Joyce smiled, the grin making her look like an idiot, but he realized she was nothing of the sort. "This is your rescue, Halud."

"Joyce?"

She waved him out. "You too, Amelia. Come on. The fighting has already started in the square, and we have work to do."

TWENTY

GAL'S HEAD THROBBED AS HE started to regain consciousness. Something pulled off his face, and light hit his eyes just before he was struck across the jaw.

He blinked and spat. His hands were tied to the back of a chair, his legs and torso strapped down as well. In the four corners of the large office stood glowing blue orbs, an uncomfortable hum emanating from them.

And Hap Lansford's sneering face loomed over him. This wasn't good.

The Speaker hit him again, his head swinging the other way. As he blinked, he saw Rayne, also tied to a chair, a dark sack over her head. Definitely not good.

"What are you doing?" he hissed at Hap.

Hap roared, his face turning an unpleasant red. He reeled back and struck him again.

When his ears stopped ringing, Gal pushed down his instinct to beg for Rayne's life, and forced himself to laugh in the Speaker's face. "The revolution has begun. You'll never stop it, not like this."

"This is the punishment for disobeying the Gods!" Hap yelled. The next impact caused Gal's chair to teeter on one leg. "They are angry with you!"

Gal spat again, this time mostly blood. He made himself stare defiantly into the eyes of the Speaker, someone he'd once called friend. "The only one angry is you. The only one disobeying the Gods is you."

Hap's meaty fist struck him again.

His head spun, and his eyes wouldn't focus anymore, but if there was one thing Gal knew--that John P knew--it was that he was getting to the Speaker. And he had to keep going. "You're just like your father!" he roared, bracing for another hit. But it didn't come.

Hap yelled out, and stumbled away, leaning on his giant oak desk. Rayne's head was still covered so he couldn't see her expression, but he could see the subtle movements her fingers made as they worked back and forth over the knots.

Hap suddenly turned. "How could you have ever gone so wrong? How could I have ever let you go so wrong?" He placed his hand on his chest. Then he pressed in his five fingertips and started to pray.

"Give it up, Hap," Gal snarled. Maybe he could keep him distracted long enough for Rayne to break free.

The Speaker's eyes flashed open in anger.

"You haven't believed in the Gods since we were kids," sneered Gal. "I know they don't speak to you."

"They do." His voice was ice.

"You forget we were friends once. You told me they didn't. Not in the way you wanted, not in the way you thought."

Hap drew himself up to his full height. "I misjudged you, Galiant. I thought you were a reasonable man, an educated man who thought well. You were never my friend. I pity you, your mind cracked and twisted in a way that it has made your thoughts dark. You see demons everywhere you turn."

Gal felt a pang—there had been a lot of demons.

Hap stalked back over to him. "The lies you spread are the sins of the Gods." He struck Gal hard enough to tip his chair and send Gal sliding across the carpeted floor, knocking into the legs of the other chair.

Rayne shouted out in surprise, her voice almost a wail as she yelped his name.

Roughly, Hap grabbed Gal and set him upright again with one arm. With the other, he jerked the mask off Rayne's head.

"No!" Gal lunged forward, but the restraints held him to the chair.

Rayne sucked in air, her eyes wide as she stared up at the Speaker. Her mouth worked like she was preparing to yell, but Hap stopped her, a hand wrapping around her throat. "How disappointing you must have been, Commander Nairu. Your father had so many hopes for you. Cherished you, taught you. And here you are with this rebel, same as your cracked mother."

Rayne made a terrible choking sound. "M-mother?"

"How unfortunate for him to lose two of you to this madness." He laughed once.

Her eyes went wide. And then she jerked up, her head catching him under his massive chin.

Hap staggered back, blood trickling from his mouth.

"What did you do to my mother?" she shrieked.

"She was a rebel too." Hap pressed his meaty hand into Rayne's face, completely covering it, and he pushed.

Her chair teetered on its back legs for an instant, and then toppled over backwards.

"You're a fool, Hap," Gal shouted. He stared down at Rayne, terrified as she moaned and lolled her head.

"And you! You were supposed to be my friend!" Hap sprayed him with spittle from his red-purple face. "Instead you're here, trying to turn the folk against me."

"No, Hap. I was your friend, I really was. I tried to open your eyes. You were always so smart, but you could never see the truth. You abused your power, just like your father did. For years I tried to help you, tried to show you the truth so you could see. Your father started the Augment program. You never had to finish it. You had a chance to do good. Real, honest to Gods, good work. Instead, you chose to be blind." Hap stared at him, murder in his eyes. Gal knew it would be the end of him, but he was too far in to stop now. He reached for whatever part of the young, reasonable, caring boy that Hap had been that might be left. "The Gods may speak to you, as they speak to all of us, but you don't listen. You are as deaf as you are blind. You've chosen your own needs, your own good, over the good of the folk. This isn't the work of Gods. This is the work of a man afraid, a man looking to save himself over those around him. A man who knows that any change, any shift toward something different will dethrone him and send him spiralling. You don't listen to the Gods. And now you have to be afraid."

Hap growled. "I am Hap Lansford, First Speaker and direct descendant of Strength. I have the power of the Gods within me. I hear their words. I speak for them." He swung his massive arm.

When Gal came to again, he was toppled over on the ground. He couldn't have been passed out long, his lungs still struggling to catch the breath that had been knocked out of him. "You've got it wrong, Hap," he wheezed. "Strength was never physical. It was *mental*."

Hap lunged, pulling something off his desk, thrusting the data tablet into Gal's face. "It doesn't matter what you say. You've already lost."

Gal stared, a scene playing out on the data tablet of the Central Square directly below them. The giant vid screens uncharacteristically blank. The rebels, the folk with their defiant swatches of colour, fighting against the overwhelming greyness of soldiers descending upon them.

And yet there was another group. Beaten and bent and brought back from death. "There's Augments down there, Hap. Your soldiers can't beat them."

A sickening grin spread across Hap's face. "I know this. But the rebels brought everyone to the Central Square. All the rebels. All the Augments. Anyone who might oppose me. All in one convenient location."

Gal's blood ran cold. One variable had hadn't considered, one thing he never would have expected, even from Hap.

"There are detonators surrounding the square, charges built into the cobblestone. A heavenly blow from the Gods to strike down the Augments."

Perhaps the man did speak with the Gods, how else could he always be one step ahead?

"You'll kill your soldiers," Gal tried. "The folk."

Hap shrugged. "I can't be selfish. If I remember correctly, it was you who once told me a true Speaker must always consider the needs of the folk first."

"Hap, no!"

* * *

A laz-bolt bounced off the stone wall a foot from Kieran's head. "Sarrin!" he called.

She paused a minute before answering. "It wasn't going to hit you."

He thought to argue that she couldn't possibly know that, but then, he supposed she did.

He hauled himself onto the ledge of the window on the sixth floor. Thank Jesus these people valued light so much. He cut a hole through the glassine with his lax-torch, and squeezed through. The broadcast room was just down the hall, the door was open, the room unoccupied.

So, the rebel's operative had come through. That was lucky.

Sarrin stepped in behind him. Her face was grey and tired.

Her eyes swam.

"Thank you," he said.

She leaned her head against the wall and exhaled.

Kieran set to work, pulling the cables from his pack and lining them up in the massive machine that was the broadcast computer.

"You okay?" he asked.

Sarrin nodded once, crawling over to sit by him. "Tired There's a lot going on below us."

He patted his hand on her thigh and smiled. "I'm glad you're here."

She nodded again.

He finished calibrating the machine, waiting for the inputs to switch over. The screen blinked on. "Let's see if Gal is ready. He should be set up by now."

But he wasn't. Kieran frowned, flicking the switches. But the feed from the camera in the rebels' lair was tipped on its side, looking up at a couple cargo tainers, the room empty.

Sarrin's eyes had taken on an unsettling glint.

"Maybe they're still setting up," he said, but even as the words left this mouth, he knew something was wrong.

"Where's Gal?" Sarrin asked quietly.

He shook his head, checking the connections again, but it was no use. The problem wasn't in the wiring. "I dunno. He's not there."

"What do we do?"

"Maybe the fight in the square is enough of a distraction. Maybe we just need to go find the Speakers."

She shook her head, staring desperately at the feed. "Gal was going to explain it. That was the plan. He was going to stop the fighting, and make them see. Without him, they won't know the truth. They won't see we're not monsters."

Kieran pressed his lips together. He looked at the sideways room in the view screen. "You'll have to do it."

Shocked, she turned to him.   Her pupils were too far dilated, a bead of sweat breaking out on her forehead.

"What? I can't."

"You have to.   He was going to tell your story.   But who better to tell it than you?"

She swallowed heavily. "How?"

He pointed at all the wires and transmitter.   "There's a comm channel. And a security camera. We'll use that."

She glanced up at the micro-lens in the ceiling, pressing her mouth into a thin line.

He pulled the lens down and dug into the computer's programming, while Sarrin sat quietly, unmoving. She looked close to cracking when he finally held up the lens and pointed it in her direction.

"Are you okay?"

Her blue eyes pleaded with him. "You do it."

"I'm sorry." He shook his head. "It will be better from you.   I'm just an Observer, some guy who got caught in all this."

"They hate me. They're afraid of me."

He shook his head. "They don't know you. This is your chance."

She stared at the floor.

"Sarrin?"

"What should I say?"

"I don't know. Just tell them the truth, right. Make them see." He tapped the controls on the computer, sending the feed from the little security camera to every view screen in the city, and every messenger ship in the system. "Go ahead," he told her gently, "like it's just you and me."

She stared at the floor, unmoving for a long time.   He thought maybe it was too much, that she'd finally broken, she was so still, and then she lifted her head and started: "My name is Sarrin DeGazo. I've been a prisoner since I was three years old."

She stripped off her cloak, revealing the lines of scars and the UEC barcodes burned into her skin. And haltingly, piece by piece, she told her story from the beginning through to the end.

Kieran fought to keep the camera steady, even as his pulse pounded in his veins. He loved her, he really did, for the person she was under everything that had happened to her. He hoped one day she would see it too, all the incredible things that were Sarrin, that had had the strength to resist everything they tried to make her.

Finally, she looked up, meeting his eyes, and nodded to tell him it was done.

He pressed the button to transmit the whole of General Nairu's database to every ship and computer under the stars, then let the camera fall. Heard it smash into the ground, and caught the flicker of the feed shorting out on the little screen. He took a step forward and wrapped her in his arms.

She didn't pull away, and he pressed himself into her. The hug was nothing like his mothers, but it didn't have to be. He was home.

"Let's go find the others," he murmured.

She nodded against his chest.

The floor shook under their feet.

"What was that?"

Her face paled, her tiny body shaking in his arms. "Omega."

* * *

The ground shook under Halud's feet, and he reached out, grabbing Joyce to steady himself.

"Explosion," muttered Amelia, looking around, her face hard. "A big one. No survivors."

"How do you know?" asked Halud.

"I could feel them. Now I can't."

Joyce's wide eyes blinked furiously.   "This wasn't the rebels."

"It must have been Hap," Halud surmised.   "He's been more and more cracked.   We have to get to Sarrin.   Is she okay?"

Amelia nodded.   "Yes, I think so."

He pushed toward the main corridor from the narrow one they were in, but Joyce put a hand on his arm.   "We have to get to the top of the tower.   Who knows what happened to the others.   We have to take down the Speakers, if we can."

Halud paled.

"I'll help," said Amelia.

Joyce spun abruptly, her skirt flaring out so it hit him in the knees.   "This way."

They climbed narrow service stairs, Joyce riffling through her over-stuffed ring of plastic keycards.   She seemed to know the warren of service tunnels like the back of her hand, pulling out card after card to open the locked doors in their path.

"You've done this before?" he asked.

She pulled out a keycard and opened the door in front of them.   "Yep."

"I never suspected," he said apologetically.

She shrugged, flashing him the same simpleton-smile she had given him day after day for years, a smile that suddenly was very different.   "That's the point, isn't it?"

The path Joyce led them on was so convoluted, Halud thought they were on the top floor of the compound, somewhere near where the tower jutted out, stretching above everything around it, but he wasn't sure.

"Wait," Amelia called, shouldering her way in front.   She pressed her ear to the door Joyce was about to open, and held up her hand.   "I'll go through first."   Without waiting for a response, she opened the door and slipped through.

"What's she doing?" Halud went to push through the door, but Joyce stopped him. "You know she's not entirely stable, she's been brainwashed, she might be running back to Hap right now. We have to follow her."

"She's a victim like the rest of them. I thought you would understand that better than anyone."

They heard two thumps on the other side, and Amelia poked her head back through. "Okay."

Halud followed Joyce, running past the two armed guards slumped on the ground.

Up another staircase, down a corridor. Down a staircase, another corridor. Up two stories, and up and up and up.

Joyce stopped. "This is the end of the service corridors. Beyond that door is the grand staircase that leads to our offices, Halud, and then the spiral stair to the Speakers' offices." She checked her little laz-pistol. "When we reach Hap's office, we can't hesitate, okay." She looked directly at Halud. "He's strong and he's vicious. But if we catch him by surprise, we might have a chance."

Halud nodded.

"There are guards on the other side," said Amelia. "I'll take care of them."

"Oh." Joyce handed her the laz-pistol, but Amelia pressed it back.

"No, you'll need it for Hap. There's a lot of guards. I can't — I'll lead them away, keep them distracted as long as I can."

"No, Amelia, you don't have to."

"After all I did…." HHer gaze fell to the side. "Just don't waste time." Amelia grabbed the keycard Joyce held in her little hand, and pressed it to the panel, the door popping open. She lunged out, moving with her enhanced Augment speed, the flimsy hospital gown flapping around her legs.

Halud gaped as at least twenty elite guards descended down the stairwell, laz-bolts flying as Amelia dodged and led them away.

"Come on." Joyce grabbed his arm.

He pulled after the soldiers disappearing down the corridor. "We have to help."

"Don't be stupid," said Joyce, her voice uncharacteristically hard. "We have to keep going." She sprinted up the stairs, the laz-pistol held out in front of her, but the landing where her little desk sat was empty. She sprinted up the spiral stairs, right into the circular room with its five doors for each of the Speakers' offices.

"Ready?" She nodded, not waiting for him to answer, and pushed the door open.

* * *

"What are you doing?" Gal shouted, lurching forward in his chair, but it was too late. The floor rumbled under them as the entire Central Square detonated.

The First Speaker laughed, a terrible, deep laughter. "The Gods have made their opinion clear, Galiant. No more Augments. They were too wild anyway, completely uncontrollable, unpredictable. We have our vaccine, and while it will take longer than I had hoped, we will have our army to do what my father never could! We will eradicate the Uruhu and claim Etar as the birthplace of humanity. A perfect world for a perfect civilization."

"You're cracked." He fought the ropes, but what could he do? It seemed Hap had him.

Rayne met his gaze, her wide eyes reflecting his own fear. She seemed to know as well as he did that if Hap spun it that way, the folk would go along with it. They wouldn't even question. That was the problem, it had been all along: blind faith in the Speakers and the Gods.

It was all happening again.

The door to Hap's office opened, and in burst a short, pleasant looking woman. He blinked twice to be sure of what he was seeing: it was Hap's receptionist. She held a laz-pistol in front of her with both hands. And behind her was the Poet.

Her sudden entry must have surprised Hap even more than Gal because he jolted upright, yelling, "Joyce?" Then he scoffed at her pistol. "Do you even know how to use that thing?"

Her eyes narrowed. "Yes." But she must have been out of practice because the shot she let off went wide.

Hap laughed. "You see, the Gods protect me!"

She let off another shot, but Hap was already moving, sprinting in her direction, and dodged the bolt easily. He grabbed the pistol, wrapping her two hands and the weapon in his fists. The laz-gun clattered to the floor, and he spun her violently, lifting her into the air.

"Joyce!" the Poet shouted, but he was too slow. Hap pushed him into the wall, hard enough to leave a dent and rattle the glowing blue orb beside him. Halud slumped to the floor.

"Joyce," Hap growled, carrying her across the room while she struggled. "All these years, I didn't suspect a thing." He let out a cracked laugh, and dropped her behind Gal's chair, tying her unceremoniously to its legs.

"You're cracked, Hap," Gal shouted, but the way the Poet was groaning and rolling around on the floor made him panic. "We can still fix this. We can work together. I never thought you were a bad person, just misguided."

"I am guided by the Gods! And they have made their opinion clear by smiting down the Augments, the rebels, and all who opposed me."

"The Gods didn't do that, you did, Hap!" Out of the corner of his eye, he saw Halud push up onto his knees and shake his head clear. If he could just distract Hap…. "But hey, it wasn't your fault. It was your father's."

It hit the nerve Gal knew it would, and Hap leaned right into his face, spittle flying all over Gal. "Don't speak ill of my father. He communed with the Gods, a direct descendant of Strength."

"The bloodline is too weak. It's been thousands of years, a hundred generations. How diluted are the genetics, Hap! You're entirely human. And that's okay. So am I. We make mistakes. We fix them." Hap pushed away, and Gal bit his lip. Halud was staggering around on the far side of the room. Maybe he could get Joyce's pistol and shoot Hap if Gal could just keep him from looking over. "I know he used to hit you!" he shouted.

Hap whipped his head back to Gal. "What did you say?"

"You thought I didn't know, but I saw it, when we were at the summer cabin. He shouldn't have done that. What kind of God hits his son? But it wasn't your fault, Hap."

Hap screamed in his face. "He hit me to make me strong!"

"No, Hap. He wasn't a God, not even a Speaker. Just a mean, old man. But you don't have to be the same. I was your friend, I know how much pain you were in, but you have a choice here. You don't have to continue this cycle."

"That's enough," Hap roared. He struck Gal across the face hard enough to send the chair flying backwards. Joyce screamed as Gal flipped over her, and the chair shattered.

Across the room, Halud staggered forward. "It's over, Hap."

Gal struggled, but the mess of shattered chair and restraints and Joyce held him prone on the ground.

"The camera is on, broadcasting," said Halud. "The feed is being transmitted to every viewscreen under the stars. You might have killed the folk in the square, but there are more. And every man, woman, and soldier will see what you have done."

Hap turned to Halud, and Gal thought they had him. But

Hap let out a barking laugh. "The folk see me for what I am, a saviour! I speak the words of the Gods." He lunged, grabbing Halud, and throwing him across the floor.

"Hap!" Halud cried out.

"Sometimes Strength is needed, Halud. You seem to have forgotten. He pointed to the mural painted on his office wall. "Sometimes a river of blood is needed for peace to prevail. *War is great for the changes it brings.* You said that, Halud. And I am the war.

"The folk see me, someone with Strength. I am only doing what is necessary to ensure the future of humanity, to follow the Path. And if I have to put down the corrupt Poet and his rag-tag bunch of criminals, then so be it!" He wrenched a piece of the splintered chair out from under Gal, and lurched towards Halud, the sharp piece raised for a killing blow.

With the piece no longer tangled to him, Gal wiggled out of the restraints and jumped to his feet. "You're wrong, Hap! With that transmission, my engineer sent out the full database from General Nairu's computer. Every experiment, every torture you authorized at Evangecore; everyone knows. There's the proof that your father engineered the virus, released it in areas with lots of kids. The Red Fever, the war, the greatest loss of life in our history, it was all created by a human being. Not a god. A corrupt, evil, misguided human being. Do what you like to us here, the Speakers are dead. Everyone under the stars knows. The folk will rise, and the Speakers are dead." Gal opened his coat, the circle with two chevrons displayed wide, right to the camera. "It's already begun. It began years ago. You're just too stubborn to see it. You've lost, Hap. John P, the rebels, the Truth has already won."

Hap took a step back, his face suddenly pale as he stared at the symbol on Gal's shirt. "It can't be. How? All these years?"

"Because Hap, you underestimated me. You always underestimated me. You underestimated Halud. You underestimated Joyce. You underestimated the folk. Here, in your tower, you underestimated the strength of the people, the strength of one man. Not a God, not a Speaker, but a farm boy from the back woods of Indaer.

"I am John P. Kill me now, if you like, it doesn't matter. The folk will always win. Strength, Fortitude, Knowledge, Prudence, and Faith will always win, but you're none of those things. You're nothing but a shell."

TWENTY-ONE

TEARS BURNED AT THE CORNER of her eyes, and Sarrin clenched her fists, staring over the unrecognizable Central Square, now nothing but a mess of broken con-plas and bodies.

"Oh my God," Kieran gasped, coming up beside her.

Through the thick cloud of dust, and the black tendrils wrapping around her vision, she could make out orderly troops working their way across the rubble. They stopped to pick up a figure, a humanoid figure, with mottled grey skin. Grant. Her breath caught in her throat.

The viewscreen flashed, a transmission coming through. It was Hap's office, and the First Speaker grabbed Halud, throwing him across the room. Gal and Rayne lay tied on the floor.

For once, she didn't fight the monster. Everything was lost. She's been given these terrible gifts for a reason, and the Speakers wouldn't see the end of the day. Save Halud, she told the monster, her vision completely black as she scaled the side of the tower like a wild animal. Kill the Speaker. Save Halud. Kill the Speaker. Save Halud.

Far below her, someone shouted, "Sarrin! Don't lose yourself."

But this was her. It was what she was built for, trained for. A monster. She would save her brother. And kill the Speaker. He would be omega, like all the folk in the Central Square. It was the only way.

Her body tensed. Years of training, flashed through her mind, her thoughts blending with the monster's, finally coming together into one cohesive whole. This anger, she knew, this was her. She wasn't lost to the monster, she was the monster.

What Hap had done to her, to all of them, wasn't right, and he would pay. The ends justified the means. If one good thing could come of all her time at Evangecore and in the secret labs on Selousa, it was this.

It was what Gal had encouraged her to do, what the rebels wanted, and the Augments. The cameras were on, broadcasting what happened in the First Speaker's office to every bien under the stars. She would be the one to do it, to use his own weapon against him, to bring peace. It was all coming together, in this moment.

She lifted her bare fist, smashing it into the thick glassine of the First Speakers' window. Like an animal, she beat and smashed until the unbreakable substance shattered. She had done it before, when she broke into the researchers viewing room in Evangecore, she would do it again.

She leapt in as the glassine shattered, landing ready. Through the darkened edges of her vision, she saw the room clearly before her: the painted mural with its rivers of blood, the dead animal trophies, Rayne tied to a chair, Halud and another woman on the floor, Gal standing. And Hap Lansford.

But as she took a step forward, a devastating despair opened up in the hollow of her chest. Her body was suddenly devoid of strength.

"Ah," Hap smirked. "I thought you might be joining us."

He nodded at the four glowing blue orbs around the room.

"You did this," she ground past her clenched jaw. She tried to stay upright, but the pulse dropped her to her knees.

"005478F, in the flesh," said Hap, and she grimaced at the identification. "What an honour. Galiant here was just telling me what a monster I am, but I think the folk will disagree when they see an Augment, here to kill me, no doubt, dropped to her knees in my presence. The Gods speak through me, and they are good!"

She groaned, another wave of despair rolling over her, turning her insides to ice. Across the room, Hamid meet her gaze. "I'm sorry," he mouthed.

Hap Lansford retrieved the staff of Strength from over his doorway, and lugged back across the room, towering over her. The 600 pound staff had belonged to Hap's ancestor the when the Gods descended from the heavens to help humanity, and he wielded it over her now, ready to drop a crushing blow. "The Gods protect us all."

She nearly laughed out loud. Hap wasn't a God, he wasn't even descended from one. He was human just like the rest of them. And the heavy stick looked like it was going to topple him over.

She lurched wildly to her feet. Her heart thumped in her chest, the pain nearly unbearable as the bio-pulse weapons drained her. But she couldn't give up now, not when they were so close. "I have a name," she grunted through her clenched jaw. "It's Sarrin."

Hap, his eyes wide, swung his club, but she caught it in her hand.

"Evangecore taught me, trained me. You made me this." She pushed with all her might, sending him flying backwards. The staff landed on top of him, and he struggled out from under it.

She almost pitied him. He didn't know he wasn't a God.

He didn't know he'd been a fool.

He didn't know they'd rescued hundreds of Augments. Or that the explosion in the square wouldn't staunch a rebellion, but fuel it.

He didn't know that while the bio-energy pulse was powerful and designed specifically to affect her unique physiology, it was her who decided what she felt, what she allowed in. He didn't know that she came from the inside, unaffected by the constant shifts of the outside.

He didn't know what she was capable of.

She pushed out e way Roelle had taught her, sending the blue orbs toppling to the ground. Their pulse continued to glow, but she didn't let it in.

She took a step forward, and then another, and she was running. She leapt through the air, pinning Hap Lansford, all 300-kilos of him under her forty. Willing him to feel the pain she felt through her hands where she held his soft, weak flesh.

She lifted her hand up, preparing the final blow. She could kill him, knew the exact spot, knew exactly how much pressure was needed to drive his cranium into the front of his cerebrum and break the base of his skull to lacerate his brain stem and stop his heart.

Knew exactly how to do it because he had ordered it to be taught it to her.

She stared into his fat face, watching as he struggled, his eyes wide with terror. He deserved to die.

And that was why she wouldn't kill him. Arm raised, she paused. She breathed out. Don't lose yourself. This wasn't her.

She let him go.

He rolled around on the floor before he could find his way to his knees, and then to his feet.

"Run." She pointed to the door.

When he was gone, Gal turned to her. "What did you do?

You had him right in front of you. The cameras are rolling."

She looked from him to the camera. "Then let them see that I won't be what they made me. I've been trained to be a monster my entire life, but I won't kill. The cycle of violence ends now." She shrugged. "The folk will decide his fate. I won't lose who I am because of what he's done."

Kieran stood by the window, smiling at her.

Halud came to her side, placing a warm hand on her arm just for a second. He turned to Gal. "Well, it looks like I picked the right ship after all, John P."

"Yes, I think you did, Poet." Gal smiled and bent to untie Rayne.

The short, pleasant-looking girl peered out the broken window. "They're coming out into the square," she said. "Folk from all over."

"Shall we?" Halud gestured to the camera, inviting Gal to stand with him.

Gal nodded, jogging over. "What do we say, Poet? It's a real mess out there. Even John P doesn't have a plan for this."

Halud shrugged. "Have faith in the folk, they're stronger than we know."

"We'll have to tell them we need to leave this planet, it isn't ours. They won't be happy."

"The colonies?" Halud asked.

"All dead. And I won't ask Cordelia. She's done enough."

"Who's Cordelia?" Halud frowned. "Nevermind. We'll take to the stars, all of humanity in all of our starships. I have to believe that if we just keep looking, we'll find a home. A real one."

"Actually." Kieran stepped forward. "I think I know a place."

Gal and Halud both turned to him.

"Earth is out there, the real one we left millennia ago. Hoepe said it, all the zinc deficiency, the mineral imbalances, they happen because we don't live on a planet we should. But we have a planet. One we forgot. One we didn't take care of and had to leave. But I think it's time. And I know how to get us there. Actually," he grinned at Sarrin again, "you do."

"What?" she frowned at him, suddenly aware of all the attention on her.

"The starchart in my room on the Ishash'tor. I watched you study it for hours; I know you memorized it. It was a photo I took it the last time the Observer ship passed through the Milky Way. All we need to do is follow it and we'll be home."

"Huh." Gal rubbed his chin. "You've always been weird as anything, but I don't think I've ever said quite how much I appreciate that." He turned to Halud. "Ready, Poet?"

Halud nodded and together they stepped in front of the camera.

Kieran stepped back, pulling Sarrin with him. He held her shoulders in both his hands, studying her. "God, I'm glad you're all right."

He pulled her to his chest, wrapping his arms around her. And she let him, pressing her cheek into his chest, above his beating heart. Because for the first time, she was all right. Not a monster, not a weapon. Just, Sarrin.

TWENTY-TWO

GALIANT IDIM STOOD AT THE crest of the hill, overlooking the forests of Indaer, the planet where he was born, the forests where he learned what he would become. It was the last time he would see them, the lush blue-green against the purple hued sky.

He smiled.

"What is it, Gal?" Rayne smiled at him.

He still found it surprising to see Rayne without her grey Central Army uniform. If possible, she managed to look even more beautiful in the flowing coloured garments sourced by the Artist Laureate, her arms marked and painted by the Uruhu.

It had been two weeks since the Speakers had fallen. Their fate was unclear, as was the fate of her father. She said it didn't matter. But the far away look she sometimes got told him that it did.

Most of the Augments had already left the planet for Cordelia's ship. They had had no trouble in sourcing the medical supplies, and food rations, and clothes for the journey home.

Across the knoll stood Halud, his hands gently brushing his sister's arms.

Seeming to know he was being watched, Halud lifted his head, and greeted Gal with a nod of his head and a knowing smile.

Perhaps without the Poet, Gal would have been trapped in himself forever.

Halud clapped a hand on Kieran's shoulder. Then, a final laugh, and they parted.

Kieran and Sarrin stepped to the front of the knoll, vanishing as Cordelia pulled them up.

Still smiling, Halud came to stand beside him.

Rayne gave Gal a quick kiss before she herself stepped to the front of the knoll and disappeared.

"You're sure, Poet?" asked Gal.

Halud nodded. "The world is in turmoil. They need a leader. Perhaps one day before I am too old I will make the journey too."

"You're not that old."

"No, but there is a lot of a work to do." Halud grinned.

"I hope you do."

"It might be hard to find room on a ship. People are eager to go. It seems they feel the pull, as though they know this place is not right."

Gal nodded. "The Uruhu say that's how it is with them. Hoepe says the human race has been in decline, that once we were all just as fast and strong and smart as the Augments. He thinks we'll feel it once we are connected again, and that with time we'll be just as strong again."

Halud gazed out over the landscape before them. "There will be poems written about you, Galiant."

Gal snorted once. "Poems?"

"I am the Poet Laureate." He laughed. "Perhaps I should just say, 'thank you.'"

Gal stretched a hand out to the other man. "No, I should be thanking you."

"You make little of what you've achieved."

"What we've achieved. Without you, I would still be hauling freight."

"Without you, who knows what would have happened to my sister. To the Uruhu."

"Will you miss her?"

"Every day." Halud turned, calling out over his shoulder. "Good luck in the old world, Galiant."

Gal took one last look. There was no one else on the hill. The only one left to board Cordelia was Gal.

And yet he hesitated. How to let go of the fight that had been such a piece of him for so long? There was still something unfinished, if he turned his back on it now, would it eat at him forever?

Aaron stood quietly, leaning against a tree at the perimeter of the open grove.

It was Gal who strode over to him. "I guess I'll never be rid of you, then?"

Aaron smiled, a broad, toothy grin, and he shook his head. "It's time for you to go, Gal. This is goodbye."

"Goodbye?"

"You've done it. I always knew you would. Because you never gave up, never forgot what you knew. Even when the Army came for us, when they tried to destroy us, when you nearly killed yourself with drugs and alcohol, your heart was still true. You are strong, Galiant. That's why I went with you every single time, right up to the end. Don't for a second think it wasn't worth it."

And for the last time, Aaron faded away into nothing, his voice carried away on the winds, his smile glowing in the heat from the trinary suns.

Galiant stepped to the front of the knoll, a tingling, whooshing sensation filling him as Cordelia lifted him up.

* * *

"Have you ever seen something more beautiful?" she asked, staring ahead of her.

Kieran spread his hand on her back, the heat rippling through her flesh. "No." She realized he was gazing down at her instead of the planet before them, and bashfully realized she had been smiling.

Cordelia hd transformed herself into a large observation platform, it stretched nearly a hundred yards, long enough for everyone on board to stare at the uninterrupted view of the planet below: blue and green and brown and white swirled together like something that could only have been painted by the Gods.

It spun slowly in front of them, mesmerizing.

Kieran rubbed a slow circle on her back.

The clothes had been given to her by the Artist Laureate himself, and were in the highest fashion, with a high front and drooping back, all of her marks exposed.

At first she had refused to wear it, but then there had been a certain freedom in it, in embracing who she was and where she had come from.

She closed her eyes and remembered the feel of Kieran tracing each one, asking what they meant, never bothered by an answer, never bothered when she refused to answer.

She recalled the way he doodled with his finger in the open spaces, making up his own symbols and telling her what they meant. Sometimes he wrote her name, or sometimes just a large 'S'. He said it was all part of her story.

One time he had leaned down and kissed her skin, and proclaimed, 'Now, I have been here too. I am on you, Sarrin, part of your story. Forever.'

She had scars. Scars that would never go away, but they could fade. They could turn into something else.

She would never get her childhood back, never spend the summers running in the orchards with her brother. But it was part of her. And without it she never would have met Kieran. And she certainly never would have been able to save his life.

The past wasn't pretty. It wasn't what she had wanted it to be. But it didn't haunt her. Not anymore. It was the Path that she was made to follow, good and bad, right and wrong. The experiences made her her, and she was herself and no one else.

The planet below called to her, its vibrations and frequencies rattling around in her bones, heating them from the inside. The others must have felt it too, their grins spreading.

Gal wrapped his arms around Rayne, kissing her on the neck. They stepped forward, ready to drop down to the planet. They hadn't told anyone yet, but their child would be the first born on Earth in millennia.

A deep, booming laugh echoed across the bay. The sound, so unusual coming from Hoepe's throat, still surprised her. He rested his hand on Isuma's shoulder, Leove on her other side, laughing just as loud. If she had to guess, their child would be the second.

There would be a lot of children on Earth—all the Augment babies had come with them. There was no telling what the future would bring for them. Would they have more abilities Sarrin had never heard of? Would they be stronger on Earth, or weaker away from the Uruhu?

Either way, she would be there to teach them the way Roelle had taught her. So they wouldn't be afraid. So they would grow feeling confident and secure and knowing who they were.

Kieran's hand slid off her back for a second, startling her from her thoughts.

He watched him reach his arms around an Augment named Arnie and hug him quickly. He'd been thrilled to find Arnie, his great grand nephew, and even more thrilled to find him alive and well, after Hoepe had pushed some colloids into him and some real food.

A lot of Augments had survived. A lot hadn't. They wouldn't be forgotten, Kieran had made certain of that. They'd been part of the journey, there and then not, but still a part of what they had done, and what they had achieved.

Kieran turned back to her and smiled. "Time for us to go too."

She nodded, staring at the view screen, committing the jewel to memory.

It would be theirs forever. Kieran and Gal had already come up with the plans, combining Gal's knowledge of farming and terraforming, with Kieran's unmatched understanding of human history to know what had worked and what hadn't. They would attempt to avoid the mistakes of the forbearers who had brutalized planet after planet.

This was Earth. There was only one.

But as Kieran said, they were ready. Ready to look after it and each other.

They thanked Cordelia, who gushed profusely in her excitement to be able to return home. And then she kissed Kieran squarely on the mouth, and thanked him for that uniquely human experience as well.

Sarrin landed on the soft ground, her bare toes digging in to the grass. A magic she'd never known shot through her.

She felt the urge to run. Pushing with her legs, she dragged Kieran by the hand. The energy surrounded her, swallowed her and ate her whole. She was alive in a way she hadn't known was possible.

Kieran pulled back, laughing and gasping for breath as he told her to go on.

Ahead of her, a herd of ungulate creatures from her dreams lifted their heads and started to run with her through the thick, unmarred forest.

She was free.
She was home.

* * *

Thank you for reading!

Human is the final book in the Red Fever Trilogy. It has been a wonderful ride, taking us from the desolate planets of the Deep Black, to the magical planet-being of Cordelia, to the Uruhu inhabited forests of Indaer. And I want to thank you, from the bottom of my heart, for joining me.

If you enjoyed the story, or even if you didn't, I hope you'll take the time to leave a review. A review means a huge amount to a self-published author like myself, and I would be extremely grateful if you'd consider writing one. It's a good way for us to communicate (yes, I read every single one!), for you to tell me what you liked and where I need to keep improving, and it helps other readers know if a book is one they should pick up or pass by.

Don't forget to join my author newsletter at thewritable.com to hear about new projects and releases (plus pick up some sample chapters and a free short story).

Scan this QR code with your phone
to access the author newsletter!

About Charlotte R MacFarlane

Oh, hey there!

It's cool you want to learn more about me.

I am an award winning author of short stories and poetry, a writing coach, editor, and lover of fiction. I also teach people about happiness and authentic living at happy-ology.com.

Probably the best way to truly learn about me is to read the words on the page, but here's a few things you might not know:

1) I have a wicked sense of humour, and a passion for coming up with irregular sayings ("well, float a log down the stream, you've probably already seen in this in the writing)

2) I love to read and write science-fiction and fantasy novels (duh!) To me, they're more than fiction. The

alternate worlds provide a perfect way to make commentary on the human condition using vast and interesting metaphors. For the same reason, I love Star Trek.

3) I am a classic over-achiever. With awards in writing, horseback riding, math, physics, leadership, and all-around good-person-ness, I often don't know when to stop.

4) I don't like TV (the one exception being Star Trek). It's not tactile enough for me, and doesn't stimulate my imagination as much as a good book.

5) I hate socks, but they are a necessity here in the frigid North, which I also have a love-hate relationship with.

6) I am most afraid of.... Pomeranians. As a former veterinarian, these are some of the hardest dogs to read their body language and hold onto, meaning I've had more tangles with Poms than any other breed. They are cute though, I guess....

Thank you for checking out my fiction, and I hope you'll leave a review and sign up for the newsletter (and buy more books!) It's an honour for a writer to be able to share their thoughts, and I'm so glad I got to share them with you.

More of Charlotte's work can be found at

www.thewritable.com

@CharlotteRMacFarlane